INKING THE WOLF

A WOLF SHIFTER PARANORMAL ROMANCE

STEFFANIE HOLMES

BACCHANALIA HOUSE

Get a free bonus epilogue, plus exclusive previews, free books, fun giveaway, and more cool stuff when you sign up for the Steffanie Holmes VIP Reader's Club: http://www.subscribepage.com/inking_bonus.

❀ Created with Vellum

1
———

BIANCA

"—that my granddaughter, Bianca Sinclair, shall inherit the entire Primrose Estate, including all associated lands and chattels, to do with as she pleases with the exception of sale, on the sole condition that she be married to a man before taking possession of the property."

I tossed the letter on the table in disgust, picking up my pint and drowning the last of my beer in one gulp. My mind buzzing with rage, I snatched the letter up and read it over again, unable to believe the audacity of its content.

My grandmother, June Sinclair, died six weeks ago. It wasn't one of those really sad deaths – no one would cry at her graveside the way they would over a child in a car crash or a mistreated kitten. Of course, part of that is my upper-class British "stiff upper lip" relatives doing what they do best, but personally I think it's because even my terrible family couldn't stand June, who was the worst of the lot. I'd barely seen the woman since my parents kicked me out of their house seven years ago. It was just as well, since I didn't exactly get on with her when we did have contact. My grandmother embodied everything I hated about my upbringing – the pretentiousness, the godly superiority complex, the stubborn refusal to move beyond 19th-century repression.

To her, I was an abomination – an ill-mannered wild child who dishonoured the family name by becoming an *artist* and dating other women. June detested me so much my own mother broke her three years of silence to call me and forbid me to attend her funeral. It was just as well – I didn't own any black skirts of the appropriate length.

Which was why I'd been so surprised when June's lawyer called in at my tattoo shop to inform me June left me something in her will. I was even *more* surprised when the lawyer handed me a handwritten letter and explained that Grandmother June's *entire estate* was mine, provided I met her provisions.

I couldn't believe my luck. My grandmother owned Primrose House, a beautiful Victorian mansion on the outskirts of Crookshollow, nestled right into the edge of the trees at the border of Crookshollow Forest. The house had been in our family for two-hundred years, and still contained all these enchanting original features – a wraparound porch, a hexagonal turret with a giant window and balcony at the top, lots of tiny rooms adorned with garish wallpaper and dark wood panelling, even an enormous ballroom hung with crystal chandeliers. Primrose House made me think of Shirley Jackson's *The Haunting of Hill House*, only instead of weird noises and supernatural forces, it was haunted by my disapproving grandmother who was always telling me to get my grubby hands off her antiques.

Two years ago, I'd been travelling across Europe, doing tattoo residencies and staying in squats and squalid backpackers, and meeting and shagging as many interesting people as I could. In Berlin, a sculptor I was shacked up with at the time took me back to her squat – a decadent Grand Guignol in a converted bunker where artists, DJs and tech entrepreneurs partied for weeks at a time. I stayed there for months – long after the relationship with the sculptor turned stale – enchanted by the wild, creative community that congregated there. Ever since, I'd had the dream of creating my own space just like it – a place where artists and other travellers could stay and collaborate. Part hostel, part gallery, part classroom and events centre. All awesome.

I'd saved a bit of money, and had even started looking at places, but even if I could afford the kind of property I dreamed of (which I couldn't), none nearby had exactly the vibe I wanted. Except ... except for Primrose House. It would be absolutely *perfect*, and now it was tantalisingly close to being mine. But the only way I could get it was to do one thing I absolutely was never going to do ... get married.

"Bianca Sinclair," a deep voice purred from across the table, the rich Scottish accent making my name sound like the heroine of a romance novel. "Disappointing family since 1989."

I didn't need to look up. I knew exactly who it was. Robbie slid into the seat across from me, a fresh pint in each hand. He pushed one across the table to me, and took a sip from his own.

Robbie was a new friend of mine, but over the three months since we'd known each other, we'd become incredibly close. He came from a shifter pack in Aberdeen, but he'd abandoned his family to align with the Lowe pack here in Crookshollow. Since I was an honorary member of that same pack, and I'd all but abandoned my family as well, we had a lot in common.

All my life – except for the time I was overseas – I'd lived in Crookshollow. I admit I kind of believed the local legends of witch hunts and strange creatures hunting in the woods. As a kid, I loved all the spooky stories about supernatural goings-on around the village. My mother forbid that kind of blasphemous talk and so of course I couldn't get enough. Even so, it wasn't until last year that I discovered for myself that shapeshifters were real, and now one of them was my closest male friend.

It all started when my best friend and tattoo apprentice, Elinor Baxter, moved to Crookshollow and fell in love with the ghost of a guy I happened to go to high school with – Eric Marshell – who had since become a famous rockstar. I rescued Elinor from some evil drug dealers and helped bring Eric back to life. (Well, I found a person who knew how to do it, which is practically the same thing). Ever since, my life has been inundated with strange creatures, from my friend Belinda's fiancee Cole, who could transform into a raven, to the famous fox-shifter artist Ryan Raynard, who was marrying my friend Alex. And, most recently, Caleb and Luke – two werewolves who'd come to Crookshollow, found their mates, discovered they were long-lost cousins, and brought all of us together to form a new kind of pack.

Robbie was the adopted brother of the pack leader, Caleb, and he'd abandoned his own pack in order to join with the Crookshollow Lowes. He was also the only one in the entire pack – apart from me – who wasn't paired up in a nice couple. It was nice to talk to someone without having to deal with their goo-goo eyes and lovey-dovey shit. Robbie and I hung out most days after work and on the weekends, unless it was the full moon and he had to run off into the forest.

Which was why as soon as I read the letter I'd sent Robbie a text and told him to meet me for a drink at the *Tir Na Nog* pub. Like any good friend, here he was, with a cold beer and a sympathetic ear.

"It's ridiculous," I said, taking a long gulp from my drink and slamming the glass down on the table. I shoved the paper across to Robbie, and he picked it up, his big brown eyes darting across the handwritten words. "She *knew* how much I loved that house, and that I'd do anything to have it. This is all part of her plot to force me to become a 'real Sinclair lady.' Even when she's dead, that old hag is still trying to run my life."

Robbie took a long time reading the letter. I ground my teeth with frustration waiting for him to finish. Finally, he tapped his fingers against his glass as he set the paper down.

"Well?" I demanded.

"You're right. It's ridiculous. I love how she specified you had to marry 'a man'."

I snorted. My bisexuality was the inciting incident behind my parents kicking me out. When I was sixteen, they went away to Bruges for the weekend, so I took the opportunity to invite my current squeeze for a sleepover. Sally-something ... I don't even think I liked her that much, but she was soft with big, innocent eyes, and she was the only lesbian at our school who hadn't already dumped me, so she was my best option. Of course, we thought we'd do what all teenagers did when their parents were away – drink our way through the liquor cabinet and shag in their bed. It was during the latter part of the adventure that they burst in and caught us.

The memory sent a fresh wave of anger through my veins. I glared at the paper as though my gaze could somehow melt June's icy heart all the way down in hell, where she'd no doubt ended up. "Her lawyer said this will was drafted up several years ago. I guess Grandmother June was hedging her bets in case gay marriage became legal. Which, by the way, it did." I jabbed my finger at the letter, as though June could somehow hear me from beyond the grave. *Take that, you homophobic cow.*

Robbie smiled. Robbie had the best smile. When he wasn't smiling, he looked all quiet and serious, like he was thinking really hard about everything that was going on around him. But when you made him laugh, his whole face collapsed with childish glee. He was actually kind of adorable. When you combined that with the Scottish accent and the fact he was probably the nicest guy I'd ever met (the kind of guy that turned gay girls straight), I was surprised the female population of Crookshollow weren't falling over themselves to date him.

"So, what are you going to do?"

I sighed, and tossed the letter into the middle of the table. "Nothing. I can't get the house unless I'm married. That's it. That's the end of it. Bye-bye art house. Bye-bye dream. My parents inherit it and they'll move in there and it will stay a stuffy, repressed shrine to Colonial oppression. Do you want some chips? I'm starving."

Robbie picked up the letter and scanned it again. "Don't give up, Bianca. This seems like an amazing opportunity. You've said so many times how perfect Primrose would be for your art house. And then this just falls in your lap? It's like it was meant to be. Don't give up just because of this one clause."

"What are you suggesting I do?"

"Find someone to marry."

I snorted. "That's not going to happen. I've been so busy chasing all the wonderful Crookshollow women, I haven't even been near a man in years. And even if I *was* seeing someone, I'm not getting married. *Ever.* It's a stupid, archaic concept designed to shackle women to domestic servitude and I want no part of it—"

"Yeah, yeah, I know." Robbie had heard my anti-marriage rant a few times now. "It doesn't have to be a real marriage, though. You could have a fake marriage."

"A fake marriage?"

"Yeah. You get married on paper, all legal like. But you don't have to *act* married. You wouldn't even have to live together. Plenty of people have sexless marriages – yours would just be honest about it. Whose business is it of anyone else's what you and your husband do?"

I leaned forward, heart pounding. Robbie was right, a

marriage on paper would fulfil the requirements of my grandmother's will. There was no stipulation that I had to be *in love* with my husband, or stay faithful to him. In fact, in my family, that sort of arrangement was practically frowned upon. I could keep my life of freedom and adventure *and* keep the house.

The idea had merit. But there was one key problem. "Just where am I going to find someone willing to fake-marry me so I can get a house?"

Robbie raised an eyebrow.

Shit.

"No," I said.

"Come on, Bianca. It's a dead pure brilliant idea. I think we'd make a great fake couple."

He grinned that silly grin of his. *Fuck. This was crazy.* Was he right?

"I don't think it's such a good idea."

"You did a moment ago. Am I not good enough for you?"

"Don't be silly. I just—" I stared at him, searching his eyes for what he was really thinking. Was he being serious?

"Do you think I'm not the strong, protecting, husband type? I can husband with the best of 'em. You dinnae want to miss out on these bad boys." He held out his arm and flexed his bicep. I dissolved into giggles. He looked ridiculous.

"See? I made you laugh. That's a fine quality in a husband. My Ma told me that."

"You do, at that." My mind whirred with the possibility. Could I *really* marry Robbie? Would it ruin our friendship? Was it not somehow wrong to ask him to do this for me? If he met someone, and wanted to get married for real, that could get really complicated. "I don't think you've thought this through. Why are you so keen on this?"

Robbie shrugged. "Ryan's house is nice and all, but it's way too big. I get lost on the way to the bathroom. Plus, listening to

Alex and Ryan discuss art for hours on end while making googly eyes at each other is driving me barmy."

I nodded. *I get it.* Ryan and Alex were getting married in a few months, and they were still very much in their honeymoon phase. They were both artists, and they talked this weird language of "post-structuralism" and "movement of light and shadow," that made me want to crawl into a hole and die. Alex was always asking for my opinion "as a fellow artist," but I drew skulls and half-naked women on people's skin for a living. I knew nothing about post-structuralism except I wanted to get as far away from it as possible.

"That's it? That's the only reason you want to marry me?"

A strange, sad look passed over Robbie's face. I opened my mouth to question him on it, but as soon as it appeared, it was gone. I wasn't sure if I'd imagined it or not.

"I just want to help. Is that so hard to believe? You've been talking about this art house ever since I first met you. I want to see it become a reality."

My stomach flipped. *I can't believe he's agreeing to do this. Robbie is amazing. I couldn't ask for a better friend.*

I placed my hands on top of his. A warm flame rushed through my arms, wrapping my body in a cosy heat. My eyes stung with emotion. "Are you absolutely *sure* about this? It won't be easy. We'll have to do some pretending. With the house on the line, I know my mother will be checking up on me, making sure I am *really* fulfilling Grandmother's wishes. She'll try to force us to get married in a church. She'll try and give you some title. She'll never shut up about grandchildren. I couldn't ask you to—"

"I'll deal with her. Just think, Bianca, it *could* be perfect. I need a place to live. You need someone to be your fake husband. We could both live at the house, tell your mother we're fucking ten times a day to make her a million grandchildren, and I can help you do all the work you need to do in order to get it ready. I'll even help run the place, if you want me. I need a job."

"You're making this sound so *possible*—"

Robbie turned his hand over, so his palm was against mine. The warmth of it seared through my skin. Why did touching him feel so good? He rubbed his thumb across my knuckles. With his other hand, he picked up the last onion ring from the basket on the table, and held it out to me. "Bianca Sinclair," his voice rumbled, "will you fake-marry me?"

This is crazy.

My heart pounded in my chest. *I can't get fake-married, especially not to my friend.* It would be wrong. It would be—

But the wheels were already starting to turn in my head. It *could* work. Robbie *was* handy – it would be great to have his skills to get the house made up the way I wanted it. We already got along great and we both drank the same beer, so living together would be a breeze. We'd basically be flatmates with the right to receive medical information about each other, which honestly could come in handy one day. It was just the kind of crazy stunt that would make the perfect backdrop for the art house I wanted to create.

Besides, Robbie with his lower-class Scottish speech and his tattooed sleeves was *exactly* the kind of husband my mother would hate. My grandmother's letter only stipulated I had to be married. It said nothing about the nature of my relationship, nor the kind of man I could be married to. Having Robbie for a son-in-law would drive her insane, and that alone was worth considering it.

I stared into Robbie's gleaming blue eyes, thinking how secure I felt around him, how much I'd come to depend on his friendship. If I had to fake-marry someone, he was the best possible choice. "Let's do it."

Robbie grinned. At the sight of his wide, toothy smile, a

warm feeling spread out from my chest, through my whole body. I stretched out my finger, and he slipped the onion ring on.

I grinned, raising my hand to my lips and taking a bite out of my engagement ring. "I love it. It's perfect."

Robbie's brown eyes regarded me intently. That sad expression flicked across his face again. This time, I was sure I didn't imagine it.

"You okay?" I held out my ring to him. "Do you want a bite?"

He shook his head. "I'm fine. It's just been a long day. There's surprisingly little to do in that big old house if you don't read books or paint things. Are you sure you want to do this? It's not exactly conventional."

"I'm not exactly a conventional woman."

"Aye, right. That I know well." Robbie drummed his fingers against his glass. "But, you willnae hate me if I cause a rift in your family? If your mother really is the way you say—"

"Trust me, she's even worse, but she doesn't scare me. She has no power over me anymore. Are *you* sure about this? It's a big ask, fake-marrying me. It's all fine for me – I'm anti-marriage – but what happens if you met a girl you wanted for a wife?"

"I dinnae think I'll ever marry anyone else," he said, then quickly added. "I mean, I never saw myself getting married, and it's hard to find a woman who could deal with the whole shifter thing."

"That's going to change once you guys reveal the existence of shifters to the world. Ladies are going to fall at your feet."

"Because I smell so bad?" Robbie lifted an eyebrow.

"Because you've got that whole broad-shouldered, wild-man of the forest thing. Ladies dig that, trust me."

Robbie shook his head. "They're going to be sorely disappointed. I'm not a wild-man of the forest or even an alpha like Luke or Caleb. Under my old pack law, I wouldn't even take a mate. I nae expected I'd marry, either."

"So you're good?"

"I'm good," he said firmly. "We're doing it, Bianca. You've told me so much about this art house dream of yours, I feel like it's my dream, too. If I can help you make it happen, I'm gonnae do it."

"Okay." I placed my hand over his. Heat soared down my arm again. *It must be the excitement kicking in.*

I can't believe this is really going to happen. I'm really going to be the owner of Primrose House. I'm really going to make my art house a reality.

The sides of my face hurt from grinning so much. Robbie's face mirrored my own, his entire face alive with excitement. "This calls for a celebration." He stood up and dug his wallet out of his jeans. "No more beer for us. We need a bottle of champagne."

"And some chips!"

"Bubbles and chips?" Robbie's grin made my heart skip a beat. "You really *are* my future-wife."

I watched my friend and future husband leaning over the bar to place our order. He ran a hand across his buzzed hair, and the fluorescent lights under the bar illuminated the scraggly tattoos across his lower sleeve. The heat of his hand still lingered against mine. I rubbed my fingers, but the heat didn't go away.

My stomach flipped again, but this time, it wasn't excitement. It was nerves.

What did I have to be nervous about? It was just a fake marriage between platonic friends. It would only become a problem if I had feelings for Robbie, but I didn't. I didn't see him as anything but a really good friend.

Didn't I?

2
———

ROBBIE

*B*ianca and I are getting married.

We're *getting married.*

I stared across the table at my new fiancee, watching her gorgeous lips move but not hearing the words coming out of them.

This is a really, really bad idea.

Bianca had no clue how I felt about her. To her, I was a good friend she could chat to over a pint. We clicked instantly, because we're the only two single members of the pack and we both have crazy families that had scarred us. She talked to me the same way she'd talk to any girlfriend, with that easy confessional air that meant she'd decided I was safe.

She had no idea that every time we met up, I spent the whole time desperately trying to work up the nerve to ask her out. I listened so intently to her because I kept getting distracted from what she was saying by how divine her lips were. She had no clue that my skin sizzled with heat whenever she was near, and that I was drawn to her like a magnet to one of the enormous metal spikes in her ear. She had no idea that she was my fated mate.

And now I was going to be her husband.

Er, *fake*-husband.

Ever since we'd started hanging out, I'd been dreaming about something like this. Bianca was like no other girl I'd ever met before. Everything about her was tiny and pixie-like. If we stood side-by-side, her head barely reached to my shoulder. Her enormous blue eyes dominated her heart-shaped face, framed by long lashes that tangled together when she closed her eyes. She kept her white-blonde hair cropped super short, so it framed her face in light feathers, often coloured with bright streaks. Her ears were tiny and filled with piercings, her fingers long and neat, her feet dainty, although she usually had them stuffed inside an enormous pair of black Doc Martins. The tattoos that encircled her arms, chest, stomach, legs, and back were intricate and feminine – skulls and flowers and delicate maidens with diaphanous wings and exquisitely rendered drapery.

If everything about Bianca's appearance was pixieish, her personality was the exact opposite. You had to be tough to survive as a female tattoo artist, but I think even if Bianca was a butterfly botanist, she'd still be exactly the same. If Bianca wanted to say something, she'd bloody well say it, consequences be damned. She was anti-marriage, anti-monogamy, anti-sexism, anti-religious, anti-just-about-anything conservative. Add the multiple piercings, odd hair colours (currently, it was streaked with blue), and tattoos over every inch of her skin (I assume), and you got a hint into her real nature.

All the girls I'd met in Aberdeen – and there were a few (mostly my brother Angus' cast-offs) – cared about were clothes and celebrities and what their friends said about them down at the pub. They didn't have an original thought in their heads. Although, it was much easier to watch a film with them. Bianca talked over any film we tried to watch, mostly ranting about various plot inconsistencies or the evils of organised religion. And then you put *Wall-E* on, and she'd cry.

All I wanted more than anything in the world was to hold her every night and listen to her crazy rants. Now, we were going to be husband and wife.

I drowned my champagne glass in one gulp, the sickly sweet fluid churning in my stomach. I should tell her how I feel. It was the right thing to do. She clearly didn't see me as anything other than a friend, and she should know the truth before we did this crazy thing. It might change things for her.

And yet ... I really *did* want to help her. I loved the idea of the art house almost as much as Bianca did. The place sounded magical, like something out of the storybooks my Ma used to read for me when my father wasn't around. It was so far from the harsh gang environment I'd grown up in. I loved the idea that all around the world there were these safe houses for misfits to congregate, and even though I could barely read and didn't have an artistic bone in my body, I wanted to be part of that.

Plus, we'd be flatmates, cooking together, having a beer together before bed, fixing things around the place, sharing a toothbrush cup ...

It's your one chance to show her how you feel, how good a husband you could really be. I knew it was pointless to hope, but I hoped anyway. I hoped one day she'd wake up and see me as more than a friend. That maybe *I* could be the one to change her mind about marriage and commitment.

I didn't want to say no and have her fake-marry someone else and wake up one day and realise *that* guy was really her fated mate.

So I remained silent, and listened with half an ear while Bianca talked about how we would go about the whole thing. We finished our chips and champagne and left the pub. Bianca said she should probably get back to the shop. She lived in a small apartment over her tattoo studio, *Resurrection Ink*. I offered to give her a ride on my way back to Raynard Hall, but she shook me off.

"I prefer to walk. I want to stare at the stars and dream about my art house some more." She stood on tiptoes and grabbed my shoulders, forcing my head down so she could reach it. She kissed me on the cheek, her lips like fire on my skin. "Thanks so much for this, Robbie. You're the best friend a girl could ask for."

"Any time, my betrothed."

"Don't you start with that shit, or I'll have the divorce papers signed before we're even down the aisle."

I waved her goodbye, and watched her blonde-and-blue head bobbing away around the corner. Sighing, I got in my crappy falling-apart Lada and drove around to Marcus' place. I didn't feel like going back to Raynard Hall immediately.

Marcus was a vulpine – a fox shifter – and Ryan's fraternal twin. He was also a mutt, which meant his shifter genetics didn't work properly. He couldn't control his shifting, especially when he got emotional, and he had an aggressive streak that flared up at the worst possible times. We had a lot in common – I wasn't great at controlling my shifts, either. I'd spent most of my childhood in my wolf form, acting solely on my instincts. It was hard to remember to rein things in. Hell, sometimes it was hard to remember to put pants on before I went outside.

Marcus lived in a small flat just off the high street with his fiancé Kylie, but she was a nurse who often worked night shifts. I was hoping I'd have Marcus to myself that night. I needed to talk to a guy.

I knocked vigorously on the door, and a few minutes later, Marcus threw it open. "Come in. Kylie's at work and I have pizza and beer and a huge stack of action films to get through before she gets back."

"Sounds perfect." I slumped down on the couch next to him.

Marcus went to the kitchen to fetch me a beer, but I told him not to worry about me. "I've been at the pub with Bianca. We had champagne, and it isn't exactly agreeing with me."

As if in response, my stomach churned.

"Champagne." Marcus made a face. "Why the fuck would you drink that piss?"

"We were celebrating."

"Celebrating what? Did she finally get her clit pierced?"

"We're getting married," I said.

"You ... *what?*" Marcus slapped three beers down in front of us, and shoved the pizza box toward me.

As I stuffed down a piece of Meatsplosion pizza, I explained about the house Bianca had just inherited, and the stipulations her grandmother placed on it. "I haven't seen it yet, but apparently, it's this beautiful old Victorian place with dozens of tiny rooms. Bianca thinks it's perfect for her art commune, so I said I'd—"

Marcus shook his head. "No. Don't do it. It's a bad idea."

"The art house? I think it's brilliant."

"Of course you do, mate. You think it's brilliant because you're in love with Bianca, which is exactly why you shouldn't marry her."

Panic seized my chest. How did he know? Had I got drunk one night and spilled the beans? "I'm not—you cannae say—"

"See, you can't even deny it out loud." Marcus shot me a sardonic smile. "I've been watching you pine after that girl for months, yapping around her heels like some lovesick pup. She hasn't noticed."

"That's not what I—"

"Don't marry her, Robbo. End of story. It's a fast pass to getting your heart trampled all over by her shiny black Docs. Now, do you want to know what happened while you were out courting? Ryan called about an hour ago. He's back from

London and he's made some progress on the location of the Benedict ring."

Ah, the Benedict ring – an ancient ring of power that had been gifted to the Lowe clan by an infamous witch way back in the dim dark ages. The ring with which our pack and our allies, the Bairds, intended to reveal the existence of shifters to the world, just as soon as we found it.

We thought the whole plan was so simple when we'd cooked it up a couple of months ago, back when I'd first joined Caleb's pack. The ring *should* be hidden in the Lowe caves – a network of tunnels and caverns in the Crookshollow Forest that the Lowes used to use as a den. But we'd searched every inch of those tunnels and hadn't found any trace. Caleb had started to think the ring might be somewhere else, so he sent Ryan down to London to look up old chronicles at the British Museum. He was hoping there'd be some other account of the ring that might tell us where else it could be. It sounds like Caleb's hunch might have paid off.

"Oh yeah?" I leaned forward. "Ryan found something?"

"Yep. Another historical account of the ring. According to this new info, the ring wasn't kept in the caves at all. It would've been nice to know that before I tore up my knees hunting around in the mud for two months. Ryan said he's going to tell us more about it at our tattoo session tomorrow."

I groaned. I'd forgotten about that. Caleb insisted that all of us should get a tattoo to mark our allegiance to the pack. Tattoos are important to shifter society, as there weren't that many ways we can identify ourselves to other shifters while keeping the whole turning-into-an-animal thing secret. If we were going to be in the media after the big shifter reveal, we were going to need some kind of emblem around which other shifters could affiliate. On paper, a tattoo seemed like a good idea, and a good excuse to spend some time with Bianca in her natural habitat. The only catch was the fact that I *hated* being tattooed.

My arms were covered in the things, and I detested them. Needles freaked me out. When I'd gone to get my Maclean family crest done on my eighteenth birthday, I fainted. The annoyed tattooist told my brother Angus to take me home. The next week, Angus took me to a much less-scrupulous friend of his to finish the ink. My second tattooist misspelled *Maclean* and his dirty needle gave me an infection. My arm turned all green and hurt like hell for weeks. The tattoo looked like shit – an appropriate symbol of our family if ever I saw one.

All the tattoos on my arms were done for the benefit of my brother, Angus. Looking at them now, I couldn't understand why I'd agreed to any of them. Angus would always mock me, calling me a feardie. So I gritted my teeth and had them done just to shut him up. I didn't like any of them – not the grinning skulls nor the Viking hammer or the growling tiger with the crooked legs. I especially hated the message written across my shoulders in a cursive font I couldn't even read. They reminded me of the person I was before, a person who didn't always do good things.

"I'll hold your hand if you like," Marcus sneered. "Although maybe you'd prefer if Bianca—"

"It's fine," I mumbled into my chest. "I'll be fine. Maybe it'll be different this time."

"You mean, maybe you won't make a fool of yourself in front of your hot soon-to-be wife?"

"Yeah, that exactly." I grabbed a beer from the table and gulped it back. There was nothing like a little liquid courage. Tattoos were Bianca's life. If she thought I hated them, then she'd never want me. I'd be over before I even began.

3

BIANCA

I barely slept a wink. My mind whirred with a thousand possibilities for Primrose House. I made lists in my head of all the people I had to contact, and how I would get started jazzing the place up and turning it into the art house of my dreams. I couldn't believe it was going to be mine, mine, mine. And it was all thanks to Robbie and his crazy plan.

I must have finally fallen asleep in the early hours of the morning, because I was thrust rudely from slumber by Macavity – my recalcitrant ginger cat – throwing my mobile phone off the side of the bed.

"Merrrw," he commanded, raising his paw to do the same thing to my stack of books. *"Merrrrwwwww!"*

"All right, all right," I grumbled, fumbling for my mobile phone. The sun streamed across my bed, cruelly informing me that I'd massively overslept. I checked the time. 9:43 a.m. My alarm had apparently rung seven times already. Yep, definitely overslept.

I fumbled my way to the kitchen, my eyes still not ready to fully open, and set down some food for Macavity. He snaffled away, his whole body shuddering with contented purrs, while I made double-strength coffee and tried to force my brain online.

Under my feet, the sound of the metal gate sliding open and furniture being moved around the shop told me that Elinor was already hard at work. Elinor was one of those annoying people who leapt out of bed at 6 a.m., instantly awake and coherent. I was the opposite. I usually spoke in grunts until at least 11.

I couldn't afford that today, though. We had a busy day in the shop. I had a regular client booked for colour-touch ups in the morning, and in the afternoon a very special event we'd be closing the shop for: the Lowe pack were all getting their tattoo.

The whole pack hadn't been together for a couple of weeks, when we had drinks at Raynard Hall before Ryan left for London. Excited butterflies flipped in my stomach when I remembered I had something amazing to tell everyone. I'd been talking about the art house idea for as long as I'd known the pack. They'd flip when they found out it was going to be a reality. With that in mind I stuffed a breakfast bar in my mouth, guzzled my coffee, hurriedly applied some makeup and found my least rumpled jeans and favourite Ramones singlet, and rushed downstairs.

"Well, well, what time do you call this?" Elinor looked up from the drawing table where she was working up stencils of the Lowe tattoo in preparation for this afternoon. I couldn't believe how lucky I was to have Elinor Baxter in my life. She'd been a highly-paid, swanky lawyer in London before she came to Crookshollow on an assignment, and loved it so much she decided to stay. Her hot rockstar fiancé Eric Marshell definitely had something to do with that decision. I admired her so much for choosing an unconventional life over her cushy, parent-pleasing job, although I wished she'd left her punctuality back at the law firm as well.

Elinor didn't look like your typical tattoo artist. She had

straight brown hair cut in neat layers around her face, and a pair of black-framed glasses that accentuated her large, dark eyes and bow-shaped lips. With her prim outfits and sexy curves, she looked more like a PA than a tattooist, especially since she didn't actually have any visible ink. Six months ago, I'd given Elinor her first ink – two beautiful wings across her back, the fine bones and sinews poking from her shoulder blades, curling into an elegant arc with the feathered tips ending right above her pelvis. Elinor drew the design herself – she had a real talent. I'd been trying to convince her to get sleeves done, but so far, she wasn't keen.

Now, she was my apprentice, as well as being my best friend and one of the other human members of the pack. I'd given her the job of designing the Lowe tattoo – it depicted a wolf staring thoughtfully up into the full moon, the branches of a spindly tree framing the scene. The pack's new motto, AMOR VINCIT OMNIA – Love Conquers All – arched around the bottom in gothic script.

Ever since I'd discovered that shapeshifters were real and ghosts could be brought back to life, business at *Resurrection Ink* had been booming. Word spread around the shifter and super-natural communities that Elinor and I were part of the Lowe pack. Shifters had been travelling from far and wide to have their pack tattoos designed and inked by me and Elinor. We'd gained a reputation for exquisite work, and discretion for our less-than-human clients. Soon, our handiwork would become one of the most recognised symbols of the shifter community. I felt a stab of pride as I admired Elinor's finely drawn lines and perfectly rendered wolf.

"You're running this place so well, I don't have to get up before lunch." I yawned as I leaned back in a chair and grabbed one of her stencils for a closer look.

"Don't you dare." She rolled her eyes. "Sometimes, I think

you and Eric would be perfect for each other. I have to go upstairs and yell at him several times to get him to roll out of bed."

I stuck out my tongue as I handed back the stencil. "I could never date Eric Marshell. He may be a sexy gothic rockstar now, but I knew him when he was the scrawny, pimply teenager who loved Star Trek. He'll always be that teenager to me."

"I'm glad I never knew him then." Elinor laughed. "It might shatter my dream."

"So, you won't believe what happened to me yesterday," I said as I wiped down the table with disinfectant and placed fresh covers on the clip cords and power unit.

"Does this have anything to do with that lawyer that came by yesterday about your mother's estate?"

I grinned. Elinor used to be a lawyer herself – she was whip smart, and nothing ever got past her.

"It does indeed." I pulled over an image of the client's tattoo and started assembling a line of inks across the top of my tray. "It turns out, I've inherited my grandmother's house. It's crazy, because my grandmother hated me, but it's right there in the will, totally legit. Wait till you see this place, you'll absolutely love it. It's a Victorian manor just outside the village. It's got loads of tiny, dark-panelled rooms and a big turret and there's even a secret passage leading from the back of the kitchen to the attic bedrooms."

"That sounds *amazing.*" Like me, Elinor had a love for the gothic. She'd have to, being engaged to the musician who single-handedly made the classical violin cool again. "What are you going to do with it?"

"I'm going to move in, of course. And then I'm going to Bianca-ify it. It's perfect for my art house. I'm going to take out all my grandmother's stuffy French antiques and ugly Victorian portraits, replace it all with junk-store finds and crazy art, turn the bedrooms into a hostel, and the parlour into an art venue for shows and readings and classes. Can you believe it? I'm actually going to make the art house happen, and all I have to do to get it is to get married."

"Wait ... what?" Elinor's pen froze in midair.

I shrugged. "Yeah. I have to get married. My grandmother placed this crazy stipulation in her will that in order to take possession of the house, I had to be legally married to a man. She actually specified it had to be a *man*, can you believe it?"

"But Bianca, how are you planning on getting married when you don't—" The bell on the shop door tingled. Elinor leapt to her feet. "Finish this story later?"

"Sure." I watched Elinor flounce over to meet our walk-in – a mousy-girl with soft blonde curls and wide, frightened eyes. She stared at the skulls and dragons I'd drawn on the walls with an expression of utter terror. Elinor started to talk to her about the tattooing process, while I shoved the Lowe stencils under a pile of drawings so she wouldn't see them.

A few minutes later, the girl was sitting behind the barrier, nervously wringing her hands while Elinor worked up a sketch for her. I glanced at the clock. My client was due in fifteen minutes, so I started prepping my gun and needles.

"What are you getting done?" I asked the girl while I worked. I loved hearing the stories behind people's tattoos. What you chose to have inked on your body said so much about you as a person. My tattoos, mostly inked by friends from stencils I'd drawn, represented different stages of my life and travels – maenads battling satyrs from my time squatting in Greece, blood-red roses from my trip to Countess Bathory's castle in Slovakia, an elaborate hieroglyphic frieze from my trip through Egypt. They were symbols of the life I'd carved for myself and the independence I'd earned.

This girl didn't look like the usual "type" to get inked, but tattoos were so common now you could no longer make judgements like that. I knew whatever Elinor was drawing for her, she'd love it.

"Oh, um ..." The girl's eyes widened as she took in the huge gun in my hands, like a deer trapped in headlights. Her face paled. "I'm ... um ... getting a rose, on my stomach."

"Cool. Roses are popular, and Elinor does a great job with florals." I pointed to a vivid pagan goddess on my forearm I'd done myself a couple of years previously. "I've been teaching her everything I know. I like to try and make tattoos look like old paintings."

The girl smiled meekly, but her eyes betrayed her horror. "I could never have something like that. It's nice, though."

I laughed. "Don't worry, we're not going to make you look like me. Although, I have to warn you, everyone starts with something small and then they get hooked. Before you know it you'll be in here every week begging for your next fix."

"... oh, I don't know ..." The girl hadn't taken her eyes off the gun in my hand. She was so scared, it was adorable.

Actually, it was more than adorable. Those big doe eyes, that dark hair, those juicy lips ... this girl was just my type – a sweet, innocent ripe for corrupting. I wondered if she was a local girl, and how she'd respond if I asked her out for a drink.

I patted her leg, letting my hand linger just a little longer than necessary. "It's okay to be nervous. Most people are their first time. It doesn't hurt as much as you'd expect, er, what's your name?"

"Willow," the girl practically whispered.

"Nice to meet you. I'm Bianca." I extended my hand.

"Hi." The word was practically a whisper. She placed her trembling hand in mine, her fingers long and thin and delicate.

"What do you do, Willow?"

"I'm ... I'm a wedding planner."

This meek girl is a wedding planner? In movies, wedding planners were always bossy, perfectionists types who bustled around in too-high heels and pretended to care about table centrepieces. I couldn't imagine Willow yelling at caterers who messed up or frantically trying to find twenty metres of hot pink bunting at a moment's notice.

My heart raced. *How intriguing.* Now I really had to get to know this girl more. On the plus side, if I kept Willow talking, she might be distracted enough that she wouldn't faint before Elinor had even begun.

"That's so cool. Elinor's planning her wedding right now, aren't you?" I grinned as Elinor came back from the drawing table with a small square of paper depicting a beautiful, delicate rose, the petals shaded with intricate cross-hatching. Three drops of blood dripped from the thorns on its spindly stalk.

Wow, that's a bit morbid. I wondered what had made Willow choose that particular design. It really seemed out of place. But that terrified look in Willow's eyes told me now wasn't the time to ask.

"I've already told Willow she should coordinate it." Elinor handed the drawing to Willow, who took it in shaking fingers and stared at it as though it might eat her alive. "She's just moved to Crookshollow and doesn't have many local clients yet. She was telling me she's worked on some big deal weddings in London, lots of celebrities and reality TV stars, even one for the royal family."

"No way. That's pretty impressive." *So she's just moved to Crookshollow, and she must be single because if she was that scared of needles, any decent partner would have come along to support her. I bet she could do with some friends ...*

Willow glanced up, her pale face flushing. "Um, it's not really ... I just ... I mean ..." She handed the image back to Elinor.

"This is perfect. Can I get it done now? I ... I think if I have to come back, I'll completely chicken out."

"Sure," Elinor sat back down at the table to make a stencil. "My next client isn't until this afternoon. But you sure you definitely want this? It's quite large and it will go over your ribcage, which means it will hurt a lot."

Willow winced, but fixed her face into a look that I guessed was as close to determination as you could get when you were shaking with terror. "I'm sure. What do I do now?"

Elinor helped Willow up onto the table, and got her to roll up her shirt. She placed the stencil on her side, adjusted it and stuck it in place. Willow checked the placement in a mirror and nodded. Elinor got her to lie down, arranged a couple of pillows to make her comfortable, and then went out back to wash her hands.

Willow gazed around the shop, that terrified expression never leaving her face. I followed her gaze, trying to see the place the way she might see it. Of course, it was impossible. Before I'd taken up the lease, *Resurrection Ink* had been a laundromat. I'd cleaned out my entire bank account to paint the concrete floor a glossy black, wallpaper it with a garish Victorian floral print, build a waist-high wall and gate between the waiting area and shop floor, and deck it out with the best tattoo gear I could afford. The skull-themed art in faux-gilt frames and constant buzzing of tattoo guns might seem terrifying to some people, but to me, this place was home.

Looking at Willow, I wondered if I could think of another topic to distract her. *I want to know more about why she moved to Crookshollow, and about the kinds of weddings she plans ... hang on, wedding ...*

"Hey, you could do my wedding!" I exclaimed. "Elinor's is still months away. Mine won't be as flash, but it's going to be in the next month or so, and I want something pretty crazy."

Elinor's head popped around the corner of the wall. "You're really getting married just to get that house? Who's the lucky guy?"

"Robbie."

Elinor's lips pursed.

"What? He offered." I didn't like the look she was giving me.

"Bianca, I'm not sure that's a good idea."

"Why not? It's not a real marriage. He's just doing a favour for a friend. He's desperate to get out of Raynard Hall. I'm going to give him a room in Primrose House for his trouble—"

The bell rang. I whirled around. Curtis, my client, stood in the doorway, his impressive bulk blocking the light from the street. "Hey, Bianca," he said, removing his sunglasses and shrugging off his leather jacket to reveal a tight black t-shirt and two full-sleeve tattoos of evil, naked mermaids slaying fish-monsters with deadly tridents. Curtis was a regular – a construction worker and Harley Davidson enthusiast from Crooks Crossing who spent every spare cent he didn't put into his bike on covering his skin in ink.

"Hey, Curtis." I patted the table. "Come on back, I'm ready for you." To Willow, I said, "Leave your card with me when you're done, and I'll give you a call."

Oh yes, I'll definitely give you a call.

"Thanks," Willow said, wincing as Elinor's needle met her soft skin. Elinor glared at me. I turned back to my client, grabbing the disinfectant to clean his arm.

What's Elinor so upset about? Is she worried my fake marriage somehow overshadows hers? That's not possible, and she should know that. So what's her problem?

~

As soon as Willow and Curtis left, we put up the "CLOSED"

sign and set about prepping the place for the afternoon's session. I tried to bring up the subject of the my fake-marriage again, but Elinor just held up her hand and said, "I don't want to talk to you about it just yet. Why don't you tell the others this afternoon and see what they say. Then I'll feel safe giving you my opinion."

I fumed as I disinfected the shop and changed the needle on my gun. *I thought we were friends. Why does she not think I trust her opinion? And what's there to even have an opinion on, anyway? It's not as if this is a big deal. I thought she'd be happy for me.*

There wasn't any time to confront Elinor again before the pack arrived. Belinda Wu was the first to walk through the door, which didn't surprise me in the slightest. Belinda was the baker at *Bewitching Bites*, the best place to eat in Crookshollow. She knew the importance of getting timing just right.

"I brought treats." Belinda tucked a strand of her black hair behind her ear and yanked the lid off a box filled with fresh Cornish pasties and slices of her signature dessert – Heaven and Hell cake.

"Don't bring those behind the barrier," I warned. "We've just disinfected. But we'll totally eat out in the waiting area."

"Way ahead of you." Elinor vaulted over the gate in her haste to snap up a still-warm pastie. "This is amazing, as always. I'm gonna have to introduce you to my last client, Willow. She's a wedding planner and she just moved to Crookshollow from London, so she'll need contact details for the best local caterer and cake-maker. I've already told her she has to plan my wedding."

"And my fake wedding," I piped up, as I joined them in the waiting area. I sank my teeth into the thick pastie. Warm meat and spices exploded on my tastebuds. My stomach rumbled with appreciation, and I realised I hadn't eaten since my breakfast bar.

"Your fake wedding?" Belinda looked confused.

Succinctly, I explained about Primrose House and my grandmother's will. "Robbie offered to marry me so I can get the house. Isn't that awesome?"

Belinda suddenly become very interested in a tattoo magazine on the table. "Yeah, sure, Bianca. It's great."

I glanced at Elinor, but she was also avoiding my eyes. *What is with everyone? Why are they not excited about this?*

A terrible thought struck me. *Maybe they all think the art house is dumb. Maybe they've been talking about it behind my back, laughing at how silly I was to think it could work.*

Anger flashed through my veins. I stuffed the rest of the pastie in my mouth and bit down hard. *So what?* Sod them all if they thought the art house was stupid. Robbie believed in me, which made him a better friend, didn't it?

I didn't have much time to ponder the question, as Caleb's voice boomed down the corridor. I rushed forward to hug him. Caleb was our leader – a boisterous hulk of a guy with a mop of ginger curls, a wicked smile and a mischievous nature. He was dragging his fiancee, Rosa, by the hand. His cousin Luke, dark-haired and serious, pulled up the rear.

"Anna decided to stay at home," Luke said, giving me a gentle squeeze. "Little baby Colin didn't have a very good night last night, so they're both trying to get some sleep. I'll come in with her later to get hers done."

"No problem. Give her and Colin my love."

"Will do. Oh, cake!" Luke bounded off to join the others.

More bodies filed into the shop. Eric arrived next, looking like a completely different person from the dweeb I knew in high school, with his long dark hair, brooding eyes, and chiseled features. He wore a high-collared black trench coat pulled close around his face, probably an attempt to avoid being recognised on the street. Elinor rushed forward and embraced him, and he whispered something in her ear that made her face light up.

A giant raven swooped in through the corridor, folding its jet-black wings around its body as it settled on the back of the velvet chaise lounge. The raven's body contorted – its body bulging outward, wing bones snapping as they folded back in on themselves. The feathers retracted into its skin, and the long talons that dug into the fabric slid down the back of the seat, forming toes and ankles and shins. The raven tossed its head back and let out a discordant "croak!" as its face shifted, the beak curling back into lips. A few moments later a stark-naked man sat on my sofa, his long black hair draped over his shoulders and a sardonic grin spread across his handsome face.

"Cole!" Belinda admonished her fiancé. "Why did you come like that? Now Bianca has to tattoo you naked."

"I know. It's her lucky day." Cole grinned, spinning Belinda around until she squealed in delight. I rolled my eyes. Sometimes all the love around here could get a little tedious.

I turned back to the door just as Robbie and Marcus walked in together. When Robbie's eyes met mine, a surge of something like relief rocked through my body. I stuffed the last bite of cake into my mouth and rushed over, giving him a hug.

"Hey." His face broke into the most gorgeous smile. "I take you havenae changed your mind about what we talked about last night?"

"Not on your life," I said, rubbing his arm. I couldn't wait to get my needle onto Robbie's skin. His current tattoos were appalling – wonky lines, dribbling ink, crooked lettering ... there was even a spelling mistake in his Maclean crest. He looked like he'd been attacked by a scratcher who was both drunk and blind. I knew by the way Robbie always wore long sleeves that he was embarrassed by his ink, and honestly, he should be. His was the only stencil I'd insisted on drawing myself. I had something special planned for him. "Come on in, Belinda brought life-giving cake."

Over Robbie's shoulder, I noticed Elinor and Marcus exchange a pointed look.

Ryan and Alex arrived last, rushing down the hall, their clothes covered with flecks of paint. Irvine trailed behind them, looking a little annoyed. Irvine wasn't officially a member of the Lowe pack – he had his own pack, the Bairds, back in Scotland. However, he and Caleb had an alliance, and to seal that pact, they were both getting each other's crests inked on their skin. Shifter politics were *weird,* but I wasn't about to complain about all these new customers.

"Sorry," Alex puffed, rubbing at a smear of forest green streaked across her cheek. "We were in the studio and lost track of time."

Elinor groaned. "I don't know how I can stand hanging out with so many bloody *artists.* I need to buy you all watches."

Alex lifted up her wrist, showing a cheap beaded bracelet that was speckled with paint. "A watch will be unreadable inside of a week. Come on, let's see this design you're going to poke into my flesh."

Now that everyone had arrived, I went back to preparing the inks and guns, while Elinor showed them her stencils.

"It's awesome." Caleb grinned, holding up the stencil. "You've perfectly captured what our pack is all about."

"It's so big." Belinda bit her lip, rubbing her arm.

"You'll be fine," Elinor reassured her. "It doesn't hurt as much as you expect. And I've made you a slightly smaller one."

Belinda looked relieved. On her tiny Asian body, the large crest would look really out of proportion.

"Right." I patted the chair next to me. "Who's first?"

"Not me." Belinda shuffled toward the back of the group. Alex joined her, shooting a nervous glance at Ryan.

Caleb slapped Luke on the shoulder. "What do you say, cousin? Let's show them how it's done."

Luke slid into Elinor's chair, and Caleb plonked down beside me. "I presume you want me to disrobe, or will that be too distracting?" He grinned.

"Keep up that lip, Caleb Lowe, and I'll replace your wolf with a beautiful big bumble bee," I responded, as I flicked the switch on my power unit and pulled the foot pedal toward me.

Caleb didn't flinch as I touched the needle to his skin. Because he was already heavily tattooed, I was reworking the edge of a previous piece into the Lowe crest, with the smaller Baird crest incorporated beneath it. Caleb kept up a steady line of chatter about the pack and their plans while I worked on him. He kept gesticulating with his free arm, causing his whole body to shift, including the canvas upon which I worked.

"Hold still," I growled at him for the tenth time, after he shifted again just as I started to draw a particularly difficult line.

"Sure," he said, lowering his arm. A few minutes later, it was back in the air again.

I sat back in defeat. "This is ridiculous. Robbie, come over here and hold his arm down."

Robbie pushed his way through the gate. I pulled over a chair next to Caleb and patted the cushion. Robbie slumped down, clamping his hands over Caleb's forearm. I picked up my gun again and continued the tattoo.

As I leaned in close to work on Caleb's arm, I couldn't help but notice the atmosphere had changed. With Robbie here, the air around me charged with a nervous energy.

Robbie's eyes burned in the back of my skull as I worked. Why did my body feel so odd, all tingly and weird? Maybe I was coming down with something. I traced the lines on Caleb's skin and wiped away the blood, my hand shaking a little. I had to pull my hand away before I messed up the line.

Whoah, that never happened. I glanced over at Robbie, and

saw he was focused on Caleb's arm. Was I imagining it, or had his skin paled?

Don't think about it. Just focus on the work. I managed to work through the weird feeling. I added the final flourish of colour, and wiped away the last of the blood. "All done."

Robbie dropped Caleb's arm. Caleb stood up and struck a pose for the rest of the pack, who cheered. "This is the beginning of something epic, you guys. As soon as we find the Benedict Ring, this symbol is going to be known the world over as the symbol of shifter freedom."

"I have some news about the ring," Ryan said. "But I don't want to try and explain it now with all the tattoo guns going. Instead, you should all come over for dinner tonight to celebrate. Simon's cooking a big roast lamb."

"I'm in," Marcus said automatically. Everyone laughed.

"Bianca's got some news as well," Robbie said.

I glanced at Elinor, suddenly nervous. "I don't want to overshadow Ryan's dinner," I said.

"You don't have Simon's roast potatoes, so that's unlikely," Marcus growled.

"Go ahead, Bianca," Ryan said. I took a deep breath, and told them about my aunt leaving me the house, and the stipulation in the will.

"That's so crazy!" Rosa said. "How could you grandmother possibly make such a ridiculous stipulation like that? Surely it's not legal."

"It actually is," Elinor said. "I worked on some pretty bizarre probate cases back in London. This is by no means the weirdest."

"There's nothing else for it," Caleb declared. "You're going to have to find some poor schmuck to marry you."

Silently, Robbie raised his hand, grinning shyly. I smiled and threw my arm around his shoulder. "Robbie's agreed to do the honours."

Silence. Ten faces stared at us in gape-mouthed horror. Robbie's grin froze on his face.

Finally, Alex said, in her most falsely-bright voice. "That's … that's great."

My jaw clenched with annoyance. I slid my arm off Robbie's shoulder. "Don't congratulate me all at once," I said, louder than I'd intended. "You're all invited to the wedding, if that's what you're worried about. I might even ask Simon to bring a batch of roast potatoes."

"It's not that I'm not happy for you," Rosa said, her dark eyes darting between us. "It's just that it's very, um … unconventional."

I gestured to the room. "I'm not exactly conventional."

"Exactly," Rosa said. "You said you'd never get married."

"I'm not getting married. I'm getting *fake*-married. Big difference."

"Not to a court of law," Belinda said. "Or the church. Don't they excommunicate people for this kind of thing?"

I threw up my hands. "Since when would I care what *the church* thought? You guys are acting like we're destroying the sanctity of marriage or something. I can't believe I even have to defend this to you. People get married for all sorts of reasons, and it's not like my fake-marriage has any reflection on all your real lovey-dovey marriages. So could you all hop off the judge-ment express and just be happy for me?"

Ten faces exchanged pointed looks. Belinda stared at her shoes. Rosa folded her arms. Only Caleb met my eyes, a ques-tioning look in his friendly gaze.

An awkward silence fell. Finally, Elinor stepped forward, placing her hand on my other shoulder.

"We're ready for the next two now," Elinor said. "Bianca and

I just need to wash and change our gloves. You guys decide who's going to go next."

Elinor and I crowded into the tiny washroom at the back of the shop. I elbowed her as she lathered up. "Okay, I waited to see their reactions. They look more like I invited them to a funeral than a wedding. What gives?"

"You *really* want my opinion?" Elinor asked, scrubbing her arms all the way up to the elbows.

"I really do."

"Don't marry Robbie."

"I'm rather confused. I thought you loved my art house idea."

"You know I do—"

"Right. Well, this is how I'm going to make it happen. It's the *only* way I'm going to make it happen in this century."

Elinor sighed. "I just ... do you think fake-marrying *Robbie* is such a good idea?"

"Why wouldn't it be?"

"Because he's madly in love with you."

I snorted. "Don't be ridiculous."

"It's true. He's been crazy about you ever since he arrived in town. We can all see it. I can't believe you're so oblivious; you're usually so clued into this stuff."

"It's not true. Robbie's never made a move."

"Have you *met* the guy? He may look tough, but he's so shy I doubt he even knows what move to make. He probably thinks he's not good enough, you being the daughter of a Lord and him being from the wrong side of the tracks. That's why he's agreed to marry you. He wants you to notice him."

I peered around the corner of the washroom, out across the shop. Robbie sat on my bench, shirtless, swinging his legs as he waited his turn. His eyes darted nervously around the room, then settled on mine. His face broke out into a big, gorgeous smile, and my stomach flipped a little.

Does he like me? I'd never got that vibe off him, that "I want to bed you in a manly fashion" vibe you got from guys who just saw you as a conquest. Robbie and I were friends. We drank beer together and watched movies and ranted about the world and farted openly in front of each other. I didn't even think he realised I was a girl.

But then ... he would always drop everything to hang out with me. He laughed at all my stupid jokes. He even came clothes shopping with me and let me chatter all the way through every film we saw ...

"But you don't feel the same way, do you?"

"I ..." For once, words failed me. I felt utterly flummoxed. It had never even occurred to me that Robbie might fancy me. What about the other night, when he walked me back from the pub? There was this moment, when I thought he was going to kiss me, and I *wanted* it?

But he was *Robbie*. He was my friend. And I did not date friends. I didn't date, period. Dating always led to serious relationships, and I didn't do serious. That wasn't my style. Robbie knew that – maybe that was why he'd never said anything. He was more of a "wife-and-three-kids" kind of guy. He'd told me so on several occasions. His mother used to read him these happily-ever-after stories when he was a kid, and Robbie still knew every single one by heart. There were always happy families, wife and husband and cheeky little kids. That's was Robbie's dream, but it made me want to retch.

Sure, Robbie was hot and all. And I guess we got on well, but I couldn't give him what he wanted. I shook my head. Elinor sighed.

"Then what you're doing is leading him on. It's cruel." She dried her hands, flinging the towel down on the side of the sink, and stormed out.

I sighed. Gripping the edge of the basin, I stared into my

reflection. A deranged-looking woman stared back at me, ears heavy with metal piercings, colourful tattoos snaking up her skinny arms, tiny breasts snuggled inside a Ramones shirt with the neck cut out, eyes wild with the revelation of her friend's feelings.

If Robbie looks at this and sees his future wife, then he's crazy. Elinor's right. He shouldn't marry me if he can't be honest about the reason.

But but but … if Robbie didn't marry me, I could kiss Primrose House goodbye. The idea sent a sharp pain right through my chest. I couldn't lose this chance. I just *couldn't*.

There has to be a way to get the house without hurting Robbie. There just has *to be—*

My phone buzzed. I swiped it from my pocket and brought it to my ear without even checking who was called. "What?" I barked into the phone.

"Bianca Sinclair, that's no way to address your mother."

Great. My whole body stiffened as her grating voice screeched in my ear. *Because this day couldn't get any worse.* "Yes, of course. Look, I'm very busy in the shop at the moment, so—"

Of course she wasn't listening. "You should begin your salutation with a polite address, then identify yourself, *then* ask how you can assist the caller. 'Good morning, Bianca speaking. How may I help you?' Really, Bianca, you've been taught better manners than this."

I rolled my eyes at the ceiling, the knot of tension already forming in my stomach. It had been months since we'd last spoken, and her first words to her only daughter were a lesson in manners. "I can't talk right now, Mother. It's loud here in the shop. What do you want?"

"What do I *want?* Is that the appropriate response for a daughter to give her mother while she's in mourning? Your father and I have barely heard from you these past three years, but I would have thought you'd call after a member of your own family is buried."

I rubbed my temple. Has it really been three blissful years of no contact before her call last week?

"You made it very clear I wasn't to attend the funeral. I felt faking interest in it would seen disingenuous."

"Bianca!" I held the phone away from ear as her screech echoed around the tiny bathroom.

"Kidding, Mother. I was going to call ..." I started to say, but she cut me off.

"The lawyer has been to speak to us about June's will. Now, I assume you'll be passing on her kind offer of Primrose House in order to continue your heathen lifestyle, and I'll need you to contact the lawyer with your statement so your father and I can continue probate—"

"I have no intention of giving you that house, Mother."

"You don't have any choice, dear. You cannot circumvent her conditions. She disapproved of your bohemian lifestyle just as much as I. I want to make it absolutely clear that one of your *women* will not be welcome in Primrose House. It is for bringing up a family, and you can't—"

"Two women who love each other and decide to adopt are just as much a family as we are," I explained through gritted teeth. "And I'd argue even more, since at least they have mutual respect, which you've never given me."

"Children do not demand respect from their parents. They must earn it, and not by deserting their families to live a life of debauchery—"

"You can stop the tirade right there, because I am getting married. To a man. With a penis. Your puritan fantasies will be fulfilled."

"Excuse me—"

"I've been seeing this guy, Robbie, and he's great." I peeked out the door again. There he was, still swinging his legs, deep in conversation with Caleb and Rosa. He caught my eye and gave me a nervous smile. Elinor's words twisted in my gut, but I ignored them. For once, I wasn't lying to my mother – Robbie *was* great. He'd be fine. I wasn't going to let *her* get her hands on the house. "We were going to get engaged anyway, but Grandmother's letter made the decision for us. Robbie asked me last night, and I said yes."

"Bianca Sinclair, this isn't how these things are done. We haven't even met this man of yours yet. He hasn't formally asked your father for his blessing. We don't even know what family he's from."

Even though she was scolding me, she couldn't hide the delight in her voice. She'd been waiting her whole life for the day I settled down and became a proper lady who liked men the way proper ladies did. She was so pleased it wasn't a woman, I imagined her doing a little dance right there in her drawing room.

"I've been living on my own since I was sixteen. I don't need Dad's permission for anything."

"Very well, I guess it's too late now. Oh, Bianca, I can't tell you how pleased I am. I've kept June's engagement ring for you, just in case this day ever came. It has a beautiful emerald that will set off your eyes. And my wedding dress, if you think you'd like to wear it—"

Sixteen feet of Indian lace and a bodice so heavy with beads it would need a whole roll of duct tape to secure it to my non-existent tits? No thank you. "I've already chosen my dress, and Robbie's given me a ring." A delicious deep-fried ring, but I didn't bother explaining that to her.

"Well, then. I expect you'll want the wedding soon, so you can get into your new home. I shall set up a meeting with Father

Henry. He'll be delighted to have another Sinclair wedding in the cathedral—"

"Robbie and I aren't very traditional. I don't think we'll be getting married in a church."

"You *must* get married in a church, Bianca. Marriage is a sacred bond that should be given in the house of the Lord."

I rolled my eyes as she railed through one of her religious sermons. She paused to take a breath and I managed to get a word in. "No church, and that's final. If it will make you feel better, I'll get one of my friends to dress up in a Cassock and—"

"Well," she gushed, switching to her tactic of ignoring anything I said that didn't fit her picture of how she wanted things to be. "You shall have to come over for dinner next week, we have a lot to do if we're to start plans for your wedding. I'll call the Devonshire Club, but I understand they're booked up years in advance. Perhaps Ryan Raynard may let us use his ballroom. After all, Raynard Hall was the original seat of our family."

I snorted. "Ryan turned his ballroom into a painting studio. That marble floor is covered with paint splatters. I did actually want to ask you ... I know June's will stipulated I couldn't move into the house until I was married, but I wondered, if I could perhaps have the wedding at Primrose House?"

"You mean, a garden wedding? A little unconventional, I suppose, but then, that is you, isn't it dear?"

I knew exactly what my mother was picturing – a marquee on the lawn, waiters in tails handing out little trays of disgusting raw fish things, a string quartet in the corner, four-hundred pretentious wankers I didn't even know talking about their horses and how England was going to the dogs because of all the immigrants. All things I abhorred.

But fine, she could think that if she wanted. Anything to get her off the phone. "Yes, that's it. And you don't need to worry about any of the details – I've hired a wedding planner. Her name is Willow and she did a royal wedding. So I have everything under control."

"But—"

"I'll send you a Facebook invite!" I cried, jammed my finger on the END CALL button, and tossing the phone against the wall.

Great. I'd hoped to keep the wedding a secret from my parents for as long as possible. They could throw a huge spanner in the works. They were the ones who had to believe in my marriage to Robbie, or they'd contest the will and get their hands on Primrose House.

My only chance of convincing them I was serious was to keep them as far away from Robbie as possible, but I guess that was wistful thinking. She'd never stop hounding me until I took Robbie to meet her. Yikes. Poor guy.

I glanced at him again. Elinor was cleaning his arm, ready to do his tattoo. He bit his lip, his eyes darting nervously to my gun sitting on top of my power unit. I didn't blame him; if I had tattoos that looked half as bad as his, I'd be nervous about being inked, too.

I grabbed the towel and dried my hands furiously. *Elinor's wrong. Robbie's totally fine. He'd have said something if he wasn't. Elinor's just overreacting because she doesn't like the fact that I'm getting married before her. Everyone doesn't understand that just because they've all paired off into happy couples, that doesn't have to be the way everyone else is.*

I'll talk to Robbie, lay everything out for him, make sure we're still on the same page. That's the right thing to do. I can still keep the house. It'll be totally fine.

Satisfied, I tossed down the towel, and pulled on another pair of sterile gloves. Time to ink some wolves.

4

ROBBIE

Ryan's butler, Simon, flung the huge oak door of Raynard Hall open before I'd even rung the bell. "You are late," he said.

"I ken."

I'd gone back to Marcus' after the tattoo session, my head spinning from contact with the needle. Only Bianca's presence at my elbow prevented me from passing out. I'd barely even glanced at the beautiful job she'd done, incorporating two of my crappy tattoos into a perfectly-shared howling wolf, turning my embarrassing ink into a work of art.

At Marcus', I ate an entire block of Cadbury chocolate and drank three beers and passed out on the couch. I woke up to find the house empty and a note from Marcus pinned to my chest.

LEFT ALREADY. TRIED TO WAKE YOU UP BUT YOU BIT ME. GET YOUR ARSE TO THE HALL ASAP.

Ten minutes later, I was standing on the ornate stone steps of Raynard Hall. Simon gave me a disapproving glare as he held the door open for me. I leapt inside and kicked off my boots, then followed Simon down the twisting halls to Ryan's personal drawing room. Even though I lived in the hall ever since I arrived in Crookshollow, I still got lost amongst the twisting hallways without Simon's guidance.

Ryan looked up when I entered. The men in our pack sat around the drawing room in Raynard Hall. The only women present were Alex – dressed in a paint-splattered shift – and Anna, Luke's wife, who was cradling their two-month-old son Colin in her lap.

"The other girls have gone to watch *America's Next Top Model* and eat the rest of my ice cream," Ryan said, his drawn expression clearly indicating what he thought of their activities. My stomach rumbled. Personally, a little ice cream wouldn't go amiss.

There was also one non-pack member present – a man I'd been taught to regard as an enemy my whole life, but now had to consider an ally. Irvine Baird sat next to Caleb, his long legs draped over the side of Ryan's couch like he owned the place. His eyes narrowed when they met mine, and I glared back. I reminded myself that Caleb trusted Irvine, and as my alpha, I had to trust Caleb. But it was hard.

Irvine's eyes burned into my back as I crossed the room. Clearly, his old animosity for the Maclean pack still bubbled close to the surface as well.

I searched the room for a seat, but all the chairs had been taken. No one seemed to notice my lack of a seat. In my father's pack, one of the women or the visiting wolf would have got up for me. Here, the pack dynamic was so different. These guys had come together as friends, and most of them had known each other for months or years before I showed up. They were all mated pairs, and Bianca and I were the only loners. We were afterthoughts, hangers-on. It didn't bother Bianca because she didn't give a shit what people thought of her.

It sure bothered me. I'd given up my identity, my whole life, to be here. No one seemed to even remember that. Apart from Marcus and Caleb and Bianca, no one had bothered to try to get to know me. No one asked about my previous life. They didn't invite me over for a beer or bring me free treats from their bakery. My arm stung from the needle. The dressing Bianca applied rustled under my shirt as I found myself a seat on the floor by the fire.

My head still spun from the tattooing earlier. It had taken every ounce of self-control I had to keep my cool while Bianca came at me with that needle. Even then, she kept telling me to relax and unclench my fists. The ordeal was over, but its consequences had only just begun: I was now permanently tied to this pack, and I wasn't sure they'd accepted me yet.

"Now that we're all here, I can tell you my news," Ryan said, dumping a stack of photocopies on the table. Everyone scrambled to grab one. There weren't enough copies, and I didn't get one. Alex held hers out so I could read over her shoulder – it showed scans of several illuminated manuscript pages. My eyes blurred over just gazing at the text. I guessed it was Latin, but I didn't really know.

No one else seemed fazed by the strange pages. Panic rose in my chest. Everyone in this room was intelligent. Most of them had university degrees or loving parents who taught them things like medieval history and multiplication tables and reading. I only had my mother, who was a learned lady herself but had to contend with my father's temper and vast mistrust of education. He never cared about Caleb, since he wasn't his son, so he got all the books, but Angus and I got our schooling in the brutal world of shifter crime, learning the ins and outs of the drug trade, and as a result, I knew exactly how to smuggle weapons but I could barely read English, and the idea of these guys finding out that I was illiterate made my stomach turn—

"Pay attention, Robbie." Alex jabbed my arm. I snapped my head up, trying to figure out what I'd missed.

"—spent the week down in London, sitting at a cramped desk in the British Museum Reading Room to see what I could dig up on the ring. Luckily, the librarians believed my story about research for a new painting, so I was able to see some rare manuscripts held in their archive, and they allowed me to bring these images back without any hassle. I've found something that has a direct bearing on our search for the Benedict Ring. Obviously, what I'm showing you now doesn't go beyond this room."

Ryan held up the first page. The black-and-white image depicted a cloaked woman with a pack of wolves. They walked together through a forest of tall, twisted trees. Slanted eyes glared at them from between the branches. Ryan jabbed his finger at the text flowing down the opposite page. "This is another retelling of the Benedict Ring legend. These accounts come from the monastery that was once part of Crooks Worthy. This story begins the same as the others, but it has an interesting divergence."

I stared at the page, pretending to be absorbed in the words as Ryan continued.

"According to the story we've all heard, about three hundred years ago a powerful witch had possession of the ring, and she was in love with the Lowe alpha. The witch hunters were closing in on Crookshollow, and she knew she'd soon be accused and killed. Rather than have the ring fall into the hands of the witch hunters, she gave the ring to her lover. According to the accounts in Clara's books, the alpha feared the power of the ring would corrupt his pack. So instead of using it, he hid the ring in the family caves, where it eventually fell out of memory." Ryan turned the page, showing another scan of medieval Latin. "Here, the monk who wrote down this legend tells a different story.

"In this retelling, the alpha wolf kept the ring on his person, and tried to use its power only for good. However, he had three sons who knew about the existence of the ring. They each had plans on how they would use the power, once they had their hands on it. They grew so hungry for the ring that it corrupted them, until they contemplated a terrible crime. The father, knowing that his sons were conspiring to kill him, and that they would use the ring for ill purposes, passed it to the Crooks Worthy monks for safekeeping. As predicted, the sons murdered their father, but they could not find the ring. Their crime was in vain."

Caleb's mouth pursed as he listened to Ryan's tale. He and Luke exchanged a pained glance. I understood why – as the only members of this pack who actually claimed Lowe blood, they didn't like to think of their ancestors committing patricide. I could relate to that. My family legacy was pretty wretched, too.

"The ring was trusted to one particular monk, a Brother Simon. Years turned into decades, and the ring was passed down from brother to brother, eventually landing in the hands of the monk who wrote this text, Brother Bartholomew."

"Does he say where it is?" Caleb leaned forward, glaring at the page as though if he thought hard enough he'd be able to decipher it. Which, probably he could. Caleb always had that easy intelligence that picked up facts and figures without a worry. A streak of jealousy coursed through me.

Ryan shook his head. "But the next page does."

Papers shuffled as everyone flipped the page over. I leaned over Alex's arm, straining to discern what I was looking at. It appeared to be a list of names in a ledger, with dates and other notations next to them.

"This is a ledger from the monastery, and it's written in Middle English, so those of us who can't read Latin will probably pick up a few of the words."

Not bloody likely, I fumed, staring at the squiggles on the page, willing them to form meaning.

"The monks kept track of the arrival of new brothers, dates the monks took their vows, and other details. Turns out, the monastery was closed in 1745 when the order decided to consolidate assets. The brothers were sent to other monasteries. Some, like Brother Bartholomew, left the order altogether."

Ryan indicated everyone should flip to the next page.

"Robbie, could you not lean your chin on my thigh," Alex said, as she smoothed out the new image. "It's quite sharp."

"Oh, sorry." I scooted back, my face flushing with heat. Ryan shot me a dirty look before continuing.

"This is a deed showing some land sold in Crookshollow. Quite a lot of land, in fact – several large farms. It looks like our monk took the name Bartholomew Winthorpe, and married himself into the nobility. His wife came with this land."

"That Lothario," Irvine smirked.

"Yeah, I can't believe it, either. Why would a noble woman want to marry a monk? But it's right here in the records. Now, obviously this land has been divided up since then. It's practically the whole town, and it even incorporates Raynard Hall and most of its original holdings. Back then, this family would have been one of the most powerful landowners in the county. I've had a look into Raynard Hall's records, but unfortunately many of them were destroyed by my grandfather, so we don't have much to go on there. It's my belief that we should continue our search for the ring in their home and property, if we can identify them."

"You reckon the monk took the ring with him, and passed it down through his new family?" Cole asked.

"Look at that map. This family was pretty damn powerful back in the day. That could have been a result of the ring's power."

"It's definitely worth looking into," Anna said, holding baby Colin over her shoulder and rubbing his back so he burped. "If the Winthorpes are as powerful as you say, they won't be difficult to locate. I can help with the local research. I've done plenty of this type of work for my degree."

"Aren't we getting ahead of ourselves? How do we know this story is even true?" Irvine demanded.

"We don't. They could both be true, or neither of them," Ryan said. "That's the problem with treasure hunting from these kind of sources. But we have to try."

"It's better than bashing through those muddy tunnels," Marcus piped up.

The room buzzed with excitement as everyone started talking at once. An idea started to form in my head. Finding the Benedict Ring was the most important task for the pack right now. Caleb may have *said* he accepted me, but that didn't mean the pack had, not yet. If I could find out where the ring was, maybe even lay hands on it first, then I'd instantly be accepted. Everyone would treat me the way they treated everyone else. They'd be my real family.

"I want to help," I said.

No one acknowledged me. Ryan, Irvine, Anna, and Caleb were all shouting over each other. Alex shuffled through the papers, frowning at the ancient images. Eric and Cole bent their heads together, their lips moving through rapid discussion.

I stood up, cleared my throat, and spoke again, "I want to help."

The room fell silent. Heads rolled toward me, eyes focusing on me.

"I'd like to volunteer to help with the research," I said, fixing my gaze on Caleb. "I really want to help find the ring."

"Um ... Robbie. Why is this so important to you?" Alex asked, her words stinging.

"Yeah." Irvine's eyes narrowed. "Why do you care so much about the ring?"

"Because I'm part of this pack," I said, glaring at Irvine. "You guys took me away from the Macleans and all the shit that was going on there. You trusted someone from the outside with this huge secret. I want to show you I'm worthy of that trust. If the ring is important to you, then I will find it."

"Surely Anna would be a better choice?" Alex asked. "She's doing her masters, so she knows how to conduct historical research. Robbie, I don't mean to sound like a bitch, but have you even been in a library before?"

Her words weren't meant to be cruel, but they made a deep flush creep up my back and flood my face. I kept my head down, hoping no one had noticed it. "Of course I have. It's the place with all the books, right? Anna and I could work together. I can do all the grunt work, and she can be the one pointing me in the right direction."

"That actually would be quite good," Anna piped up, bouncing baby Colin on her knee. "I can't exactly work for hours in the library with this little guy."

Caleb sighed. "Fine. Robbie, I'm putting you in charge of leading the local investigation."

"But—" Luke started, but Caleb held up his hand.

"Please use the expertise around you. Anna will be of invaluable help, and Ryan would probably also be useful, as he's done all the London research. I expect daily updates." His eyes met mine. "Don't disappoint me."

I rubbed my arm, where the sting of my tattoo still itched my skin. "I won't."

5

BIANCA

"Down there." I jabbed my finger at the windshield. "Turn left!"

Obediently, Robbie yanked the wheel hard around, and we managed to swing into the drive without hitting the ornate iron gate. Robbie groaned as the Lada's wing mirror clipped the stone gate post, and clattered to the ground.

"Flippin' wonderful," he moaned as the back wheel crunched over the mirror.

"Hey, I think it's an improvement. Gives you more manoeuvring room without that ugly thing sticking at the side of the car."

"All the people in this car who *dinnae* drive can shut up now."

Grinning, I slapped him on the shoulder. "I'll buy you a new one, husband. It's the least I can do."

"Aye, damn right."

I stared out the window, in awe of this beautiful property that would soon be mine. A wrought-iron arch over the gate depicted the house's name: PRIMROSE HOUSE. Silver birch branches scraped along the roof of the car. The trees tangled together over our heads, creating a tunnel of foliage so dense and knotted, I couldn't see anything beyond the bend in the drive ahead. A few hazels mixed in with the birch, their nuts littering the ditch on either side of the drive. I imagined sculptures hidden in the trees, Chinese lanterns strung from the branches, leading the way to an artistic sanctuary. We turned the corner, and I gasped.

Primrose House rose up in front of us; a grand old lady, bedecked in the lace of early Victorian grandeur. A wide porch circled half the house, white lattice details framing the house like a delicate lace petticoat. The roof jutted out at stark angles, punctuated by grand dormer windows. The turret dominated the front facade, leading my eye up to that gorgeous hidden balcony. Immaculate boxed gardens lined a pebble path leading up to the sweeping steps.

"Wow," Robbie said, his gaze leaping across the house before focusing on the turret.

"Yeah." I grinned, leaping out of the car before it came to a complete stop.

Last time I'd been inside this house, I was fifteen. My mother and I weren't speaking (which wasn't unusual), but she forced me into the car for our monthly visit with Grandmother June. June started the evening by telling me I was to take my nose ring off at the table, then refusing to allow me to eat after I removed the stud but replaced it with an enormous spike. I stormed out of the gate, called my then-girlfriend Sally-Sandy-Sarah-something to come pick me up, and spent the rest of the night smoking weed and snogging up at the Witches Cemetery. Mother kicked me out a few weeks later and I hadn't spoken to my grandmother since.

To think that now I was about to step inside Primrose House again, to remove from it the stain of her oppressive tyranny, and give it the life it *really* deserved.

I couldn't wait to get my hands on this place, strip off all the stuffy English details, and fill it with art and eccentric people. *The first thing to go will be that hideous gazebo,* my mind whirled, as I stood on the steps and gazed out across the garden at the flimsy wooden construction where the garden met the edge of Crookshollow Forest. *In its place, we'll put in a fire pit, and maybe an outdoor natural spa pool...*

June's lawyer was already waiting for us on the porch, her thin mouth frowning at her watch as I jogged over to her. "You were supposed to be here thirteen minutes ago," she snapped. "I'll be billing you for this extra time."

I rolled my eyes. Elinor was exactly the same, always ridiculously punctual and chastising anyone for being late. I guess it came from having to bill time in three-minute increments.

Not even the threat of additional legal fees could destroy my mood today. I beamed as the lawyer tossed the keys into my hand. My stomach fluttering with excitement, I bounded up to the door and shoved the key into the lock.

The key turned. I pushed the heavy mahogany door open, revealing the familiar front hall. Drab floral wallpaper covered every wall, hidden in places by neat rows of dreary paintings of the English countryside. My Docs sank into a deep Persian rug. At the end of the hall, beside the door leading to the rest of the house, a grandfather clock clacked, the only noise in that silent home.

The *clack clack clack* of the clock took me back. Suddenly, I wasn't 23-year-old Bianca anymore, I was six years old, tugging desperately on my mother's skirt, trying to get her to go back to the car so we could go home.

"No, Bianca." Mother prised my fingers off the hem of her skirt, dusting down my itchy frock and using the corner of her handkerchief to wipe dirt off my face. "You're going to sit in that house and behave yourself."

"But I don' wanna!" I plonked myself down on the porch steps, staring into that dark hallway like it was the mouth of hell. "I don wanna see mean lady."

Six-year-old me wasn't exaggerating. Grandmother June was one mean octogenarian – a fairy-tale wicked witch in the flesh, who made my mother look like a saint of the first order. June believed children should be seen and not heard.

Ideally, if she couldn't see us either, I think she'd have been happier. She would make my brother and I sit straight-backed on the uncomfortable sofa, not fiddle, not say anything for hours. She had no toys in the house, unless you counted her collection of porcelain dolls in one of the bedrooms upstairs that we weren't allowed to touch. For hours we'd sit there, dying of boredom, while she lectured our mother on manners, our schooling, my marriage prospects, the family holdings, and all manner of dull dull dull topics until my head felt like it was going to explode.

Sometimes, she babysat us while Mother and Father went to functions down in London. I dreaded those weekends. June would lecture us for hours on Bible stories and force us to memorise Psalms, rapping our knuckles with her walking stick when we messed up. She'd send us to bed with empty stomachs and stories about the fires of hell, then get us up at six in the morning for church service, and force us to eat spoonfuls of cod liver oil before every meal. And the food ... my stomach turned at the memory of piles of over-boiled cabbage and tough roast beef. And while all this torture was going on, that grandfather clock *clack-clack-clacked* in the background.

I stepped back, my blood running cold. Stale air wafted across my nostrils. Age and furniture polish and un-aired rooms, mixed with notes of June's gardenia perfume. So much hatred in this house, so many bad memories. Had they infected it some-how, seeped into the walls, ready to taint my artistic vision?

A warm hand fell on my shoulder. Robbie's face appeared out of the corner of my eyes, his kind eyes wide with concern. "You okay? You look a little freaked out."

I gave him a small smile. "I'll be fine. I was just remembering coming here as a kid."

"It wasn't a trip to the sweet shop, right?"

"Not even close. I'll tell you all about it one day, when I'm really, really drunk. Come on." I placed my hand over his and squeezed it. A strange electric pulse ran down my arm. That had been happening a lot lately. *It's just your nerves playing tricks on you.* "Let's go see our marital home."

Robbie grinned. I screamed with glee as he swept my legs out from under me, lifting me into his arms. "Not so fast. We need to do this properly. My future-wife should be carried over the threshold. Otherwise, our whole marriage is cursed. My mother told me so."

I burst out laughing. Robbie approached the door, but with my legs dangling over his arm, I was too wide to fit through. He frowned. Instead of simply turning himself sideways, he tried to tip me up, dipping my head down toward the verandah. I screamed as I grabbed at his neck to hold on, my shrieks dissolving into laughter.

"I'm billing you for these shenanigans," the lawyer snapped. This only made us laugh harder.

Finally, Robbie managed to squeeze me through. He carried me across the entrance hall and plopped me down at the base of the stairs. From here, I could see through into the formal dining room to the left of the front door, and the ladies drawing room on the right. The dining table was set with my grandmother's fine china, the crisp white tablecloth perfectly square, the napkins neatly folded at each place, and all the silver out on the sideboard. At any moment, I expected her to appear at the door like an apparition, scolding me that if I couldn't sit quietly at the table like a proper lady, I could go to bed again without any dinner.

I'm going to order a feast of takeaways to eat at your table, I thought gleefully, my stomach rumbling just thinking about it. Indian food, Turkish kebabs, sushi … all the ethnic food you refused to eat because you couldn't abide those horrible foreigners on English soil. I'm going to drink a beer straight from the bottle, without a coaster, and there's nothing you can do about it.

"This place is insane." Robbie touched one of the dining chairs as he stared up at the high beamed ceiling, his eyes bugging out of his head as he took in the crystal chandeliers, the heavy mahogany furniture, and the grim portraits of long-dead relatives that crowded the walls.

I crossed the hall and stepped into the drawing room, my combat boots making a loud *clap clap clap* as they left the rug and hit the oak floor. I ran my hands along the high back of the Chesterfield sofa. Two matching chairs on either end faced inward, all the furniture turned away from the tall windows obscured behind thick drapes. Behind the settee, in front of the marble fireplace, the tea table was set out with June's Royal Doulton tea service – a crocheted doily lining every plate. More drab portraits and boring British pastoral paintings adorned with walls. There wasn't a television in sight, nor a used coffee-mug on the table, nor even a book lying half-read on the chair arm.

The whole place remained frozen, a time-capsule of my childhood terror. My grandmother lived every day in this house, but to look at it now, it appeared as though she'd never lived at all. It was a mausoleum to her stupid English snobbery, her need to cling to some glorious colonial past that had never really existed at all.

That's all about to change.

As I glanced around, the possibilities whirled through my

head. I imagined the chairs gone, replaced by funky Scandinavian furniture and bright throws. I pictured the walls painted white, hung with artwork, and the dark mahogany bookshelf in the corner bursting with books about art and tattoos and really filthy romance novels. I pictured a little bar in the corner, and a stack of board games under the coffee table, and people in bright clothing filling the space with fun and laughter and possibilities. I pictured a bra hanging from the crystal chandelier after an absinthe-fuelled night of debauchery with some divine international artist ...

At the back of the sitting room, a low arch led into the dark-panelled study, with its gleaming marble fireplace and window seat. Leather-bound books that were never allowed to be opened and priceless ceramic vases lined the shelves on either side of the fireplace. My grandmother had barely used this room – it was a "male" domain and when Grandfather George died, she kept it only as a shrine to his maleness. The room even smelled like him – stale tobacco smoke and racism.

A door in the living room led into the hallway. Directly behind the entrance hall was the door to the ballroom – my favourite room in the whole house. I'd only been allowed inside once, and even then I wasn't to touch anything. June never held a single ball or event, which was a glorious waste of owning a ballroom in the first place. I planned on remedying that as a matter of great urgency. Excitement fluttered in my chest as I shoved the door open.

Darkness clung to the vast room, shrouding its features in gloom. A damp smell flooded the hall. I coughed as I entered, stumbling along the back wall, pulling open the curtains and flinging open the tall windows to allow fresh air and afternoon sun to permeate the space.

And what a space it was! Here, the high-beamed ceiling was painted white, accentuating the vastness of the room. Striped wallpaper adorned the walls above the wood panelling, marred only by thick cobwebs hanging from the corners and dangling from the chandeliers. The delicate carvings on the marble fireplace on the opposite wall were completely obscured by a thick layer of dust.

"Wow." Robbie spun in a circle, his eyes wide as he took in the place. "This is dead pure brilliant, it is. This room wouldnae be out of place at Raynard Hall. How awesome is it that it's yours?"

"I know!" I jumped into his arms and he spun me so my feet flew out in a wide circle. The room was so big there wasn't any danger of my feet hitting the walls.

Robbie set me down. Exhilarated, I raced into the hall, eager to check out the rest of the house and delve into the corners I'd never been allowed in before. "Come on," I yelled to Robbie. "I want to show you something awesome."

He followed me down the hall into the kitchen. The kitchen was in a separate building – built of brick instead of wood to make it more fire resistant – and connected to the main house by a dark corridor. An old meat store and milk room were accessible by a short garden path. I pointed them out to Robbie through the window.

"This place is brilliant," Robbie said, walking over to inspect the stove.

"You're telling me." I moved around the table in awe. I'd been in this room once or twice before, but only when I'd wriggled out of my mother's grasp and chased my brother in here. My grandmother, who had a live-in maid to clean and cook her meals to torment with cruel remarks about her Romanian heritage, didn't believe women "of our breeding" should set foot in the kitchen. From what I remember of the kitchen, it had been right out of the Victorian era, complete with an old wood-fired Aga.

Now, it was completely different. This must be the only room in the whole house my grandmother had modernised – a gleaming gas Aga replacing the old wood-fired model, gleaming modern surfaces polished to a high shine. I flung open the door to the butler's pantry, hoping what I wanted to show Robbie was still there.

"Ah, hah!" New shelves lined the walls of the pantry, still stacked with cans and cartons. But in the back corner, the outline of a narrow door, with only a thumbhole for a handle, could be seen against the wood.

"What is it?"

"A secret passage." I tugged the door open and showed Robbie the staircase inside. "The servants used to use it to move between this floor and their attic bedrooms without using the first floor hall or main staircase. In the early days, the family had a lot of guests, and they didn't want them to accidentally run into a maid during their time in the house."

"Did your grandmother ken this?"

"Oh sure. June would sometimes let my brother play in here," I said, remembering his squeals of delight from my place at the tea table. "But never me. Girls shouldn't run inside."

Robbie swept a hand toward the staircase. "What she don't ken ..."

Grinning and giddy with mischief, I leapt up the stairs two at a time, excited to see where they led. At the top of the stairs, a small door was bolted shut from the inside, I guessed so the lady of the house could lock the maids in the attic as punishment.

It took a bit of wiggling to lift the bolt, but finally I shoved the door open, and crawled into the small, dark space.

The walls sloped steeply inward, and were lined with thick planks of rough wood. It took me a few moments to realise I was in the roof of the house. A tiny dormer window at the end of the room, thick with dust, let in a faint stream of light across a small brass bed, a narrow stool and a tiny wooden trunk.

"What is this place?" Robbie asked, as he twisted his shoulders to fit through the tiny gap, and collapsed into the room.

I sneezed into my hands as clouds of thick dust, disturbed by our presence, curled around us like smoke machines at a EDM gig.

"These were the servants' rooms," I said. I crossed the room to where there was another low door. Sure enough, it emerged onto a narrow hallway, the sloping roof on the other side creating a space so small you'd have to crawl through it. I noticed two more openings further along the hallway. "There are three rooms up here. Isn't this insane? They're kind of creepy, like something out of a horror film."

"I think it's cosy," Robbie crossed the room to the window, staring down at the back garden. "Did people really live up here?"

"Of course, although not while I was alive," I said. "When my mum was growing up, I think she said her nanny lived up here. She was also the family cook. June had a cook and cleaner, too, but I think she had one of the first floor bedrooms. You can't ask someone to live in the attic these days."

"This is all so ... *Downton Abbey*."

"Tell me about it. And remind me to mock you for watching *Downton Abbey*."

"Alex loves it. I used to watch when I lived at the Hall."

"When you live with me, you can watch whatever you want." I ducked down and crept out into the hall, peeking into the other two bedrooms. At the end of the hallway, I followed another narrow staircase down to the rear of the first-floor landing, hidden around a corner so it couldn't be seen from the main staircase. The narrow boards creaked beneath my feet as I shuffled down backwards to keep my balance.

Robbie followed me down. He started throwing open doors, peering in at the dark bedrooms, his face wrinkling. "Every one of these is more hideous than the last."

"Gee, Gok, I didn't know you were so into interiors."

Robbie shrugged. "I've never been inside a house like this before."

"Never?"

"Well, Raynard Hall, but Alex and Ryan have done so much redecorating that place doesn't really compare. This house seems ... frozen in time."

"There are literally hundreds of frozen houses like this all over the country. You seriously never went to see a National Trust house when you were in school?"

"I didn't go to school."

"What?" How could he not have gone to school? Wasn't that illegal? "You never told me that."

Robbie stepped into a garish pink bedroom, a weird expression on his face. He fingered the edge of a lace curtain. "Angus, Caleb and I were all educated – if you could call it that – in the pack. Our mother taught us to read and write and do basic maths. My father didn't place much value on learning, so he gave us no assistance. We had no resources, no field trips, no books apart from the pack ledger. None of us took our O levels."

"Yikes." That was horrible. Robbie didn't talk much about his childhood in the pack. From what little he'd said, I gathered it was pretty tough. But not even going to school? I placed my hand on his shoulder, but he shrugged it off.

"I don't want your pity, Bianca. Especially not today. Forget I said anything. Focus on the house." He rapped a mahogany door with his knuckles, the sound like a gunshot through the hall. "This house may have some hideous wallpaper, but I can see the potential – everything you imagine for this place. It's gonna be a lot of work, though."

"You have no idea." I pulled him down the hall. "Just wait until you see the master bedroom."

At the end of the hall, a short staircase led up to a secondary landing, where a pale blue chaise lounge stretched beneath a bay window. This was another part of the house I'd only ever seen once, and only because I'd snuck up here one night when I was supposed to be sleeping. As I headed up the final mahogany staircase toward the thick door leading to the room beyond, I hoped it was as ghastly as I remembered it.

I threw the door open, excitement clenched in my gut. *Yes.* It was *exactly* as I remembered.

From beside me, Robbie's eyes widened as he took in the spectacle. Roses covered every surface of the turret bedroom, from the garish rose wallpaper to the roses splashed across the carpet and the rose duvet covers and pillows. Even the dresser mirror had roses carved into the frame. I crossed the room and drew back the rose drapes, revealing the door that led out onto the secret balcony, hiding in the slope of the roof.

"What do you think?" I grinned, stepping onto the balcony and throwing my arms wide.

"It's ..." Robbie screwed his face up.

"Yes?"

"I have no words."

"Try me."

"It's right pure brilliant, if you like roses."

I snorted. "I'm going to have terrible nightmares of roses crawling out of the walls to strangle me in my sleep."

"Don't be daft. All it needs is a little paint, a match, some lighter fluid ... and it'll be perfect for us."

My head snapped up as his words registered. When I looked at his eyes, something there made me start.

"Robbie, you remember this is a fake marriage, right? We're not sharing a bedroom."

"Aye, right. Of course I ken." A shadow passed over his face, but then he smiled again. "I absolutely *do not* want this room."

"Good. You have your pick of the other rooms on this floor. Now get out here and look at my balcony."

After a short walk around my balcony, we toured the rest of the rooms on the first floor. Robbie's face twisted with terror as he took in the froufrou wallpaper, frilly valances, and lacy curtains. "I think I'll take the attic bedroom," he said. "The one with the secret passage down to the kitchen."

"The servant's' room? You can't. Robbie, that's in the attic. It'll be freezing up there. And the bed's tiny. You are ... not tiny. You'll hardly have any room for your stuff."

"I know. I just ... I think I'll feel more comfortable there. I can't really deal with all this ... rich people guff. Besides, I have direct access to the kitchen for midnight snacks. I cannae pass that up."

"If you're sure ..."

"Aye, I'm sure."

Downstairs, the lawyer waited in the hall, tapping her foot impatiently on the hardwood floor in time with the grandfather clock. "Sorry," I said, in a voice that didn't contain an ounce of remorse. "We got lost in the attic. What else do you need from me?"

"I just need you to sign these papers," she said irritably, waving the stack under my nose. "Your mother has given you permission to take the keys and enter the house to make any necessary preparations and to store your chattels. As soon as the marriage is officially registered, you can move in."

I bent down to sign the papers. A scrawl of my signature, and it was done. Primrose House was mine, pending our marriage in just thirty days time. I shoved the papers into the lawyer's arms, and she left in a hurry, leaving Robbie and I to stare at each other across that huge, empty entrance hall. Robbie took my hand and squeezed it.

"We going to do this, and it's going to be amazing." he said, grinning that beautiful smile at me.

I grinned back, but this time, my smile was forced. As I stared into his eyes, all I could think about was that sparse attic room and the way his face had contorted as he'd told me that he'd never been to school.

I'd never realised before that there was so much about Robbie I didn't know. *What you're doing is cruel.* Elinor's words drummed against my skull. But this wasn't supposed to be about Robbie, it was about the art house. It was about making my dream come true, and creating a safe place where people like me and Robbie could come when they didn't have family who supported them. I should have been ecstatic, so why was my stomach flipping with nerves?

6

———

ROBBIE

With the papers signed, it was time to celebrate. Down in the kitchen, Bianca ordered a stack of Indian food, and messaged Elinor and Eric to come and join us for a celebratory dinner. While she bustled around the living room, trying to make her grandmother's stuffy furnishing somehow comfortable, I went upstairs to check out the attic again.

From the moment I'd stepped inside it, the attic room drew me in. The narrow brass bed, the tiny dormer window, the simple wooden chest coated with decades of dust ... all of it so different from the ornate furniture crowding the rest of the house. I sat on the bed and gazed out the tiny window. It looked out over the back of the house. Neat rows of box hedges extended across a flat garden, extending down a steep set of steps and retaining walls toward the canopy of the forest. The towering trees shaded most of the beds, where squat bushes and sickly-flowers suffered under their cloying presence. The only real colour came from the canopy of purple primrose flowers spreading out from between the trunks, creeping over the edge of the lawn, like a purple army marching toward the house.

Am I making a big mistake?

Being here at Primrose House with Bianca, I could *see* her vision, as clear as if she'd placed a photograph in front of my eyes. She was a great shining star, a woman with purpose and creativity and spark. Under her watch, this house would be an amazing place, a hub of artistic activity.

What was I? Nothing – a lowly wolf from the wrong side of the tracks, an outcast even among the pack that had chosen me, a stupid man who could barely read or write. I wanted Bianca so bad, but I knew now more than ever that I could never have her. I wasn't worthy of her.

That's why I'd taken the attic room. I would marry Bianca, because it would make her dream come true, but I needed to remember who I was, and what my place here was. I ran my fingers along the dusty window frame, looking down at the forest that would shroud me during the full moon. At least here, I would be near to the wildest place in Crookshollow, the only place I probably really belonged.

My hand trailed across the wall, leaving a smudge in the dust. I lifted the lid of the wooden chest, coughing as a cloud of dust wafted across my face. Inside, there were a few threadbare wool blankets, riddled with holes, a woman's wool coat and hat, a linen apron, and, nestled right at the bottom, a book.

I picked the book up in my hands, staring at the words in the hope they would suddenly reveal their meaning. I sounded out the letters, the way my mother had taught me. "Fa-fa-fairy ..." I muttered, until I figured out it was a book of fairy tales. I held the book up to my face, sniffing the musty paper. A flash of memory overcame me. A similar book, held in my mother's hands, as she stroked my fur and read to me in a harsh whisper, as quiet as possible so my father wouldn't catch her. We huddled together in a forest clearing far from the pack's territory, open to the cold moon. The story was of a princess trapped in a tower, waiting for her prince to rescue her. I remembered that as much as I wanted to be the prince, riding in to save the day, I knew I had more in common with the princess. I was trapped, too.

I stroked the cover of the book, imagining the girl who lived in this room reading these stories by candlelight, staring out the tiny window, wondering if her prince would come to rescue her. I was here now, but I was still no prince. I'm just as trapped as always.

Even though I'd never know any of the maids or servants, I had more in common with the women who'd lived in this room than I did with any of the people in my life right now. Even Bianca. We were all young and uneducated, with few options for the future other than to keep working hard and hoping life had a little joy in it.

I set down the book, and continued my investigation of the room. My fingers brushed a crack in the wooden wall. A whiff of cool air hit my palm. I bent down to investigate, and realised it wasn't just a panel in the wood. It was another hidden door.

I took the woollen blanket from the bed. A cloud of dust puffed around me as I balled it up around my hand and used it to wipe away the thick layer of dust and cobwebs. My fingers poked through moth-holes as bits of the blanket fluttered away. I cleaned along the crack, revealing a large rectangle. A faint draft emanated from the behind the crack. The surface was completely smooth – there was no handle or finger hole to open it.

There might be a spring. I pressed my fingers all round the edges, searching for some pliant part of the wood. In the top right corner, I hit the jackpot – the wood shifted under my fingers, and a soft click echoed through the tiny room. A gap appeared in the right of the door, swinging inward to reveal a small set of shelves crowded with objects.

A secret cupboard. This house sure was dead pure brilliant.

I reached inside and pulled some of the objects out into the light. They were covered with a thick layer of dust, and the musty smell suggested they hadn't been disturbed for many years. The top shelf held a few small pieces of silver – a miniature chalice, a sugar bowl, a few mismatched spoons. The kinds of objects a servant might pilfer from her masters to sell off for some quick cash. There was some jewellery too – faceted gems glinting even through the layers of dust.

From the bottom shelf, I lifted a leather-bound book, wrapped in a thin leather strap. I took it down, holding it gingerly as I wiped the dust from the cover. A date embossed in gold on the cover read, "1836."

Gingerly, I sat down on the bed, and opened the book. It was a scrapbook, with fabric swatches and photographs and thin lines of journalling written with exquisite loopy script. I'd never in a million years be able to read it. Two words were lettered on the first page. After ten minutes of squinting and sounding out aloud, I figured out they were the name, "Silvia Sinclair." Bianca's family name. It must be the girl who owned the book. But why would one of the family's scrapbooks be up here in the attic?

A photograph on the second page caught my eye. A severe-looking girl of maybe sixteen posed without smiling, her black gown buttoned right up under her chin. She clasped her hands in front of her chest. On her finger, she wore a large, garish ring. A family heirloom, I didn't doubt.

It made me think of the Benedict Ring. It was now my job to find it. I *needed* to find it. I had to prove to Caleb and Luke and all the others that I could be trusted. The rest of the pack had so much history together – they'd helped each other through all kinds of situations. But I was new, and until a few months ago, Caleb considered me his enemy. Irvine still did.

I had to make sure my position was well established before

the pack put their plan to reveal shifter existence into action. If the pack kicked me out, I'd never be able to come back to Crook-shollow, and I'd never see Bianca again.

That was not an option. All I had to do was follow the clues to find the ring. Anna would tell me where to find the documents. She'd do the difficult stuff. I'd just have to read titles and search through shelves. It might take me a long time to figure out the words, and I probably didn't know what they all meant, but that's what dictionaries were for. How hard could it be?

"Robbie!" Bianca's voice called up the staircase. "Where are you? The food's here!"

"Coming!" Folding the photo album under my arm, I shut the hidden door again, clicking it into place. I couldn't do much about replacing the dust, but I wanted to leave it for Bianca to decide what to do with. It was her house, after all, and her treasure.

"Bianca," I cried as I burst into the living room, holding the book up. "You won't believe what I've found."

THE GIRLS PAWED over the scrapbook while they ate their curry. Eric and I sat opposite them, on either end of the couch, politely eating our dinner – butter chicken for me, some weird spicy beef thing for him – without speaking.

Eric intimidated me. He stood nearly six-feet tall. Dark, gleaming black hair streamed down his back. He dressed like a Victorian dandy in frock coats and cravats in lush fabrics. He had money, fame, talent. He read books with unpronounceable titles, and could recite poetry on command. He had nothing to say to an uneducated, uncouth wolf like me.

"This is so cool," Elinor said, her fingers carefully turning the pages. "It's a snapshot into your great-great-grandmother's life."

"That's your great-great-grandmother?" Eric asked.

"Yeah." Bianca grinned. "I don't know much about her, but my mother made me memorise five generations of our family tree as a child. That shit is burned into my brain."

"I wonder why the book was in the attic," I said. "If she was part of the family, she wouldn't ever go upstairs."

"I wonder, too. You said there were other things in the secret cupboard?" Bianca tossed her empty curry container down on the table. She leaned back in the chair, her combat boots resting on the edge of the fancy table, beer gripped in her hand. She burped. I loved the fact that even in the presence of a celebrity like Eric, Bianca was comfortable enough to be completely herself.

"Yeah, some jewellery and silver. I wondered if a maid who lived in the attic room might've stolen them. They were all quite small objects, easy to slip into pockets ..."

My voice trailed off as I noticed Elinor giving me an odd look, a look that said, "How come you know so much about robbery?" My face flushed, and I stared down at my hands, not wanting the conversation to shift towards my past.

"Odd that this maid left those behind, or that she'd have stolen this book. It might be sentimental to Silvia, but it wouldn't be valuable." Bianca flipped another page. "Silvia mentions a maid here."

She started to read. "'Mother is angry with Hattie again, because she was teaching me her tarot cards. I don't understand what concerns Mother so. The cards are a harmless game, another of Hattie's fancies. But I do so enjoy her games and stories, much more than that hideous Martha and all her prim and proper lessons. Mother says Hattie will not be long with us. I hope she does not force Hattie away. She has been saving money to rescue her brother, who is locked up in Bedlam. If she cannot find work then she will not be able to pay the fee to free him.'"

"Does it say anything else?"

Bianca turned another few pages. "Yes. here. The writing is really messy, and she's pushed her nib really hard. 'I am so angry! Mama and Hattie had a terrible row. Mama said Hattie has been stealing from us, but from the way she was shouting ... I do not believe that was the true reason at all. I believe she has caught us.' Caught them doing what?"

"You've missed a ton of entries; it's probably back there somewhere." Elinor jabbed the page. "It looks like Hattie might be our thief. Look at this one. 'I'm weeping as I write this, my tears smudging the ink. There's been a terrible accident. Mother and Father went away for the night. Hattie and I were playing cards in the drawing room, when there was a rapping on the window. Hattie opened the window, and there was Ben, the gardener's son. Hattie helped him to climb in the window. I couldn't believe it. Ben came and played cards with us, and he and Hattie drank some of Daddy's brandy, and they danced silly dances while I played the piano for them. Hattie pretended to propose to him with a ring of Mama's. It was so silly. Of course woman don't propose. It was the most fun I've ever had in my entire life.

"'I went to bed at ten, but I could hear Hattie and Ben laughing downstairs. Then, there was a sudden commotion. The front door slammed. Mama's voice boomed through the house, reaching my ears even through the thick walls. She screamed that Hattie had sinned in her house, and she'd no longer be welcome within these walls. Hattie was screaming and crying, and I think Mama was dragging her by her hair because Ben was also crying out for her to stop. Then there was this horrible crash, and Mama started to scream.

"'I ran down the stairs and found Mama and Father and Ben on the front steps. Ben wore only his breeches, and the pale skin of his chest glowed under the moonlight. Father was trying to comfort Mama, who was hysterical. I squeezed past them. Ben tried to drag me back, but I saw her ... Hattie, my beautiful Hattie, naked apart from my Mama's mink coat. She lay crumpled at the foot of the steps, her eyes like glass beads, her neck bent at a horrid angle.'"

"Whoah," Eric said. "That's intense."

"I wonder what happened next?" Elinor asked.

"What do you mean?"

"Well, Hattie died because she fell down the steps. But was it an accident? Or did the mother push her? I wonder if there's any records of a trial."

"I'm going to the library tomorrow," I said. "Anna's going to help me try and find more information on the Benedict Ring. I'll have a look for information about Hattie and Silvia, too."

"That'd be awesome, thanks Robbie." Bianca grinned. "I can't wait to learn more about them."

Elinor shut the book, and handed it to Bianca. "If Hattie was the one who stole the silver, this would explain why it was never found. I bet the family didn't know about the hidden doorway. The secret died with her."

"Then how did the scrapbook end up in there?" Eric asked, wiping the edges of his mouth with a napkin.

"We have to see this secret hideaway." Bianca leapt up, her eyes sparkling. Eric reached out and saved a takeout container before it toppled over the edge of the table.

I led them all up to the attic and showed them the little hidden cupboard. Bianca took out the objects and spread them out on the bed, her eyes alight with joy. "I love this," she breathed, holding the little silver teaspoons in her hand. "I love that this house has hidden secrets. I hope we find more."

"What will you do with these?" Elinor held up the silver sugar bowl.

"I'm not sure just yet. I think we'll leave them up here for now." Bianca's face lit up. "I know. We should hold a seance."

"No, you're joking." Elinor looked disgusted.

"I'm not. Maybe the spirit of Hattie still haunts the attic. She can tell us all sorts of fun things about what used to go on in this house. Here, help me push the bed to one side."

"I'm not sure this is a good idea," Eric said, twisting a strand of his perfect hair. I didn't blame him. He had already been to the spirit world once, and very nearly didn't return.

"Hey, you used to be a ghost. Wouldn't you have liked it if people could talk to you? Besides, I saved your arse from being a permanent poltergeist. You owe me one. "

"You'll never let me forget that, will you?"

Downstairs, Bianca found a piece of chalk down in the kitchen drawer, as well as some beeswax candles in elaborate silver holders. She piled the candles into my hands and made me bring them upstairs. Back in the attic, she made me and Eric shove the bed against the wall, and drew a series of letters in a semicircle on the floorboards. She took the largest goblet from Hattie's hoard and flipped it upside down, placing it in the centre.

"How much do you know about this stuff?" Elinor asked, her forehead creased.

"Only what I've seen on TV." Bianca crouched on the outside of the circle. "Let's do this."

Elinor grasped Eric's hand, and they crouched down in front of the spirit board. I sat between Bianca and Elinor. We all looked to Bianca. She indicated for Eric, who was closest to the door, to turn off the light.

The candles flickered, casting strange patterns of light across their faces. I moved closer to Bianca, grabbing her hand in mine, trying to ignore the electric energy that coursed from her fingers into mine. Elinor took my other hand, but no strange energy leapt from her skin onto mine.

Bianca started to chant. "Spirits of Primrose House, speak to us. Spirits of Primrose House, make yourselves known."

We all took up the chant, our voices blending together in the darkened room. After a while, Bianca dropped my hand. As she did so, a shaft of cold air blasted my back.

"Did you feel that?" Bianca whispered. "It just got cold."

"Oh yeah," Elinor said through gritted teeth. She dropped Eric's hand and rubbed her bare arm. "I feel it."

"It could just be a draft," Eric muttered, but no one agreed.

Shivers ran down my arms. Bianca bit her lip as she stretched out one finger, and placed it on the edge of the goblet. I copied her, and so did Eric. Elinor shook her head, folding her arms across her chest.

"This is crazy," she said.

"Come on, Elinor," Eric said. "It's just a bit of fun."

"You try being in love with a ghost, and tell me how fun it is," Elinor said, but she relented, and placed her finger on the goblet, too.

Bianca started to chant again, focused intently on the glass. I muttered the words under my breath, keeping my finger against the glass, wondering how long we'd have to sit here for, when the glass jerked under my finger.

"It moved!" Elinor cried. "I felt it."

"Me too," Eric said.

My stomach tightened as the goblet slid across the floor, moving across one of the letters. Bianca let out a squeal. "That's an E. This is amazing," she breathed.

The goblet touched another letter, and another. "L ... I ..."

"It's spelling something ..." Bianca said. Elinor whimpered, as the goblet swung toward another letter.

"N ... holy shit, Elinor—"

"Why is it spelling my name?" Elinor moaned.

Eric sniggered. The glass toppled over on its side.

"Omigod, Eric, you bastard!" Elinor grabbed the pillow off the bed and beat Eric over the head with it, sending a great cloud of dust.

"Sorry, my love. I couldn't help it." Eric grinned as he fended off her blows. "Your face is priceless!"

Bianca exchanged a glance with me. "Bloody Eric." She scooped up the candles, and set the goblet back on the shelf in the secret cupboard. "I was hoping we could really channel a spirit."

"Yeah," I said. "But Eric didn't make the temperature drop, did he?"

"Hey, yeah, you're right." Something warm brushed against my fingers. Bianca's hand. She slipped her fingers into mine, squeezing me tight. A surge of energy jolted up my arm, straight into my chest. My whole body hummed with want of her. All I had to do was throw my arm around her and pull her close and try to chase away the unearthly chill with the heat of my body—

But I couldn't, because it was pointless. *Because I'm holding the hand of my fated mate, but she will never see me as anything other than a friend.*

7

———

BIANCA

*B*ack in my own bed in my tiny apartment above the shop, I hardly slept a wink, my mind focused on the Primrose House and poor Hattie. At 3 a.m., I couldn't take it any longer. I flicked on the light and sat up, dragging the scrapbook over my knees. Macavity glared at me as I shifted my legs, disturbing his sleep.

"Sorry, boy." I patted his head. "This thing is keeping me awake, so I might as well see what happens next."

I flicked through the pages, past the crumbling lace samples and faded illustrated postcards of birds and flowers, my eyes flicking over Silvia's beautiful cursive. At first, her entries were quite dull, just listings of her daily activities – the embroidery she was working on, the dresses she commissioned down in London, the books she read, the teas and dances she attended.

Hattie's name started coming up more and more. It seemed the girls were spending time together while Silvia's parents were away. Silvia's entries filled with gushing prose about Hattie's wicked humour, her games, her lovely hair.

If I didn't know better, if Silvia wasn't a repressed Victorian lady who eventually married a Yorkshire earl, I would have guessed that she had a crush on Hattie.

I turned the page. The next entry read:

"I am dazzled. My stomach twists and flutters as though it is filled with beautiful butterflies. I must write quickly, so Mama does not come up behind me and see. Today, I had my lessons with Martha in the drawing room, with the curtains drawn tight so the sunlight wouldn't damage my skin before next month's ball. Hattie was dusting in the hallway, and every so often, I would look up from my lesson to see her peering in, making faces at me. I couldn't help laughing, and Martha rapped me across the knuckles. After she had set me some French vocabulary, she left to finish kneading the dough for the evening's bread, and Hattie and I were alone.

"Hattie dropped her duster and ran over to me, her smile bright and becoming. Before I could tell her that we must be quiet, for Martha could be back at any moment, she grabbed my face and pressed her lips to mine.

"Oh, diary, it was exquisite! All the words of all the great poets cannot describe the wonderful feeling that overcame me. I want to sing out to all the world that I am in love, but I dare not, for I know that Hattie and I will never be allowed to marry."

Wow. Not so repressed, after all. I grinned from ear to ear to think that in this house of repression, a forbidden lesbian relationship had blossomed. My smile froze when I remembered how it ended. I turned the page.

"Mama and Father went off to Yorkshire to visit our relatives. Normally, they would make me go also, but I begged them to allow me to stay behind so that I could attend the Winlove's ball. Last night, when I was sure Martha was asleep, I crept downstairs to the kitchen and took the secret staircase up to Hattie's bedroom. I lay with her on the bed, and under the glow of the moon we discovered each other.

"I wish Mother and Father would never return. Hattie wants us to run away together. She showed me her secret stash of little trinkets she has stolen. She says when she sells them, she'll have enough money to free her brother, and the three of us will buy passage to America and start a new life together."

My fingers trembled with excitement as I flipped another page.

"Mama and Father returned today. Over dinner, Father informed me that they had an enjoyable time with the friends of our relatives – another noble family who own a lot of land in Yorkshire. He mentioned that their son, Edmund, Earl of Dartmouth, would be inheriting an estate on his twenty-first birthday, and that he was looking for a wife. He said he'd invited the Dartmouths to accompany us when we travel to London for the Season. I believe he intends for Edmund to court me, but I am afraid. I know that I should be excited about the prospect of marrying such a good match (and a handsome man, too, if the portrait Mama brought back for me is any indication). But if I left Primrose House, I'd never see Hattie again, and the thought of it is too much to bear."

I flipped past the next few entries, searching for the diary entries after the death of Hattie. There was only two. Silvia had doodled all over the page, adding clothes and pressed flowers to an outline of a woman's body that had been printed there. The journal entry was dotted with tiny specks, blurring the ink. I realised they were tear drops.

"Everyone has forgotten about Hattie, except me. The constables came to speak with Mama, and Lord Raynard, as well. Mama keeps telling me to stop looking so morose, that I'll never find a husband if I keep up this sullen attitude. I do not care. I took some money from Father's office and brought it to Bedlam to secure Hattie's brother's release. I hope it will be enough for him to begin a new life."

On the corner of the page, just below the entry, was a ticket stub for the train to London, a first-class seat. So our narrator went down to London to free this brother herself? I smiled, wondering how it must have been for her to stand in that demonic place and free a brother she did not know.

People do such remarkable things for love, I mused. *I wonder if anyone will ever love me like that. That crazy, all-consuming love that dooms even the brightest stars.*

I flipped to the final entry. One entire page was taken up with swatches of white bridal lace and beautiful embroidered silk. An exquisitely lettered invitation requested the presence of a guest at the wedding of Silvia Sinclair and Edmund, Earl of Dartmouth. A flash of anger shot through me. I'd known the wedding happened, of course, for it was part of my family tree, but now that I knew what had occurred before it, seeing that bridal lace turned my stomach.

"So much has happened since I last made an entry; I am to be married! Edmund is everything I dreamed of in a husband – handsome and clever and kind and noble. I am sure that if she'd still been alive, he would have let Hattie come to live with us as my personal chambermaid, and everything would have been exactly as I dreamed.

"I am to move with Edmund to his residence in Yorkshire. I am not sure when next I'll set foot in Primrose House again.

After what happened to Hattie, and how her presence has haunted me since she was laid to rest in her pauper's grave, I doubt I shall return willingly.

"I leave this, my record of our time together, in Hattie's secret place. She has some things in here, silver and jewellery belonging to Mama. I'm going to leave them here. Perhaps the next maid that must endure this stuffy, desolate room will find them, and use them to buy her fortune."

I closed the book and flicked out the light, my eyes brimming with tears. *How differently their lives might have turned out if they were born today!* If Silvia had just run away with Hattie, she might never have died and they might have found a way to be together. But Silvia was too cloistered by her upbringing to see the possibility in that, which was why even though her very own dragon-slayer was right in front of her, she still went looking for Prince Charming.

"I promise you," I whispered to the darkness, my hand still resting on the cover of the book. "No one who sets foot inside this house from now on shall ever have to suffer as you did. Anyone who comes through these doors will be free to love whomever they chose."

THE NEXT DAY, bleary-eyed and mildly hungover, I stumbled downstairs into the shop. Elinor stared at me from her spot at the drawing table. "You look like shit."

"Eight beers and a bad sleep will do that to a person. Thanks for the pep talk, by the way."

"Usually you like the fact that I call it like I see it."

I scowled at her, tossing the shop phone onto her desk. "Usually, you're not directing that brutal honesty at me. Cancel my appointments today. I'm in no state to hold a gun."

"If you're cancelling on them, *you* call them."

"You're my apprentice," I growled, lowering myself onto the chaise lounge. "It's part of your job description that you assist me. Now, start assisting."

Sighing, Elinor grabbed the phone and the appointment book, and started dialling. Her immaculately styled fringe bobbed over one eye as she held the phone up to her ear and sorted through her sketches. Damn her, how did she manage to look so good? *Probably because she stopped after three beers last night,* I mused, wincing as a particularly nasty headache throbbed against my temple.

"What will you do today instead? You should probably get started on the taxes."

I groaned, clutching my head. "My headache just got worse."

"You could sweep out the—"

"Stop right there." I held up my hand. "This is my shop. I don't want to hear about any more chores. This is a chore-free day. I'm going to plan my wedding."

"Your *fake*-wedding," Elinor corrected, a hint of annoyance in her voice.

"Yes, my fake-wedding. Where was that girl's number?" I waved a hand vaguely in the direction of our desk.

"What girl?"

"The hot one who could didn't speak above a whisper ... you tattooed a rose on her ribcage ..."

"Oh, *Willow*. Right, here you go." Elinor passed me a scrap of paper. I tugged my phone out of my pocket and, steeling myself against a wave of nausea, dialled Willow's number.

Willow showed up at the store ten minutes later, clutching a big stack of wedding magazines. I noticed she lurched a little as she walked, as though one of her legs had stiffened up. Her sweater was inside out and it looked as though she hadn't brushed her hair.

"Big night out?" I grinned at her.

"Huh?" Willow placed the magazines down on the waiting area table. The stack teetered precariously. She yelped and reached out to save it, but she was too late. Wedding magazines cascaded across the floor.

"I mean you, looking a little worse for wear." I bent down to help her collect the wayward magazines. "No judgement here, I'm a little hungover, myself."

"Oh, no, ah ... I don't drink." Willow turned her face away.

"Right." So she went out in public like this without the influence of alcohol? *Hmmmm.*

Again, I wondered how Willow managed to organise all the millions of tiny details associated with a wedding. She seemed a little scatterbrained as well as horrifically shy and totally drop-dead gorgeous. "Hey, how's your tattoo healing up?"

"Oh ... good so far. Um ..." Willow set the last of the magazines back on top of the pile, then slid into the seat beside me. Her blonde curls hung over her face, hiding her expression from my view. *Dammit, woman, look at me. I want to drown in those gorgeous eyes.*

She rested a moleskin on her lap and flipped it open to a blank page. She placed a pair of craft scissors and some double-sided tape on the table. "So, let's start by having a look through these. You can point out anything you like, and we'll add it to a vision board."

"Fun!" I grabbed the first magazine and flicked through the images. *Ick ... gross ... marshmallow ... pink, eeech ... what has she got in her hair?*

"See anything?" Willow shifted, her curls brushing my arm as she leaned in to get a closer look at the magazine.

"Er ... " I turned the page around, showing a picture of a

snooty-looking bride and groom walking away from an archway made of gnarled wood. "I guess that's pretty cool."

"The archway?"

"Yeah. Only ... not with that hideous white bunting. Maybe with some fairy lights instead, or some barbed wire and black roses, and even a couple of swords hanging from the struts."

"Swords?"

"Yeah, that would be really fun. Hey, yeah! We could even cut the cake with them."

Willow looked ready to faint. "Um, I'm not sure I even know where to find swords—"

I waved my hand. "Oh, don't worry. My friend Alex knows a guy who does re-enactment. I'm sure he's got a house full of swords. Alex told me how she once chased a werewolf with a broadsword ..."

My voice trailed off. Elinor was making wild gestures at me behind Willow's back, her face white. I clapped my hand over my mouth, but it was too late. I was used to talking about werewolves and ghosts and supernatural stuff as though it was perfectly normal, I'd completely forgotten that Willow knew nothing of this world.

"Er, I mean, this was a Halloween party, of course," I said, hurriedly picking up the next magazine and opening it to some tulle monstrosity. I snuck a look at Willow out of the corner of my eye, but she was still staring at the magazines with her hair in her face, so I couldn't read her expression. "So it's settled. I'll take care of the swords. Now, let's see what else we can come up with. Not this dress, obviously, but I guess I kind of like the colour of the groom's pocket square ..."

An hour later, and we'd gone through every magazine in the stack. Now I saw what made Willow so good at her job. She didn't try to lead me on. She just sat silently, listening to my running commentary about tulle and cake toppers and little gift boxes called "favours" that seemed to be a scheme to deprive brides of a small fortune for plastic tat that no one in their right mind would keep. All the while, she cut out images and swatches and made pages of notes in her little book. Somehow, she was creating a wedding out of my insane rantings.

"I think I know what you don't want," she said at last, tucking a loose strand of hair behind her ear and dropping the magazines on the floor. The heavy pile fell right on top of her foot, but she didn't seem to notice. "Let's try to get a grip on exactly what you *do* want. Any venues around Crookshollow that you'd be comfortable in?"

"What about Club Medusa?" Elinor asked. Club Medusa in Crooks Worthy was the sole music venue within driving distance, unless you counted *Tir Na Nog* on Irish dancing night.

"Hey, yeah!" I exclaimed. "We could have like a whole show, with bands playing and fire dancers and—omigod, I just thought of the perfect idea. We should have it at Primrose House."

"What's that?" Willow asked, looking as though she was bracing herself for some other crazy idea.

"It's this house I just inherited. You'll love it. It's an old Victorian mansion with all these dark rooms and ridiculous wallpaper and it has a real honest-to-goodness ballroom. I'm going to turn the house into an artist's sanctuary and backpackers. We could easily have the wedding inside, and hey, we could even make it the grand opening of the art house!"

"Hang on, don't you have to get married *this month?*" Elinor said. "There would be a ton of work to do if you wanted to de-octogenarianify it, *and* have it ready to host a huge event. Will the house be ready by then?"

"It had better be." I grinned. "I want my wedding to be the biggest, craziest, most ridiculous art party Crookshollow and Primrose House has ever seen."

Now that I had a wedding venue, the ideas came thick and fast. A decadent Victorian gothic ball with mandatory costumes, art from all my friends on the walls, Eric's band on stage in the ballroom playing their unique gothic rock while a DJ spun dance tunes between sets. Laser lights and aerial silk performers hanging from the chandeliers. And, of course, as many swords as I could legally swing about the place.

By the time Willow got up to leave, her hand had cramped up from all her note-taking, and her face looked pale and slightly terrified. I couldn't help grinning as I walked her out to her car, letting my hand linger on her arm longer than necessary. If she could pull this off, then she really would have proved herself as a wedding planner extraordinaire, royal shindig or not.

And damn, was she still gorgeous. But I knew she wasn't comfortable enough around me yet to make any kind of move.

Since I technically had the day off, I decided to go see how Robbie was getting on with his pack assignment. He'd looked pretty nervous when he left Primrose House last night. I thought back to what he'd said about not having an education, about how he'd handed me that scrapbook filled with cursive writing, his excitement hiding the pained expression that told me he had no idea what it was about. If he didn't know the first thing about the Victorian period, how was he going to handle the hardcore library research needed to find a location for that ring?

I dragged my bicycle out from where I'd chained it to a down pipe behind the shop, and started pedalling toward the high street. I stopped in at *Bewitching Bites* and picked up some treats for Robbie and Anna. With the box of treats nestled in the basket, I biked over to Crooks Crossing, and texted Robbie to meet me outside the University Library. He stepped outside as I was locking up my bike, squinting into the English sun like he hadn't seen it for months. He took the box gratefully.

"Find anything yet?" I asked, watching him devour a Cornish pastie in a few bites.

"Not a thing, but I'm only just starting. Anna's found some old maps of the country, and a registry of landowners in the area. But without an exact year for the sale, it's taking a long time to trawl through."

"Do you need any help? I've got the day off on account of our exciting night last night."

"Thanks, but no. I'm fine." He took out a beautiful buttery scone slathered in jam and clotted cream, and pulled it into two pieces. He handed me a piece with fingers splattered with sticky jam.

"In hindsight, I probably shouldn't have brought you jammy treats when you're dealing with archival material all day." I took the scone, and bit into the delicious buttery treat. Bloody hell, that Belinda was a good baker. "I wanted to tell you all about our wedding plans. It's going to be *amazing*."

"You've planned the whole wedding already?"

"Not the *whole* wedding, but I had the perfect idea for the venue. It's going to be at Primrose House. It'll be perfect – one huge crazy party to celebrate the opening of the art house. We'll have bands, performers, living art, amazing food, a crazy out-of-control masquerade ball. And we'll say our vows right there in the ballroom. I want you to carry a sword. And, get this, I reckon we should get our celebrant to dress as the Pope—"

Robbie laughed. "Who ever thought you'd be so excited about a wedding, Bianca Sinclair?"

I jabbed him in the arm. "You're very lippy for a man who's getting a free place to stay."

As my knuckles grazed his skin, that weird tingling sensation rolled up my arm again. Robbie stepped closer, his hand reaching up to my cheek. He wiped a strand of hair from across my eye. "You okay?" he asked, his voice serious. "You look like you havenae slept a wink."

"I couldn't sleep with Silvia's scrapbook waiting to be read." I launched into a description of everything I'd read, how Silvia and Hattie had been lovers and how Silvia had left the book in Hattie's secret cupboard.

Robbie licked his fingers, and handed me back the box. "I should probably get back. Anna will be getting cranky. Once I'm alone, I'll see if I can find anything about that earl she married."

"You're a good man, Robbo." I clapped him on the shoulder, and swung my leg over my bike.

8

———

ROBBIE

All morning, Anna had been fretting about leaving her son with the babysitter, so as soon as I returned from seeing Bianca, I told her she should leave me alone to continue the research. She dashed off without even saying goodbye.

I stared down at my corral in dismay. The tiny desk was piled high with archive boxes, indecipherable maps, and a giant ledger filled with tiny cursive print that might as well have been Sanskrit for all the sense it made to me. I stared at the words on the map open in front of me, but the letters swarmed and blurred in front of my eyes, just lines on the page, devoid of meaning. My temple throbbed. A bead of sweat rolled down my forehead.

How the hell was I going to find this ring? Why had I volunteered for this job? I had an app on my phone that could scan text and read it back to me, but when I tried it on the old documents, it wouldn't recognise the text. I'd have to read every word myself, which was going at a pace that would make ice ages seem speedy.

I'm an idiot. When Caleb found out that I could barely read – which he would inevitably discover when I failed to deliver any coherent information – he'd be pissed that I'd wasted the pack's time when there were plenty of other more qualified people who could have done the research.

I glared at the map, hoping somehow the letters would form themselves into a pattern I could understand. A word jumped out at me … I sounded it out. S. I. N. C. L. A. I. R … *Sinclair*. Bianca's last name.

That wasn't surprising. With a fancy home like Primrose House, and a family that had been in Crookshollow for generations, they were bound to appear on some of these old records. I traced my finger around the property line on the map. *Interesting*. In the late 1700s when these maps were made, the Sinclairs owned most of Crookshollow. They must have sold off a lot of that land over the years, because Bianca's property was only five acres of forest and the house.

The story Bianca had told me about Silvia and Hattie spun in my head. I decided to put the ring research aside for the moment, and focus on Bianca's mysterious ancestor, the unique Silvia Sinclair and her lover, the wild maid Hattie.

From what Silvia said in her scrapbook, it sounded like her mother or father pushed Hattie down the stairs. Bianca wanted to know if either of them were ever tried or convicted of manslaughter. If I could discover that, maybe I could count at least one victory for the day.

Even though I now knew how to search the archives from watching Anna, it took me a long time to locate the historic records that dealt with crimes in that era from amongst the hand-labelled boxes in the climate-controlled room. My eyes were watering by the time I finally pulled out the right ledger – court records from the 1830s – when Silvia lived in Crookshollow.

The librarian told me that back in Silvia's day, there wasn't an established, organised police force – town authorities would employ constables to keep the peace. It was largely up to the lords to judge crimes committed on their land by their tenants, and to preside over and make judgements. Luckily for me, they kept diligent records.

Spurned on by the promise of Bianca's smile, I squinted at the words in the ledger, spelling each letter aloud. The work was agonisingly slow, but just as I was about to give up, the name Sinclair jumped out at me again.

In a notebook written by one of the Raynard Lords – Ryan's ancestors, I realised – I discovered what I was looking for. The Lord Raynard had visited the Sinclair's home to look over the death of a servant. But he wasn't there in the capacity of landowner. He was a friend, lending his shoulder to Silvia's mother, Matilda Sinclair. It took me a long time to figure out all the words, but I learned that Matilda was:

"the most formidable woman, who owned all of the county. Even much of our own property was bequeathed to us in marriage from her own estate. The Sinclair name is fascinating, for their family has a truly unique history. Matilda's ancestor married a monk – Bartholomew Winthorpe – who had left the Crooks Worthy monastery to pursue a secular life. As the monk had no fortune, and his name had no weight in the community, he instead took his wife's name. Thus, the land she brought to the marriage remained under Sinclair."

Holy shit.

My heart pounded so hard, I was sure the librarian would come over to tell me to tone it down. I had it, right there in front of me. The answer I'd been searching for. This document explained why I couldn't find any land owned by the Winthorpe family. The Sinclairs had the land under their own name.

But that means ... that means Bianca's family ... they have the ring.

~

I TRIED to call Bianca immediately to tell her the news, but the librarian gave me a stern look and tapped her red fingernails on the NO PHONES sign above her desk. Sighing, I left the archival boxes open on my corral, and dashed outside.

"Urrgh," Bianca groaned, her voice croaking. "I hate you."

"Headache getting better, then?"

"I was sleeping. The phone is *loud*."

"Set it to silent."

"Urrggh. I hate you. This better be important."

"It is." I told her what I discovered. "Can you believe it? All this time, we've been crawling around in those caves, when *your* family are the ones who had the ring all along. It might even be at Primrose House."

"I *can't* believe it. You'd have thought if this heirloom was so valuable and precious, I'd have known about it."

"Your mother has never dug it out to wear at some fancy occasion?"

"If that ring looks anything like the description, my mother wouldn't be caught dead wearing something so garish. It's much more my style. After we have dinner with my parents, you'll learn exactly why."

"When is that again?"

"Tomorrow night. I apologise in advance."

"I don't mind, really." I didn't. Bianca had talked about her parents – especially her mother – in excruciating detail for so many months, I was kind of curious to meet them in the flesh. They couldn't be as bad as my dad. At least they'd never threatened Bianca with violence if she didn't commit armed robbery. How bad could they possibly be?

"We're going to have to convince them we're really a couple. And not just a couple of people floating around the same house without ever having a real conversation, like them. They have to believe you're a guy I really would marry, which basically means you have to totally piss them off. If we're not woefully inappropriate, they won't believe I really like you."

"Define 'woefully inappropriate'?"

"I don't know, snogging on the steps, pilfering silver teaspoons, pissing on a Chippendale chair. It would also really help if you showed up stoned, with a black eye."

"I'll get right on that." I hit the END button. Talking to Bianca always made me smile. Once again, I wished like hell she felt the same way.

Soon, we're going to be spending a lot of time together. Even though I knew it was stupid, I still couldn't help but hope that maybe she'd see me as more than a friend. She *was* planning our wedding, after all. *Love is in the air, and all that ...*

But it was a forlorn hope. I stared down at my mobile phone, deflated. *Try not to focus on it. Even if Bianca never realises she's your fated mate, at least you have her in your life, and the rest of the pack, too. At least you don't have to break the law in order to earn respect. At least you've managed to contribute something useful to your new family.*

I quickly called Caleb and told him what I'd discovered. He whistled. "That's awesome. Thanks, Robbie. I'll call Ryan and tell him. He'll be stoked his research has led us this much closer, and that it was a member of his family who gave us the final clue!"

I gritted my teeth. Of course Ryan would get credit for this. Ryan was rich and influential in the shifter community.

I clicked off the phone and went back inside. As I entered the reading room, I noticed a man leaning over my desk. I rushed over, thinking it was a librarian putting away my archive boxes. As I got closer, I saw the man shuffling through the maps and files, getting them all out of order and mixing up the different boxes. I'd have a hard time putting everything back.

"Excuse me." I tapped his shoulder. "I'm still using those—"

The man looked up, his eyes blazing across my face. I staggered back as I recognised him. Rolf Hermann, rising alpha of the Wulfric pack – a notorious German gang who'd clashed heads with the Macleans in numerous occasions.

Five years ago, Rolf came to Aberdeen to intercept a shipment of weapons his clan wanted for some work they were doing in London. As my first big solo job, Dad sent me to nick the same treasure. I managed to pick up one of the cases, but Rolf sidelined me, beat me to a pulp, and took it. I had to go back to Dad empty handed, and he beat me some more, basically told me I was useless and a disgrace to the Maclean name. I still had a long scar across my stomach to testify to his brutality. Rolf had taken the prize and ever since then, he'd been spreading around shifter circles that the Macleans were weaklings.

And now he was *here*, in Crookshollow, snooping through my stuff.

"What are you doing here?" I growled, my cheeks flaring with heat.

He cast a wide smile. "Relax, Robbo. This is a public place. You do not need to raise your voice."

"Why are you in Crookshollow? Are you following me?" *Did you not humiliate me enough back in Aberdeen? Do you need to come here to finish the job with my new pack?*

"I could not give a fuck about you, you useless worm." His eyes flashed. "I am here to meet with Irvine."

"Here? In this library?"

Rolf grinned wider. "I am not familiar with the customs of your new pack, but I assume I'm not expected to reveal plans to lowly wolves?"

I grabbed the book from his hand, placing my body in front of the corral, trying to block him from looking at my work. "Stay away from me."

"It would be my pleasure." Rolf grinned again, as he turned on his heel and stalked toward the door. I glared after him, my blood boiling.

Why is he here, *now*, to meet with Irvine? As quickly as I could, I shoved the archive material back into the boxes, not caring if it was right or not. There was no way I could deal with any more reading for the day. My blood pounded in my ears, as I thought about what it could possibly mean that Rolf had decided to show up now, and that he was here to see Irvine, not Caleb.

Was Irvine up to something?

9
———

BIANCA

Breathe. Just breathe. It'll be fine. You'll be out of here in three hours, and you can go home and scrub the horrible scent of your mother's disapproval from your clothes, and you don't have to see them again for another two years ...

Ever since Mother called demanding I bring Robbie over to meet them, I'd been plotting and scheming how to make tonight go off exactly the way I wanted it. But now that I was actually *here*, standing beneath the pillars of my parent's grand Georgian home – not quite as large as Primrose House, but infinitely more intimidating because of who was waiting inside – all my childhood terror came rushing back.

"You okay?" Robbie tapped my shoulder, his freshly-shaved face twisted in concern. "You've gone all pale."

I nodded, taking a moment to look him over. He'd scrubbed up really well. Instead of his usual dark t-shirt and holey jeans, he was wearing black dress pants and a red shirt he'd borrowed from Marcus. Even his normal woody scent was disguised with cologne. His leather jacket crinkled as he placed a protective arm around my shoulders. The edges of his lower sleeve tats peeked out from the cuffs of the jacket.

My mother would not fail to notice them, or his buzzed prison-style hair, or the fact that he hadn't attended a public school. She was going to hate him on sight, which was *exactly* what I wanted. I just hated that it would make tonight excruciating for us both.

I rubbed the goosebumps on my arms, naked in my tight black body-con dress. I stared down at the beautiful ink that told the story of my life. As soon as that door opened, the stream of vitriol would begin. *You look like a prostitute. You bring shame on the Sinclair family name. After everything we gave you, you threw it all away to live in squalor and play with needles ...*

"Bianca? Do you want to just flag it? We could go back to your flat and—"

"We should ring the bell," I said. I didn't move.

This is ridiculous. I shouldn't be nervous. I'm not even introducing them to a real boyfriend, er ... fiancé. This is all in aid of getting the house. If they don't believe Robbie and I are for real, they'll contest the will. I don't care if they like him, I don't care what they think of me. All that matters is that they think Robbie and I are madly in love.

I reached up and rang the bell. As the sound of Pachelbel's *Canon in D Major* echoed through the house, I grabbed Robbie's face and pulled him down, pressing my lips on his. He reacted with surprise, then returned the kiss with vigour. His tongue slid into my mouth, toying with my tongue piercing. I ran my fingers over his face, forcing him closer.

The kiss was just supposed to shock my mother when she opened the door. I didn't expect the shiver of delight that coursed through my body – a flame of desire that arced from my lips straight between my legs. *Whoah.* I hadn't felt this kind of intense desire from a kiss in a *long* time, especially not from a guy, and *especially* not a guy I wasn't keen on in that way.

Robbie's tongue slid over mine, expertly coaxing out the

minx in me. My fingers closed around the back of his neck, and I pressed my body against his, my skin itching for his touch. *Where's all this lust come from? Why does he make my body light up like this? Goddamn, but I want him so bad right now—*

Behind Robbie, the door creaked open.

Eat this, Mother.

"Bianca Sinclair! What are you doing?" Something screeched in my ear. A spidery hand grabbed my shoulder and tore Robbie and I apart. I sucked in air, my body screaming in protest at being ripped from that intense kiss. "You do not canoodle on the front porch, where any of the neighbours might see. Especially not when you're wearing *that*." She glared down at my dress, the vein above her temple throbbing against her papery skin. She clutched a hand to the severe collar of her blouse, where a red stone cameo was clasped. "You look like a prostit—"

"Gee, Mum," I snarled, straightening my skirt. "It was just a kiss. It's not as though we were going to throw down and consummate it right here on the porch."

Her lips pursed. Robbie glanced from her to me, his face confused. If he felt anything like I did, I guessed he was still reeling from the kiss. My veins thrummed with energy, a hot fire that clouded my thoughts.

Stop it, Bianca. Don't get distracted. Focus on the reason you're here tonight.

That reason loomed in the doorway, her bony figure casting a long shadow across the porch. Her outfit looked like something out of a Dracula comic – a high-collared black shirt with cream lace inserts, and a long wool skirt that flared at the bottom and must've itched like crazy. Her fingers glittered with dozens of rings, and that cameo against her throat. She'd pulled her hair – more silver than when I'd last seen it – into a tight bun high on her head, so tight it stretched the skin at the edge of her forehead, as though the knot was what held her whole face together. Impeccably applied lipstick curled back into a disapproving frown.

Mother looked me up and down, sniffing as though the smell of me was somehow unsavoury. Robbie shifted uncomfortably from foot to foot. I glared back at her, daring her to further disobey her protocols and continue to allow Robbie and I to remain standing on the porch in the cold.

Finally, she stepped back into the entrance hall, holding the door open. "Please." She held the door open. "Won't you come in?"

Robbie jumped, a little surprised at her quick change of tone. He recovered quickly, and stepped into the house. He held out his hand.

Good idea, Robbie. Of course she doesn't shake hands.

Mother stared down at his outstretched hand, her features twitching with thinly veiled disgust. To my surprise, she didn't give him a lecture on proper protocol. Instead, she leaned forward and presented her cheek.

Robbie glanced at me, his eyes wide with panic. I nodded toward her cheek. The message got through, and he pecked my mother's cold skin.

"Your home is beautiful, Mrs. Sinclair," he said. "It's massive."

"Why thank you, Robbie. It's Lady Sinclair, if you please. It's not often I hear the word 'massive' in relation to our front hall." She frowned as he started undoing his laces. "Please don't. We do not need the smell of sweaty socks ruining our dinner. Unless they are covered with *dirt*." She spat that word as though it were actually a piece of dirt stuck at the back of her throat. "If so, I shall fetch you a pair of Charles' slippers—"

"Oh, no." Robbie quickly snapped his foot down, his laces

still half-untied. "I cleaned and polished them this morning. We're good."

"Yes, well." She wrinkled her nose. "Follow me to the dining room. As Bianca has arrived late, as usual, we shall skip pre-dinner drinks and go straight to the table."

"Damn," Robbie whispered to me as we trooped behind Mother down the hallway. "If we'd come on time we would at least have had alcohol to fortify us for battle."

"Trust me," I whispered back. "You don't want to sit around on stiff chairs trying to make awkward conversation with these people any longer than necessary. Besides." I patted my purse. "I've got a flask of whisky if you need it."

"You're an amazing woman."

"What are you two whispering about?" Mother frowned at me from behind her chair at the table. "It is rude to whisper. It leaves others out of the conversation."

"It was nothing. I was just explaining to Robbie about how Robert Adam designed the interior to reflect the classical motifs he collected from his travels in Greece."

"Robert, you sit over there, opposite Charles." Mother gestured to the setting in front of the sideboard, at the foot of the table where my brother Daniel always sat. My mother insisted on a traditional table, with folded white linens and her best Cumbria crystal glassware and an even number of men and women sitting in alternating order. Even if she'd been able to accept my bisexuality, she'd never have been able to have my girlfriends over for dinner. Heaven forbid that an extra woman would have unbalanced the table.

Father was already sitting at the head of the table, a half-empty glass of wine in front of his place. He glanced up as I sat down, pushing his glasses up his nose. "Bianca."

"Father. This is Robbie."

"Ah, Robert, it's lovely to meet you."

"And you, Lord Sinclair." Robbie extended his hand to my father to shake, but he just picked up the wine bottle and refilled his glass. I shook my head at Robbie, and he sat down. My mother signalled to her cook to fill our glasses and bring the first course.

The first course was a salmon *soufflé*. I purposefully tapped the top of mine until it deflated, then spooned the gooey contents into my mouth with relish, even adding a moan of pleasure. Mother glared at me, but I pretended not to notice. Robbie met my eyes across the table. He looked terrified. No one spoke. The mantle clock ticked away the minutes.

Maybe we'll get lucky and they won't ask him anything for the whole meal. Maybe we'll get out of here without—

"Robert, you are from Scotland?" Father said.

"Hello, Captain Obvious," I muttered.

Mother frowned at me, but didn't admonish me. "Charles and I travelled there recently, to attend a shooting party of one of Charles' colleagues. Have you ever been to Drumlanrig Castle? The Duke and Duchess of Buccleuch and Queensberry are marvellous hosts. Perhaps your family has summered with them before?"

"Oh, no, ma'am. But I've heard it's lovely."

"Robbie comes from a less reputable family," I said. "He was homeless for a while, and his dad was in and out of jail—"

"Bianca, *really*. We don't need your interjections. Your fiancé can speak for himself. Heaven knows, he'll need to learn to speak up if he's married to you."

"Aye, well ..." Robbie's face had turned pale. His spoon clattered out of his hand and fell on the table, leaving a small smudge of creamy soufflé on Mother's white tablecloth. "It's true that my family dinnae exactly own an estate, but the Maclean clan can trace our history back hundreds of years—"

"It's fine, dear." My mother patted his hand. *She patted his hand!* Like she was trying to ease his nerves. She'd never, ever patted my hand. "We do not subscribe to the idea that children take after their parents. That's certainly not true in this house."

No, it's not, because you two are stuffy, repressed bores clinging to an outdated class system, and you have a daughter who is a tattoo artist and a son who teaches skydiving in New Zealand.

"So, Robert." My father put down his spoon. "What do you do for a living? Bianca didn't say."

Ah, hah. Here's my chance to gain back some ground.

"He doesn't work at the moment," I said. Robbie shot me a panicked look. I would've kicked him under the table if I'd been able to reach. *It's okay if they hate you, remember. It's actually the best solution.*

"I'm actually conducting some research in Crookshollow," Robbie said, his hand shaking as he reached for his water glass. "I'm investigating an obscure family who lived here during the medieval period. There are some documents in the university collection I wanted to look at."

"Oh, you're an historian?" Father leaned forward. "I dabble a little myself. Perhaps you've read my piece on traditional cooperage technology. It was published in *The Chaucer Review*."

"Dad, Robbie doesn't have time to read and remember every single article in those stupid journals."

"Nonsense, Bianca. Academics remember everything they read. Isn't that right, Robert?"

"We try, Lord Sinclair—"

"Please, boy, call me Charles."

"—er, Charles, although I cannae say I recall the piece. Why dinnae you tell me what your findings were about, er, coopering?"

As the maid cleared our plates and delivered the roast course, Dad launched into a long-winded soliloquy about his research into medieval barrel-making. I poked at the carrots, astounded by the fact that we'd managed to get to the second course without any major arguments. Sure, Mother still had her nose in the air like there was a bad smell in the room, but she wasn't crossing herself frantically like Robbie might be a demon. Dad was gesticulating so much, his fork still in his hand, that he splattered gravy across the white tablecloth and didn't seem to notice.

What on earth was happening here? I bring home an uneducated, tattooed dude with a leather jacket and prison haircut, and despite my best efforts, my parents actually seemed to *like* him. At least, Dad did.

"Robert, would you like some more custard?" My mother interrupted, as she held out the jag to him.

"Aye, please." Robbie beamed at her. "This apple crumble is absolutely delicious. It's rare I get to enjoy such wonderful home-cooked food."

"Yes, Bianca isn't really one for the domestic life, although Lord knows I tried to teach her."

"Oh, I mean, because I'm so distracted with my studies, I often forget to eat."

"I've got an idea," Dad piped up, as Mother poured a generous helping of custard over his dessert, before setting it down in front of him. "After dinner, maybe you could look over my Latin translations. I have a devil of a time with the tenses."

"Oh, ah ..." Robbie begged me with his eyes to intervene, but I shook my head. He got himself into this mess, with his fibs and his charm. He could get himself out of it.

"That's a beautiful necklace, Lady Sinclair," Robbie said. "Is it an heirloom?"

I stomped on his foot under the table; he flinched, but continued to stare at Mum with a rapt expression. We'd specifically talked about the Benedict Ring before we left my flat, and

I'd told him on no uncertain terms that he wasn't to mention it to them. But damn him, he was going to ask her.

Mum touched the red garnet clasped at the collar of her severe shirt. "Why, thank you, Robbie. Yes, it was given to me by Charles on our 40th wedding anniversary. It has been in the family for four generations. Charles' mother was the last to wear it, and it was one of her favourites."

"I love the idea of jewellery being passed down like that, from father to son and mother to daughter. Do you have any particularly old and interesting pieces?"

I stomped on his foot again. This time, he nudged me back.

My mother laughed, a strangled sound, foreign in this dining room. "Such a curious man. Are you planning a jewel heist, Robert?"

"Victoria, don't tease the boy," Father croaked.

My mother, *teasing* someone? What universe have I wandered into?

She waved a hand. "Oh, Charles, don't fuss. Robert must know that Bianca's previous suitors have all been criminals."

"Excuse me?" I snarled. "That's not even remotely true—"

"No, Lady Sinclair, not planning a jewel heist here." Robbie didn't miss a beat. "My research is about medieval adornment. I'm always on the eye out for interesting pieces."

Just like that, he calmed the flash of anger in Mum's eyes. She wiped the edge of her mouth with her napkin, and touched the choker again. "We have some rosaries dating from the thirteenth century, in a case in Charles' study. There was an old family scandal in the 1700s – one of the ladies married a monk who'd left the monastery in Crooks Mallow. He gave her these as a gift, as well as a chalice, and her last name, as it carried more power than his."

There was a scraping sound as Father pushed back his chair.

"I'm finished. Let us retire now. Victoria, please ring for the brandy."

Father led Robbie and I into his study – an enormous high-ceilinged room lined with books and display cases containing various specimens. He never usually allowed me inside – afraid I might break something, probably with justification considering the number of precious things I'd broken over the years. He'd also never invited one of my "suitors" to stay for port before. *He wants to show off his collections to Robbie.*

"Wow." Robbie stared into a glass case containing some old medieval books. I made to follow them, but my mother grabbed my shoulder and shoved me down into one of the chairs.

Oh sure, let the men talk about "male things" and we'll just sit here and crochet tea-cosies.

"That's an original Chaucer right there." Father nodded proudly. "And, of course, you recognise those Bibles."

"Aye, of course," Robbie nodded in imitation of my father. I stifled the urge to giggle.

While Mother decanted port into tiny crystal goblets for us all, Father led Robbie to the display shelves along the back wall, behind his desk. He pointed to a small, golden chalice standing on its own shelf. Robbie bent in to look at it, his eyes dancing with excitement. Even I was getting curious. I couldn't believe that all this time, these objects were in this house, and I never knew the significance of them, or that they would connect in some way to the existence of shapeshifters.

"It's ... exquisite," Robbie remarked, putting on his "I'm a student of medieval adornment" voice. "I'm impressed by the craftsmanship and, ah, symbolism. And the curves are beautiful—"

"It's a cup, dear, not a centrefold," I chirped, downing my port in one gulp and reaching for Robbie's untouched glass.

The back of Robbie's neck turned red. "Were there any other things the monk brought with him from the monastery?"

"I don't believe—" Dad started, but Mother held up her hand.

"Actually, there *was* something. Charles, get the rosaries."

"Of course!" Dad set down his port and jumped up again. I snatched his glass off the table before anyone noticed. Mother – usually eagle-eyed when it came to my consumption of alcohol – didn't even see, so riveted was she by Robbie's interest in our proud family history.

"I also remember June mentioning another jewel, a ring of some kind." Robbie stiffened as she continued. "The last person to wear it was her great-grandmother, Silvia Sinclair. It went missing around the time Silvia went to Yorkshire to marry the Earl of Dartmouth. We've spoken to the family, of course, and they have no recollection of the ring, but as it was valuable, they may not be forthcoming."

"Was there ever a picture taken of the ring? A drawing, perhaps?"

"I believe so. Mother pointed it out to me once, but I don't remember where. There are many boxes of old papers in the attic at Primrose House, not to mention all the portraits. You'll be able to get your hands on them soon enough. But what made you think the monk would have brought anything else with him?"

"Oh, no reason. I'm just asking."

Mother tapped her nails on the table. "Charles might have a full inventory somewhere. Oh, we don't have any cheese. Robert, please forgive me, I'll be right back."

As soon as she was gone, Robbie leaned over and squeezed my knee. "I don't know what you were worried about. They seem fine."

I glared at him. "They aren't *fine*, Professor Maclean. They're barmy. And they *like* you. If they like you, they're never going to believe we're getting married."

He shrugged. "They seem to be okay with it."

"That's because they think you're an expert in medieval history. How are you going to escape translating my dad's Latin for the rest of your life?"

Robbie shrugged again. "Maybe I'll pick it up."

"You are impossible."

"I cannae help it. I *want* them to like me. Besides, I've managed to find out more about the ring—"

"Not everything in the universe is about that bloody ring—"

"Here we are!" Mother announced, returning with a tray laden with cheese, crackers, and tiny dishes of pate. Robbie and I sprang apart, and I hastened to straighten my skirt, before slapping my own hand down. *What is wrong with you tonight?* I didn't straighten clothes around them. I'd learned long ago that they would never accept me, no matter how hard I tried.

It's Robbie. He's thrown everything off.

While Mother handed out plates and fussed with the port glasses, Dad took one of the specimen cases from his cabinet and set it on the table in front of us. Three rosaries nestled inside, the beads dulled with time, the metal links drab with tarnish.

"They need a good clean," Dad said, sitting back in his chair and accepting his refilled port from Mother. "But there they are. I'm not sure why Bartholomew Winthorpe – that was the name the man took when he left the monastery – had them when he left the order, rather than giving them to the monks who were continuing on at other monasteries. Either way, they are fine things."

"Thank you so much." Robbie held the case in his hands, staring at the tiny rosaries as though they held all the answers in the universe. "They're exquisite. I haven't seen finer in all my research."

"Oh." Dad stood up. "That reminds me. I'll go get my translations. The conjugations are giving me a world of trouble."

Robbie's face paled. He set down his drink. "Actually, as much as I'd love to help, Charles, I'm afraid we'll need to leave shortly. I have an early meeting with my advisor tomorrow, and I need to drive Bianca back to the shop."

"Oh, you drive?" Mother held out the cheese plate, and Robbie took a cracker.

"Bianca doesn't have a car. She doesn't want to contribute to *climate change*." Father laughed, as though my lack of a car was an amusement to them, and not yet another aberration they counted against me.

"I have ... a Lada. It's a pile of shite—" Robbie stopped himself, "Er, I mean, a pile of *rubbish,* but it gets me from point A to point B."

"Oh, that's wonderful," Mother exclaimed.

Oh, that's wonderful. Robbie's Russian shitbox was wonderful? What Twilight Zone world have I stepped into? It's time to get out of here before Mother asks Robbie take her for a drive.

"Okay then." I drowned Robbie's second drink in one gulp and stood up. "So we're going to go. Um, you'll get a wedding invite soon, but there's no pressure if you don't want to come. It's going to be a bit different—"

"Nonsense, Bianca. You're our only daughter. We wouldn't miss it."

"There's no crystal china, Mother. No string quartet. No flowers or church hymns."

"I never expected there would be."

"I'm not wearing white!"

"As right you shouldn't." Mother fixed me with a pointed stare. "White symbolises a pure, virginal marriage. We will be there, no matter the date or the dress code or the number of prostitutes or clowns also in attendance. Goodnight, Bianca. Robert, it was a pleasure."

Robbie shook hands with Dad, and kissed my mother on the cheek. He waved goodbye to them from the driveway as he held my door open for me. As soon as he'd slid in the car beside me, I leaned over and rapped him over the head with my purse.

"Ow!" He rubbed the back of his head. "You still have that flask in there."

"You deserve it."

"Why?"

"*Why?* What was that ridiculous act you pulled inside?"

Robbie grinned. "I thought that went quite well."

"'Quite well'? It wasn't supposed to go quite well! They were supposed to hate your guts."

"It freaks you out that they like me, doesn't it?"

"It really, really does. You're a man of constant surprises, Robbie. And you've made your life incredibly difficult.

He shrugged. "Not as difficult as you were going to make it."

"I don't understand."

"We're getting married, Bianca. That's a forever thing. If we want your parents to believe us as a couple and let you keep the house, we have to keep up this charade for the rest of our lives. That means endless evenings just like this one. And I'd much rather do that with your parents as allies, instead of adversaries."

"It doesn't matter," I said. "I got Elinor to check over the letter and June's will. It looks as though there's no stipulation on the amount of time we have to be married. I think that since to June the idea of divorce was so abhorrent, she didn't even conceive of the idea that I'd consider it. So don't worry, you'll be free and clear of all familial obligations in a couple of years."

"Aye, right." He glanced away. "Good, I guess. I wasn't really keen on learning medieval Latin."

Is it just me, or does he seem less than enthused about the idea of splitting up our fake-marriage?

Dammit. Ever since Elinor had confronted me at the shop, I'd been meaning to talk to Robbie about his feelings for me. Or his *supposed* feelings for me, because I still wasn't entirely convinced there was anything between us other than two close friends who maybe happened to acknowledge that we found each other at least somewhat attractive. But the idea of talking about it with him terrified me. If it turned out Robbie really *did* have a thing for me, and it was influencing his decision to go through with the wedding, then … I'd have to reconsider the whole thing. And I didn't want to reconsider. Primrose House was my *dream.* We were so close, and all we had to do was make this marriage thing work for a couple of years, and everything would be fine.

But judging by the way Robbie wasn't looking at me, everything wasn't fine now. I rubbed my lips, remembering the kiss I'd sprung on him on the porch. Holy hell, that was a good kiss. If it was half as hot for Robbie as it was for me, then no wonder he was feeling a bit off.

I guess we're doing this.

"Robbie?"

"Aye?" He pulled over in front of *Resurrection Ink.*

"About that kiss—"

"I ken." He still wouldn't look at me. "That was for your mother's benefit. It's fine, Bianca, really. It donnae mean anything."

"But I—"

"Look, it's getting late. I should probably get back to the Hall before Simon locks me out."

"Oh, sure. See you tomorrow at Primrose House?"

"Aye, right." I leaned toward him, arms open, for our usual goodbye hug. Robbie didn't seem to see me. Instead, he stared at the wheel, his hands gripping the side. Sighing, I dropped my arms, and got out.

"Well ... goodnight." I waved at the window.

"Aye ... goodnight." Robbie looked up then, the sadness in his eyes so intense that I reeled. He gunned the engine, muttering something under his breath as he backed into the street. It almost sounded as though he'd said, "I love you."

10

───────

ROBBIE

After the dinner with Bianca's parents, things started moving even faster on both the ring investigation and on Primrose House, which Bianca had renamed "The Prim." My days blurred into each other as I worked from sunup until sunset. The relentless work was good, because it almost kept me distracted from the fact that I still desperately wanted Bianca, but I still saw no way to make that happen.

Almost.

In the mornings, I would head to the university library or local records office as soon as they opened to dig through the archives. Sometimes Anna would join me, giving me an hour or so of her wisdom while Luke watched the baby before hurrying off again to attend her motherly duties.

Anna's presence made me nervous. Every time she glanced over my shoulder or asked me why I was still on the same document, I panicked that she'd figured out I was struggling to read. But she seemed too preoccupied with the baby – checking her phone every few minutes in case Luke messaged her – to put it together, which suited me fine.

I made slow progress. I dug through every piece of history on the Crooks Worthy monastery, Bartholomew Winthrope, and Bianca's family, but there was no mention of the ring. I *did* discover a marriage announcement in the local paper for Sylvia and her Yorkshire Earl, as well as a pamphlet about the castle where she became Lady and gave birth to six children. I added that castle to my list of possible locations for the ring. Despite what Bianca's mother had said about the Earl's family not having the ring, I wanted to go up to York and look for it, but Caleb insisted he and Irvine would do it.

When I'd told Caleb about Rolf's visit to the library, he didn't seem fazed. "He's in town because Irvine invited him to meet with us," he said. "We've already had one discussion, and we plan to speak again in a few days. I'm not surprised he's taking the time to investigate my pack. I'd do exactly the same in his position."

"What are you discussing with a *Wulfric* alpha? You realise they—"

"—are the bitter enemies of the Macleans?" Caleb said. "Yeah, Robbo, I remember. But Irvine says they can help us, and I trust him. So does your mother. You need to trust him, too."

I was never going to trust Irvine a single bit, but there was no way I could tell Caleb that. "I'll try, man."

"You do that. And you find that ring."

The afternoons and evenings I spent at Primrose House, making repairs and painting and redecorating, readying for the opening of the art house. Bianca came after work to do her share of the work, but I didn't stick around to socialise with her. I didn't want to give myself any more false hope, and I had other work to do.

By reading late into the night, I was also able to start sorting through the boxes of documents stored in the attic. Bianca kept offering to help me, but I didn't want her to discover my illiteracy, so I took the boxes back to Raynard Hall and pored through them on my own. So far, nothing had come up connected to Silvia Sinclair and the ring, but I was such a slow reader I'd barely made a dent.

At least one thing was going right – "The Prim" had taken on a life of its own, and Bianca's dream was starting to take shape. I lived for our afternoons together working on the house, and I hated them in equal parts. Bianca's sweet scent as she bent in front of me to put more paint on her roller nearly knocked me off my feet.

The memory of her lips haunted my dreams. That kiss ... she said it was just for her parents' sake, but how had she not felt what I'd felt? The electric charge surging through my body, the heat drawing us together, like two magnets desperate to be united. The force of our destinies trying to unite us at last.

If Bianca felt any of it, she hadn't said anything to me. She kept up a steady stream of excited conversation about our wedding, the grand opening, the renovations, but about us ... about the marriage, her parents ... *nothing.* Sometimes, I'd look over at her and catch her staring back at me, her bright blue eyes focused hard, as though she were trying to see right through me.

The kiss hung between us, unacknowledged, but tainting every conversation, confusing every touch.

Despite the weird tension between us, we got a lot done on the house. Mostly, I worked during the afternoon on the manual tasks. I took some of the larger, clunkier antique furniture to *Abracadabra Antiques*, the local antique dealer, as well as some of the silver. That gave Bianca the funds to pay for the renovations, fresh bedding for the guest rooms, get a decent website built, and send out an enormous stack of promotional flyers to art communities, tattoo studios, and underground galleries she had connections with. We replaced the stiff rose-covered couches with a big squishy sofa that took up the majority of the drawing room.

Art started arriving. Bianca's network of friends from all over the world wanted to donate paintings to hang on the walls. We painted over the garish wallpaper in most of the downstairs rooms, and started hanging the pieces in every available space. Most were for sale, with Bianca acting as a dealer taking a commission. She typed up a catalogue of the work while I unboxed each piece and we argued over where to hang it.

"Where do you want the hideous cow?" I held up a picture of a giant, fat cow, her wrinkled face rendered in excruciating detail. A lolling tongue hung from her lips, dragging the British flag into her mouth to be chewed into a pulp.

Bianca tilted her head, thinking. "Above the dining table?"

"I think it will put people off their food."

"Perfect. That means we won't have to order so much food. Even with Belinda doing the catering, that shit's expensive."

I grinned as I banged a picture hook into the wall and hung the painting as straight as I could. Bianca typed "Ugly Cow" into her catalogue.

"What's next?"

I tore off the packaging on the next piece, revealing a large square abstract canvas. Black and brown lines crisscrossed a brilliant blue background, the paint so thick it stood out in high relief, it reminded me of the sitting under the trees in the forest, staring up at the winter sky through thick, leafless branches. A slash of black in the corner made me think of a raven poised to swoop down for it's next kill. "This one's dead pure brilliant."

"I agree." Bianca hopped up from her place at the table and came over to look closely. "That's my friend Odette's piece. She's this mega-hot German chick who does these incredibly gothic abstracts. I think this one's supposed to be a scene from the Black Forest."

"I love it." The image invoked the forest, all right. For a moment, a strange yearning for the wilds of Aberdeen washed over me. I'd lived in that forest my entire life, sleeping in the open air and hunting in the frigid valleys. Now, I was indoors all the time, trying to learn how to be part of society and fit myself into Bianca's life, and it wasn't exactly going the way I'd hoped. At least in the wild, everything was simple.

"Odette's coming to the wedding. I could introduce you if you like." Bianca grinned. "I bet you'll hit it off. She's gorgeous, and she is an animal in bed. I know from experience."

Don't do this to me, woman. I dropped the box of picture hooks. They scattered across the floor. I squatted to scoop them up, turning my back to Bianca so she wouldn't notice my cock springing to life.

It wasn't the idea of meeting this Odette chick making my blood run hot, but the thought of Bianca in bed with another woman, their naked bodies rolling over each other, hands caressing each other's breasts, playing with their nipples, tasting each other's juices ... I knew it was ridiculous, that Bianca's bisexuality was part of who she was, not a party trick designed to make her more desirable, and yet, my most secret sexual fantasies involved her being with another woman ...

Of course, in my dreams, I was in the room, too. And even though Bianca was totally hot for this other chick, she was really there for me. The two of them would slide their hands over my body, their tongues licking—

"Robbie, you okay?"

"Yeah, fine." I gulped, hopping over the floor to collect a hook that had rolled into the corner. "Is there ... anyone at the wedding you want to ... hook up with?"

Bianca tilted her head to the side. "You know Willow, the wedding planner? That girl is so odd and shy. I just want to corrupt her."

Think unsexy thoughts, think unsexy thoughts ... the vein on Dad's forehead throbbing as he yelled at me, the sound of police sirens getting closer when I'm on a job, Irvine clipping his toenails ...

That did the trick. The tightness in my jeans faded away, and the heat rushed out of my veins. I waited a few moments longer, fiddling with the hooks in the box, before standing up and facing Bianca again, happy that at least I wasn't embarrassing myself in front of her any more than I already had.

"Sorry, a little clumsy today." I stood up, clapping her on the shoulder the way friends who totally didn't want to touch their friend's naked bodies did. "Let's get these paintings hung."

11

BIANCA

The next two weeks passed in a blur. I worked long hours at *Resurrection Ink*, booking in as many clients as I could to fatten my coffers so I could afford some of the bigger decorating projects I wanted to do at The Prim. In the evenings, I worked on the PR for the grand opening and packed up my apartment. Luckily, the landlord had given me the okay to sublet it so I didn't have to break the lease, and Willow was looking for a place, so she decided to take it over.

Willow was an absolute legend. I had my doubts about her ability to pull off my crazy fake-wedding, but she totally delivered. She organised all the entertainment, scoured junk shops and eBay to find me the perfect vintage blue dress, managed to find a contractor who could secure all the circus troupe's aerial stunt equipment to the ceiling of the ballroom without damaging the period features, made travel arrangements for my friends from all over Europe, and scored me exclusive coverage with *London Underground* – the hottest art blog in the UK, all without raising her voice above a whisper.

And she was still fucking gorgeous, even though she never seemed to stop walking with that odd, slightly stiff gait.

Ever since he'd been all weird when we were hanging the pictures, I hardly saw Robbie. He was at the house every day, working on repainting over the hideous wallpaper and pulling up some of the more dated rugs. But whenever I showed up in the evenings, he'd disappear back to Ryan's as quick as he could.

The day before the wedding, I was doing my last appointment in the shop. I tried to talk to Elinor about it, but she refused to discuss Robbie. "I've already told you what I think about what you're doing," she said. "I'm not going to repeat myself. If you have a problem with Robbie, you need to talk to him."

"But—"

"Sorry." Elinor turned her chair around and bent over her client, the buzz of her tattoo gun covering the frigid silence that permeated my usually cheery studio.

I gritted my teeth as I focused on my own client – Kurt, the new drummer of Eric's band Ghost Symphony. Kurt had driven up from London today to be here for the wedding. Elinor and Eric's house – a Victorian gothic manor just down the road from the studio that had been in Eric's family for years – was already bursting at the seams with musicians here to play for my friends.

I should have been head banging with joy about all the awesome people who were showing up and pulling out all the stops for this shindig. It seemed like all of my friends were as excited about The Prim as I was. But all I could think about was Robbie. If I wasn't reliving that amazing kiss, I was tying myself up in knots worrying what he was thinking, how he was feeling.

If I didn't know better, I'd think he was avoiding me. But why would he do that? It doesn't make any sense. He's still planning to marry me, and we're still going to live together ... he can't avoid me forever.

He's not having second thoughts about the wedding, is he? Surely he'd say something? I mean, the whole thing is planned, everything's ready, people are starting to show up ... all he needs to do is say the magic words and sign the papers. If he pulls out now, all this work is for nothing.

I'll talk to him tonight.

When I arrived at The Prim that evening, the driveway was crowded with cars. Many of my friends were arriving from the continent. I flung open the front door, and was instantly swept up in a giant bear hug. "We have arrived," a deep German voice boomed in my ear.

"Welcome, Hans." I kissed his tattooed cheek. Hans was the Berlin tattoo artist who'd apprenticed me when I was an upstart teen. He introduced me to the underground arts scene in Berlin, took me out on 48-hour benders, and taught me everything I knew about tattooing. "Was the trip over a nightmare?"

"I had a harrowing brush with your British cuisine on *das Flugzeug*, but I managed to survive. Your friend has already made us very comfortable." Hans gestured to Robbie, who was chatting with a particularly attractive member of Han's female entourage. His shoulder muscles bulged with the weight of two giant suitcases under his arm.

At the sight of Robbie, my stomach twisted. "Excuse me for a minute." I shoved past him, and tapped Robbie on the shoulder.

He turned. At the sight of me, he jumped, dropping the suitcases on my foot. "Bianca, I'm ... I'm so sorry!"

"It's okay." I grabbed one of the cases, and thrust out my boot. "That's what steel-capped boots are for. I'll help you with these."

"Okay, sure." He picked up another case, and started dragging them up the stairs. A thin blonde German flattened herself against the wall to avoid being run over. I yanked my case up behind him.

"Dammit, Hans. What did you pack in here, bricks?"

"Surely, you did not expect me to arrive without a supply of our superior Bavarian beer," Hans yelled back at me. "Come back soon, for I have found your liquor cabinet and I am emptying it."

I grinned. It was awesome to have this house filled with *my* people. Already, the Prim seemed brighter, less oppressive.

Robbie reached the top of the stairs and headed off to the pink room. "You put Hans in there?" I asked, dragging the heavy case after him.

"Don't blame me. He *begged* for this room," Robbie said, as he set down one of the cases at the foot of the bed, beside several other rucksacks and sleeping bags. "Apparently, he'll be sharing this tiny bed with four of the lucky ladies downstairs."

"If you knew Hans, that wouldn't surprise you in the slightest. Who's that one for?" I pointed to a sleek red leather satchel slung over Robbie's shoulder.

"That's mine."

I whirled around, and my eyes met a slim girl leaning against the doorframe. Vivid green eyes stared me up and down, taking in every detail. The girl tucked an elegantly-styled curl of shiny brown hair off her face, revealing a slight smile with a dimple on her left cheek. Something about her face ... about that dimple ... looked terribly familiar, but I couldn't quite place it.

The girl reached out a hand. "Serenity Jones, blogger at *London Underground*. Great to meet you in person at last, Bianca."

Ah, that must be why she looked familiar. I'd have seen her photo accompanying articles on underground art shows and tattoo exhibitions. Elinor said she'd given Eric's first show post-resurrection a rave review. She was staying in Crookshollow to cover the wedding, and I'd let her crash at the Prim in exchange for a write-up on our accommodation, as well. If Serenity gave us a good review, we'd be golden.

I grabbed her hand and shook it. "The pleasure's all mine.

And I gather you've already met my *fiancé*, Robbie. If there's anything we can do to make you more comfortable, just let me know. Things are a bit crazy around here at the moment, so you're getting a bit of a bare-bones look at what The Prim has to offer, but we've got big plans for the future. As soon as I've got everyone settled, I'll give you a proper tour of the place."

"I'd like that. From what I've seen so far, you've done a fantastic job. This whole place just screams, 'Bianca Sinclair.'"

"What makes you say that? Are you familiar with my tattoo work?"

She tossed her hair over her shoulder. "Oh sure, I research all my subjects. I'd love to come see you at your studio as well. My photographer is with me, we could get some shots for the piece. Maybe I could even get some ink done?"

"Sure thing. Come grab me any time over the next couple of days and we can set it up."

"Excellent." She held out her hand, and Robbie passed her the satchel. "If you'll excuse me, I'm a bit tired from the drive. I think I'll go lie down for a bit. Talk to you guys later."

She turned on her heel and headed down the hall. Robbie made for the door. "I'd better get going," he muttered toward the floor. "Marcus wants to do this whole stag night thing—"

I grabbed him before he could run down the stairs. *Now or never.* "Big day tomorrow." I grinned, gripping his arm so he couldn't escape.

"Aye." Robbie's gaze focused on the wall behind me. "Look, Bianca, I should really go. I need to get my beauty sleep so I can be your Prince Charming in the morning—"

There was a hardness in his voice I'd never heard before. My stomach churned. *He's really not happy. He's going to bolt.* "Robbie, talk to me. You've been acting weird for the last couple of weeks. Are you having second thoughts?"

"It's a bit late for that, isn't it?"

"That's not an answer."

"I have to go." He tried to turn, but I yanked his arm back. I reached up with my other hand and grabbed him around the neck, locking him in place so he couldn't look anywhere but directly at me. He squirmed, but I dug my fingers in.

"Dammit, Robbie. I'm your friend. If you don't want to do this, you have to *tell* me. I'm not forcing you into anything, and I don't want you to do something you're not comfortable with. So go on, spill. What's going on? Have you changed your mind?"

Robbie started to say something, then his gaze focused over my shoulder, to something in the hall. I whirled around, saw it was Odette's painting. I turned back. Robbie squared his shoulders and sucked in a breath. His eyes bored into mine.

Energy jolted through my fingers where they touched his skin. An invisible heat rose between us, tugging my body toward his. I stared at his lips, full and hot and begging to be kissed.

Robbie blinked. "No, I haven't changed my mind. We've created something awesome here, Bianca. I want to see it through."

"Good." My voice came out hoarse and husky. "I'm glad you agree. Could you stop being so mopey, then? Tomorrow is gonna be awesome. You've worked your arse off on this place, Robbie. You deserve a party to celebrate. And I'll totally introduce you to Odette. I promise."

"Sure. Okay." he swallowed.

Just kiss me, dammit.

Despite how stupid it was with everything going on, I wanted it so bad. I wanted him. But he was Robbie. He wouldn't make the first move.

I leaned forward, my lips outstretched, ready to fall into him, to feel that electric charge jolting through my body once again. But Robbie moved, and my face hit him square in his broad chest. He wrapped his arms around my shoulders.

"Goodnight, my sweet bride." Robbie kissed my forehead, his lips lingering. A shiver of delight ran through my body, and I found myself gripping him tighter, not wanting him to move. We stayed locked like that, for several moments, before Robbie pulled away and headed for the door again.

"Wait!" I yelled.

He whirled around. "What?"

"Do you want to stay and have a drink with us? I'd love for you to get to know Hans, and Odette should be here later—"

His mouth gave a weird little wobble. "No, no. I can't. Marcus is waiting, remember? I'll see you in the morning."

Before I could say anything else, he bolted for the stairs, as though he were escaping a fire or a crazy ex. I trudged down after him, clutching the doorframe while he stumbled down the porch steps, his boots not even properly on his feet. I shut the door as he sped away, my heart hammering against my chest. My eyes filled with tears.

Hans rushed in and grabbed my hands, dragging me through the house, his mouth moving a mile a minute as he filled me in on all the gossip from Berlin. I barely heard a word as I was pulled through the remodelled ballroom. Robbie had spent a whole day polishing the marble floor of the ballroom until it shone like new. Together, we'd hung strings of fairy lights across the rafters.

My house. *My* dream come true. *My* friends here to celebrate *my* epic party tomorrow. I should have been giddy with excitement, so why was my stomach tied up in knots? Why did the vision of Robbie's crushed expression burned into my mind? Why did none of it feel the same without him here with me?

Why did my lips still ache for that kiss?

"Bianca," my mother growled, her eyes glaring with disapproval. She loomed over me, harsh light highlighting her twisted face, like some monster from a B-grade horror film. "What have you done to your dress?"

I glanced down at the beautiful blue fishtail skirt and matching beaded corset, straight out of a 1920s masquerade. Horror clenched in my stomach as my eyes fell upon the dark red stain spreading across the bodice. Trails of red dripped down the corset, dribbling between the delicate beading and turning the beautiful silk fabric into a grisly pink mess.

I swiped my hand through the spreading stain, my fingers wet with the warm, dark substance. I brought it to my lips, and tasted. *Blood.*

But why was I bleeding? Had I been shot? Why didn't I feel any pain?

I cupped my hands to my chest, desperate to staunch the wound. I stared up at my mother, ready to accuse her of this crime, but she was no longer there. Instead, Robbie stood in her place, naked from the waist up, the shitty tattoos on his chest blurred and crisscrossed with deep cuts. The jagged edges of the cuts hung down, revealing the muscles and bones beneath. My stomach turned as I realised the cuts appeared in four neat lines – claw marks. He'd been been mauled by a wild animal.

As though a wolf had attacked him.

"Robbie ... what happened?" I tried to step toward him, but my legs wouldn't budge. As hard as I tugged, my feet remained glued to the wooden floor of the ballroom. I stretched out my hands, desperate to see if Robbie was okay, but he remained just out of reach, his hands hanging at his sides. Pain welled in his eyes – intense, overwhelming pain that clouded his whole face.

"It's not your blood," he said. "It's mine. Look."

He pointed to his chest. A dark red dot appeared on the left side, the red spot growing larger and larger as more blood pooled from the wound.

"Robbie ..." I choked out. My chest ached, the horror of seeing him becoming a physical vice that clamped around my heart.

"It's my broken heart." Robbie's face drooped.

I poured my whole being into tearing my feet from the ground and propelling myself toward him. But no matter how hard I tried, I couldn't move. I opened my mouth to scream, but my lips wouldn't move. My tongue stuck to the roof of my mouth. Instead, I screamed inside my head. *Robbie, don't leave me!*

The colour faded from his cheeks. He teetered on his feet. Blood oozed down his chest, dribbling over his belt. "I guess ... our vows didn't mean anything after all," he said, a sigh in his voice like he never expected anything else.

Robbie, no!

But he faded away, his body disintegrating into the air. A smear of dark blood spread across the floor. From somewhere in the depths of the darkened ballroom, the first haunting notes of the bridal march struck.

I worked my jaw open, and screamed and screamed. I tore my feet from the floor, and flung myself at the spot where Robbie had been, my hands grasping at thin air—

"Meeeeeooww!"

My eyes flew open. My hip hit something hard. I grabbed for my chest, clutching at my own pounding heart. My eyes adjusted to the bright room, and I realised I wasn't in the ballroom, wearing a blood-soaked wedding dress. I was back in my own bedroom, at my flat. I lay on my side on the floor, the bedspread tangled around my legs. Macavity glared at me from on top of the now-empty bed.

It was just a dream.

I rubbed my eyes, and tugged my legs out of the blankets. All my stuff had already been moved to The Prim. The bare room unnerved me – I felt displaced, as though I'd never really lived here, but was just visiting. Just my bed and an empty dresser (which I'd sold to Willow), the suitcase I'd been living out of for the last week, Macavity's orange cat bed, and my wedding dress hanging from the wardrobe door remained.

I picked up my phone from the floor. 1:03 a.m.

It's my wedding day.

I took the skirt and corset down, checking the bodice for blood stains, but finding none. I moved in front of the open bathroom door and held my dress up to my body, admiring the beautiful beaded bodice, the flare of the skirt as it swished across my legs. The dress was a bright jet blue that drew out the blue in my eyes.

"It's my broken heart." Robbie's sad words echoed in my head. I thought of everyone who'd objected to our fake-marriage, all the friends like Elinor who warned me how he felt about me, who told me that I was cruel to go ahead with it. I thought of the way Robbie looked when he left The Prim yesterday, how he avoided my eyes.

Are they right? Is Robbie really doing this just to get close to me?

Knowing that, should I go through with it?

I hugged the dress closer to me, and imagined Robbie standing beside me, wearing his traditional highland dress, his eyes sparkling with love. His hand reached for mine, and I could almost *feel* the tingling of his warm skin against my bare arm. I imagined Robbie's lips brushing my neck, turning my head toward him, and his tongue exploring my mouth, the way he'd done on my mother's front step. An ache rose in my stomach, and goosebumps flew up my arms.

Was it *really* possible that I might also be attracted to Robbie? He was *not* my type. I wasn't usually attracted to men these days – women were soft and yielding and generally much more fun. When I did go for guys, it was the arrogant artist types – guys like Elinor's Eric with wild hair and waifish frames who created and fucked with intensity (so I've heard. Sadly, I'd never managed to get Eric into the sack).

Sweet little Willow made my lips ache to deflower her, but thinking about Robbie's kiss made my knees shake. I couldn't deny that I wanted more of him. Maybe I'd really felt like this all along, but I'd been determined to ignore it because I didn't want to destroy our friendship, because ... deep down I knew that I might actually have a real shot with this guy, that he might be the kind of person I could be with permanently, something I'd never wanted.

And now I was marrying him. *Way to get things all backward, Bianca.*

I sighed, and dropped my dress on to the bed. There was only one way to find out if what I was feeling was for real. I needed to embrace it. I needed to stop playing with Robbie's feelings and give him a *real* chance.

I picked up my phone, and text Robbie a short message:

HEY, IT'S ME. HAPPY WEDDING DAY. CAN'T WAIT TO SEE YOU TONIGHT, HANDSOME. I ESPECIALLY CAN'T WAIT FOR THE KISS.

I hit send, my heart pounding. He couldn't misinterpret *that*.

"Time to get married." I smiled to myself in the mirror. Feeling better already, I flung the dress over the door, and flopped back down onto the bed, where I quickly fell into a deep and dreamless sleep.

~

"Ouch! Not so hard."

"Sorry, sorry." Elinor pulled back, staring at me with concern. The eyebrow pencil – in her hands, a weapon of mass destruction – clattered against the dressing table.

I clutched at my eye. "It's going to be hard to walk straight down the aisle when I'm blind."

Elinor tapped the empty glass and ornate silver spoon beside my makeup box. "With the amount of absinthe you've drunk already, I think you're doomed either way. And don't touch, you'll smudge my hard work."

My bridal party and I were all crammed into the Rose Room at the top of the turret, which was now my bedroom and makeshift dressing room. Dresses and corsets were slung over every surface, makeup fanned out across the rug, curling iron cords crisscrossing the few remaining squares of floor space. I slouched over the back of an antique dressing chair while Elinor did my makeup. Despite some seriously misplaced jabs with the eyeliner pencil, she'd done a wonderful job – bright blue around my eyes and on my lips, a pale foundation to make my huge eyes stand out, an icy blue on my lips.

I picked up my phone to take a selfie. My eyes flicked to the message icon on my homescreen. Nothing. Robbie still hadn't replied to my text last night. My stomach twisted with nerves. In just a few minutes I'd be meeting him at the altar, but so many unanswered questions still hung between us. Would he even show up at all? Had I just succeeded in scaring him off?

"You look amazing, Bianca." Belinda grinned from her spot on the bed. I beamed back. She looked pretty hot herself. I'd told my three bridesmaids to just wear whatever they wanted. Belinda had chosen a black lace fishtail gown that made her beautiful Asian skin gleam.

I tried to stand up, but Alex – wearing a beautiful soft pink grecian-style dress – placed a hand on my shoulder.

"Wait. The *pièce de résistance*." Alex lifted an object out of a wooden case. She placed a wreath of twisted metal and black stones on my head, pulling strands of my hair over the wire so it looked so though the crystals grew from my skull.

"It took me a whole day to make this, so you'd better like it." She adjusted the tiara on my head and pinned it in place. "You like it?"

"I love it." I twisted this way and that, admiring the way the stones sparkled on the light. Against my white and blue hair, the crown made me look like a fairy princess.

"You look stunning," Elinor breathed, brushing down the red corset of her gothic-style dress. Her blood-red lips curled back into a grin. "The best fake bride I've ever seen."

"Robbie is going to flip when he sees you," Alex gushed.

"He's not really my husband, remember." I thought about the text, gone unanswered, and my stomach twisted in a knot. If he didn't show up, he might not be my husband at *all*, real or not.

Alex and Elinor exchanged a look. I braced myself for another lecture, but none was forthcoming. Finally, Alex said, "I just meant ... that you look really different, is all. You're usually in jeans and your Docs."

Grinning, I lifted up the corner of my dress to reveal my scuffed patent black Docs. Elinor snorted.

Noise from downstairs wafted through the crack in the door. People chatting, laughing, glasses tinkling, Eric playing violin quietly in the background. The door creaked open further, and Willow poked her head into the room. She looked particularly stunning today, wearing a black A-line dress with a white collar, her hair pinned back like Wednesday Addams. "All the guests have arrived, and Robbie's waiting. We're ready when you are."

A lump formed in my chest. So Robbie did show up, after all. He didn't completely hate me.

I actually felt nervous. But why? This was a fake wedding. I wasn't marrying Robbie. Well, I mean, I *was*, but it didn't mean anything. He hadn't replied to my text, so everyone was obviously imagining his attraction to me. He was just a friend doing me a favour. That was all it was going to be.

I'd misread everything, and worked myself up for no reason at all. Now it was time to go downstairs and face my fake-husband and make it through my fake-ceremony without succumbing to the urge to jump his bones.

I straightened my bodice, and the girls lined up behind me. Willow ran down the stairs, her gorgeous little ass sliding around in her silky dress, and told Eric to cue the music. The first sombre strains of Ghost Symphony's latest single, *Requiem for a Dying Rose*, wafted up the stairs. My stomach fluttered.

"Here I go." I flashed Elinor a grin, and descended the first step.

12

ROBBIE

"That's the cue." Ryan's mother Clara wrapped her wizened hand around my arm, her kind eyes staring into mine. "You ready, love?"

I nodded, my stomach twisting, as I shuffled into position at the front of the makeshift stage in the corner of the ballroom. My kilt itched like hell, and I longed to scratch my bare thigh, but as the oddly-dressed crowd shoving their way closer to get a good view for the ceremony, it didn't seem like a good time.

From a larger stage in the opposite corner, the music swelled as Eric drew his bow expertly across the strings. A single spotlight danced off his flowing black hair. Behind him, the rest of his band picked up the tune – drums marching a slow beat, bass thumping, the electric guitar swelling along with the violin. Was it a wedding march, or a funeral dirge?

As the drummer rolled the snare, a second spot lit up the doorway to the hallway opposite the grand staircase. The guests' heads turned away from me, giving me relief from their piercing judgement. Every eye in the room focused on the stairs, waiting for Bianca – my bride – to make her entrance.

I shifted my weight from foot to foot, my fingers tightening around my sporran. Half of me – the wolf half that lurked dangerously close to the surface tonight – longed to run for the open window, leap into the forest and never return. The other half kept my feet glued in place, watching the shadows dance at the edge of the ballroom, waiting for my first glimpse of her.

All day, Bianca's SMS replayed over and over before my eyes. I'M ESPECIALLY LOOKING FORWARD TO THE KISS. I'd barely been able to belt my kilt this morning, I was so hard.

My wolf snapped at my skin, spurned on by my constant state of arousal. I'd typed a hundred messages in reply, then deleted each one without sending it. I couldn't figure out what it meant. Was Bianca just teasing, or ... *was she saying she felt the same way I did?*

Eventually, I'd given up trying to comprehend it, and I showed it to Marcus. Big mistake. I'd had to wrestle my phone from his hand so he wouldn't send her something foul in reply. "She's playing with you, mate," he'd said. "You can't go through with this. She's going to mess you up."

He could be right, but ... I had to take the chance. If Bianca wanted to play ... I'd take it. I'd take anything she was willing to give—

There she is.

Bianca rounded the corner of the staircase, and swept into the ballroom. She wore an electric blue corset and fishtail skirt, embroidered all over with swirls of black beading. Her lips were a slice of ice-blue, and atop her head sprouted a crown of twisted black metal, like an ice princess or a faerie queen. Her eyes locked on mine, and her lips drew back into a dazzling smile.

I gasped, her beauty stealing my breath. The whole room faded, the colourful outfits and judging faces of the crowd blurred into background smudges, dulled by her radiance.

Bianca floated across the marble floor, her body carried by

the haunting music. She reached the stage and stepped up to stand opposite me. The bridesmaids' lined up behind her, grinning and waving to the crowd.

"Hi." She grinned, her face lighting up. She'd never looked more beautiful.

"Hi, right back." My hands itched to draw her close, feel the softness of her body against mine. I wanted nothing more than to be the one who undid the strings of her corset, revealing the smooth skin beneath. The words of her SMS flashed in my mind once more.

Camera flashes went off across the floor. Eric faded out the song. My gaze briefly settled over the crowd, recognising Caleb, Rosa, Irvine and Rolf standing together against the back wall, Ryan and Cole over near the band, Bianca's parents frowning as they inched away from a scantily-clad tattooist in the front row.

We were here. We were really doing this.

As one, we turned to Clara, who began to read from a large black book about the sanctity and ancient traditions of marriage. Bianca had written the ceremony herself, and it was filled with crude jokes that Clara delivered with gusto. In minutes, the room was in uproar.

I didn't hear a single word. I kept staring at Bianca, unable to believe this was real. She was *really* standing here with me, becoming my wife. My inner wolf clawed against my skin, desperate to reach out and claim her as my mate.

Soon, we'll kiss again.

It's not real, Robbie, I told myself, over and over, trying to calm the wolf inside me that wanted desperately to lay claim to his mate. *She's only your wife in name. She doesn't really belong to you. Hell, she's probably standing there thinking about Willow.*

Clara droned on about the symbolism of wedding rings and Viking oaths. She nodded at me and I lifted Bianca's hand, my fingers grazing her knuckles. The pull of our connection sizzled between us. Marcus handed me her ring – a tungsten carbide ring engraved with my fingerprint – and I slipped it onto her tiny finger, pushing it down over her finger tat.

"With this ring, I bind my life to yours," I repeated, the words falling from my mouth. As I spoke them, the connection tightened. "Wear it, and know that I love you."

Bianca raised her eyes to me, her irises sparkling. She pursed her lips, as though she wanted to say something. Then Clara handed her my ring – another tungsten carbide piece engraved with her fingerprint (a friend of hers made them) – and her mouth faltered. Bianca gripped my hand, her fingers like fire against my skin. She turned my finger toward her, and pushed the ring past my knuckle.

"With this ring, I bind my life to yours. Wear it, and know that I love you."

The words echoed in my mind. *I wish like hell they were the truth.*

My inner wolf growled with agony. Clara said something, but I didn't hear it. Bianca's face mesmerised me, those sparkling eyes drawing me in. *What are you thinking right now? What does this mean to you?*

"You may now kiss the bride."

I froze. The moment I'd been waiting for, and suddenly, I couldn't move. I stood, transfixed by her, utterly flummoxed by the whole situation.

"Kiss her! Kiss her!" The crowd roared, like it was a rock concert.

The corners of Bianca's lips turned up in a smile. I willed myself to shuffle forward, to take her in my arms, the way I'd always longed to do, and claim her lips with mine. To show her once and for all that I wanted her. My inner wolf howled with frustration as my feet remained rooted to the spot.

Bianca reached up, wrapped her arms around my neck, and pressed her lips to mine.

A surge of energy shot through my body, reaching right down into my boots. My arms enclosed around her tiny frame, gripping her waist. She felt so good in my arms, like she fit. Our faces mashed together, our lips enmeshed.

Bianca *kissed* me.

The ballroom erupted with applause. Bianca drew back, her breath brushing my lips. "I told you I was looking forward to this." She grinned, her arms still wrapped around me. "You can't keep me waiting, Robbo, or I'll take matters into my own hands."

"Bianca, wait. Does this mean—"

But Bianca grabbed my hand and thrust it into the air. Thunderous applause washed over us. People hooted and stamped their feet. The band struck up a raucous tune, a cover of *Eye of the Tiger*. Eric's violin screeched as he played the main riff.

Bianca's beautiful face broke into a wide grin. She squeezed my hand, and I couldn't keep an identical grin from spreading across my face. The room erupted into chaos. People swarmed around us, hugging and kissing and congratulating us. Confetti littered the air. Glitter sprayed in all directions. I took it all in with barely a glance, so focused was I on the warmth of Bianca's hand in mine, and the tingling of her presence on my lips.

Bianca kissed me. She kissed me. She feels the same way.

"THIS IS SOME PARTY." Caleb slapped me on the shoulder. "Your wife really knows how to throw a fake wedding."

Your wife. The words were so foreign, but they felt so, *so* good.

The "fake wedding" part, not so much. They snapped me back to reality. I gazed around the darkened ballroom, searching for Bianca. I hadn't seen her for a couple of hours, ever since I'd lost her to a horde of heavily-tattooed Germans. She'd be some-where in the centre of the fray, downing G&Ts like they were water and being the life of the party.

I told myself that I didn't mind that she'd gone off without me, but it was a lie. She'd barely said a word to me since our kiss.

That's your fault, you coward. I couldn't work up the courage to go find her. I'd liked her for so long, and the idea that she might feel the same way … it was everything I'd dreamed, but what if I was wrong? I couldn't deal with it, not tonight, when it was supposed to be her night, *her* triumph.

So instead, I stood against the wall, occasionally shuffling behind some brightly-dressed artist to avoid being spotted by Bianca's parents, who were currently standing in a corner looking like they needed to be rescued from Hans. The last thing I wanted was to get pulled into an awkward conversation about Latin verbs. I downed several sugary cocktails and watched people in bright-coloured costumes mosh to Ghost Symphony, and wished like hell I had some balls.

My inner wolf wished it, too. My stomach churned with the effort of holding the wolf at bay, so desperate was the desire to claim my mate. With Irvine and Rolf floating around together, the desire to leap into my wolf form was ever more present.

Now, Caleb was here, trying to make small talk like he thought I needed a babysitter. *Great.*

"Bianca's hoping she'll get written up in all the underground press in London," I said, gesturing to a group of woman standing in the corner, talking into their mobile phones. The girl we'd met yesterday, Serenity Jones, stood off to one side, snapping pictures with a long-lens camera. "If word gets out about The Prim, she'll be able to start filling the rooms and running events, and make this place turn a profit."

"Good. That's good. You guys have really done a great job on the place." Caleb lowered his voice. "Anything new on the Benedict Ring?"

I shook my head. Of course, Caleb couldn't go a single night without mentioning the ring. My failure to find it hung in the air between us, an invisible billboard screaming I'M A SCREWUP about as loud as an invisible billboard could. "I've come up with nothing but dead ends since Bianca's father showed me the jewellery."

"A ring that powerful doesn't just get lost," Caleb growled. "Keep looking. We're getting desperate. Irvine and I are on the cusp of an important alliance, but we're going to need to demonstrate our power with that ring to seal the deal."

"Who with?"

"The Wulfric pack."

My head jerked up. *That's insane.* Caleb had grown up beside me, had lived through long and bitter battles with both the Bairds and the Wulfrics. Now, my stepbrother was deliberately aligning his pack with our family's oldest and most bitter enemies.

I touched the waistband of my kilt, reminding myself that the Macleans weren't my family anymore. I'd invited my parents and my brother Angus tonight, but my mother had written me to say that my father had torn up my letter, officially declaring that he disowned me. She wished me the best, but that she wouldn't be able to get away without angering Colin.

It had taken me nearly an hour to read that letter, and not just because I struggled with the words. I couldn't go back, which meant that if things with Bianca didn't work out, and if I couldn't find the ring, then I'd really be on my own.

And now Caleb was deliberately aligning with another old enemy, with a guy he knew had it out for me. It seemed like he was already making his choice. But if he was aligning with them

... than what was Rolf doing at the library? Was he following me, trying to get a look at my research?

"Don't you think that's dangerous? You know better than anyone what the Wulfrics are capable of. And after I saw Rolf at the library going through the archives—"

"He's allowed to be at the library. There's not exactly a lot to do in Crookshollow while he waits for us to iron out this alliance."

"What if he's just biding his time while he tries to beat us to the ring? If they get their hands on the ring, they won't need an alliance."

"That won't happen. They don't know we don't have the real ring." Caleb held up his hand, where he wore a pewter ring – two snake heads entwined around a blood-red stone. It was the fake ring he'd got from Ryan's mother Clara in order to trick my father, but it was close enough to the historical descriptions that it could pass for the real thing. "This isn't your business to worry about, Robbo. Irvine and I are dealing with it. Just do your job and find that ring."

"Aye, right. Of course."

Caleb nodded. His eyes darted behind me, and his face broke out into a smile as he sighted someone he actually wanted to talk to. He ducked into the crowd, leaving me on my own.

As soon as he left, I missed him. At least he tried to include me in the pack and give me responsibilities to help me prove myself. It wasn't his fault I was failing miserably.

I scanned the faces in the crowd, searching for someone friendly. Many of them were strangers, known to me only by Bianca's animated descriptions. There was Hans, the German tattoo artist who had his entire face decorated like a panther, and Lux, a Serbian guerrilla artist who'd only recently been released from incarceration after she was caught painting her country's parliament buildings bright pink. Over in the corner was Odette, who was indeed fucking hot, and whose face would feature alongside Bianca's in many a late night fantasy of mine for years to come. The one stilted conversation we'd had at the bar – filled with too many words I couldn't understand – put to rest any possible future we might have had.

I didn't want her anyway. I had eyes for only one woman ... my fated mate.

"Robbie!" I breathed a sigh of relief as Elinor pushed through the crowd, her red dress sparkling under the flickering lights as she waved a glass of champagne under my nose. "I saw you looking a little lost, and thought I'd come and rescue you."

"You're an angel," I yelled back, accepting the glass, even though my stomach probably couldn't handle too much more liqueur. In the corner, the band had returned from their break. Any moment now they'd start up again, blasting their unique blend of industrial goth, and at least I wouldn't have to make any more small talk until their set was over.

"Killer party! Bianca really knows how to throw a rave."

"Yeah, she's amazing."

Eric's band struck up at full volume, and all conversations in the room dimmed to screaming. These guys usually played to sold-out concert venues and arenas. To get them here, at a tiny house party, was pretty crazy. Elinor grabbed my hand and dragged me toward the front. I glanced around for Bianca, but couldn't see her in the fray. People jostled against me, moving in time to the pounding beat. An elbow knocked my hand, splashing sticky champagne down my shirt.

Eric straddled a foldback, his fingers sliding over the strings as he tore at his violin with the bow. His black black hair flew around his face, and sweat streamed down his broad forehead. Girls in the audience grabbed at his legs, but his intense gaze remained locked on Elinor, who tossed her arms in the air and screamed his name.

That's love. My stomach churned, and not just because it was filled with an insane cocktail of absinthe and gin and bubbles. I wanted that kind of love so bad. I wanted Bianca to stare at me the way Elinor was gazing up at Eric, to see me as something other than the illiterate loser everyone else saw.

Every bone in my body ached to be close to her, and my inner wolf was practically clawing me to pieces in desperation to go and claim her before another wolf did. I'd barely managed to make it through our wedding day. I'd never be able to survive this marriage if I had to continue to pretend I didn't have feelings for her.

It was my wedding day, and I'd never felt more alone.

I can't keep on hiding this. The realisation hit me along with the pounding drums, the thundering bass driving my determination. *I need to talk to Bianca, and I need to do it now. I've got to tell her the truth. What she does with it is up to her, but I can't carry this bloody secret around anymore.*

I drowned the rest of my glass, and dropped Elinor's hand. She grabbed my arm and mouthed something to me, but I had no hope in hell of hearing it. I yanked my arm away and dived into the press of people.

I shoved and ducked between gyrating, moshing bodies, copping an elbow in my cheek and several slaps on my ass. Lights spun overhead, casting brilliant discs across, making their faces appear like speckled demons. My wolf senses stood on high alert, drunk on the myriad of scents and excretions that permeated the hot room.

I scanned every grinning, leering face, but couldn't see Bianca anywhere. I shoved my way toward the back of the ballroom, heading to the bar. *Where is she?*

At the bar, I grabbed another champagne, and drowned it. The alcohol buzzed in my veins, mingling with my agitation. My inner wolf clawed against my skin, desperate to free itself. I picked up a whiff of Bianca's scent, and dived back into the fray, heading toward the door to the hallway, on the other side of the room.

I reached the hall, peering around at the people standing in small circles, deep in conversation. I still couldn't see Bianca anywhere. Where could she be? I doubted she was out in the drawing room, deep in serious conversation. Bianca liked to be where the action was. I must've missed her before on the dance floor. I drew myself up to my full height, and set down the glass. Time to get back in there and—

What's that?

Something was happening on the other side of the ballroom. People gathered in a circle, cheering and thrusting their glasses in the air. Ripples of excitement spread through the crowd. As Eric finished his solo, the room erupted with the cries of, "Snog, snog, snog!"

I pushed through the throng of people, heading toward the centre of the circle. My heart thundered against my chest. *Something's wrong.* But I didn't know what.

I shoved my way between Rosa and Belinda. Belinda grabbed my arm, yelling at me to get back, but I wrenched my arm away. I pushed forward, and saw what had captured everyone's attention. My heart sank to my knees.

At the centre of the circle, Bianca had her arms wrapped around that shy wedding planner, Willow. Bianca's hand tangled in Willow's hair, shoving the girl's face against hers. Their lips were locked together in a passionate kiss.

I couldn't tear my eyes away. The room around me faded, the cheering voices dying away, until all that I could hear was the beating of my own heart, pounding against my ears.

Only a few hours ago, Bianca had kissed me like that, with all the fiery passion she could conjure up. From the text, from what she'd said, from the heat that surged between us, I'd thought it meant something to her, the way it had meant every-thing to me.

And now, here she was, kissing this girl like none of it meant anything at all. Because it didn't. She was everything to me, but I was nothing to her.

From deep inside me, my wolf dragged up a deep, furious anger – a rage so primal, it boiled in my veins.

To the furious applause of the crowd, Bianca tore her lips away, raising her hands above her head. Champagne splashed from the bottle, soaking my shirt. The whole room cheered.

Everyone, except me.

Bianca's eyes swept around the room as she drank in her adoring audience. Her eyes fell on me, and her smile froze on her face. "Robbie," her lips mouthed my name. The same lips that had betrayed me.

I threw back my head, the howl tearing from my lips before I could hold it back.

Shit, no, get back inside me.

Too late. The wolf burst through my chest, claiming my body. I roared as pain arced across behind my eyes as all the bits inside me that made me see as a human rearranged themselves, and my wolfish eyes bulged forward. My nose broke away, elon-gating to become a muzzle. Hair sprouted from my arms. The pin on my kilt burst open as my hips rotated, bending backward to become my hind legs.

Someone screamed. All around me, people backed away, their faces frozen with fear. The music cut out with a screech as Eric's band dropped their instruments and scrambled for cover.

"Robbie, please. I'll explain—"

Too late, the wolf inside me had taken control. I howled again as I toppled forward, landing hard on my palms. My fingers curled over, becoming claws that itched to tear out throats and slice skin. My skin prickled as more hair pushed through.

Everyone screamed and rushed for the exits. Glittery shoes and bejewelled capes flew in all directions as the crowd fled the room. Only Bianca remained, her eyes boring into mine, her face collapsing with pain.

I didn't want to hear her say it. I couldn't bear to know that our kiss meant nothing. I beat my tail against the ballroom floor, about-turned, and stalked from the room, leaving a wake of terror behind me.

13

BIANCA

"Robbie, wait!" I grabbed for him, managing to graze his tail. But the wolf was too quick, and he darted away toward the hallway. The surging crowd parted to let him through. As soon as he'd disappeared up the staircase, they crowded into the gap left behind, swallowing him up like the Red Sea drowning the Pharaoh.

"Bianca!" A hand grabbed my arm. Hans shook me. "You are okay, yes? The wolf, did it bite you?"

"No, I'm fine."

"What happened? I do not believe what my eyes have seen. Your friend *turned into a wolf*."

"It's fine, Hans. It's just a trick." I waved a hand at a gaggle of terrified guests by the bar, trying to put my face into a this-is-totally-normal expression, even though I wanted to curl up and die. "Tell them, would you please? It's just entertainment. I have to go."

"But, Bianca—"

I was already gathering up my skirt and running, my boots thudding across the marble floor. Robbie's stricken expression just before he shifted burned into my retinas, instantly sobering me up. Willow ... I was kissing Willow. Why had I done that?

Because she's hot and you're drunk and horny and it seemed like fun at the time. Not fun now, though, is it?

God, Robbie's face ... he'd looked so hurt. *But it was just a kiss. He knows what I'm like, especially after a few drinks. He knows I think Willow is hot.*

Shut up, Bianca. Don't make excuses for yourself. You know how he felt about you. That kiss at the altar today proved it. And yet you did this to him, on his wedding day. You're a total selfish bitch, and you don't deserve him.

I lurched in the hall, but the gaggle of reporters shoving their way up the staircase told me I wasn't going to get anywhere quickly if I went that way. I knew Robbie would head to the attic and lock himself away in that tiny room until he could change back. Luckily, I knew there was another way to reach him.

I crashed through the dining room, my hip knocking the table and causing my friend Patrice – who was balanced on top pretending to be a statue – to wobble dangerously. "Sorry," I yelled as I shoved more people aside, ducking across the hall into the kitchen.

I dived for the pantry, but someone grabbed my arm and yanked me back. I whirled around. It was that reporter from the *London Underground* blog, Serenity Jones. A salacious smile deepened her dimple.

"Nice kiss." She grinned, waving her camera in front of my face. "And the wolf ... you really did a brilliant job with the special effects. I got some great pictures. I can make this place look totally wild. This'll really stir up interest in The Prim."

"Good. That's good." My fingers itched to claw her eyes out. *Just go away.*

She shoved her phone under my nose. "Can you give me a

few quick words about the wolf stunt? Just a soundbite I can quote on our Facebook page—"

"Fuck off," I growled into the phone, then turned to the kitchen door. "Everybody, get the fuck out of this room!"

Alex and Ryan stood by the fridge, staring at me with wide-eyed concern. "What happened?" Alex yelled to me.

I waved my hands and they got the idea. Ryan grabbed Serenity and herded her out the door, while Alex started shoving other people away. I scrambled over piles of catering boxes to the back of the pantry and yanked open the narrow door that led to the secret staircase.

Heavy boots thudded behind me. Caleb's voice growled beside me. "Where is he? I'm gonna fucking *kill* him—"

"Caleb, not now."

"He *revealed* himself, Bianca. You've got a party of terrified guests out there convinced they just saw a werewolf. This is going to be all over the press, and we're not even *remotely* ready. It's a fucking *disaster.*"

"I said, not now!" I slammed the door to the secret staircase in his face. Caleb swore, but he didn't try to follow me. He wouldn't have been able to fit up the narrow staircase anyway. His shoulders were broader than Robbie's, who only just fit.

I clattered up the stairs and shoved my weight against the secret panel at the top. I expected to meet the usual resistance, but instead, the panel flew open and I tumbled into the room, tripping over the edge of the step and sprawling in a heap across the floor.

"I heard you coming." Robbie's face loomed over me, the door in his hands. "I was just about to let you in."

"Robbie, you bloody *fool.*" I gazed up at him, meeting his eyes. My whole heart poured out to him as I saw how miserable he looked. "What happened?"

He threw the panel down against the wall, and slumped on

the bed, his hands balled into fists. I tried not to focus on his naked body – the toned, trim muscles of his torso, the V-of his hips leading down to a seriously impressive cock. He wasn't a total alpha like Caleb or Luke, but damn, did that guy have the body of a superhero. "I'm an idiot, is what happened."

"You turned into a wolf, in the middle of the ballroom—"

"Dammit, Bianca. I *know*. I was there. I don't need a fucking play-by-play."

"I'm sorry, I'm just trying to understand. I'm worried about you."

He grunted.

I dragged myself to my knees, inching forward so I was kneeling in front of him. My stomach flipped. "It's true, Robbie. I *am* worried. Something upset you. Was it me and Willow?"

Robbie turned his head to the window, deliberately not looking at me. His lip trembled. Damn, the pain in his face ... *I'm making you feel like this. Oh, Robbie, I never knew how deep your feelings went ...*

I wanted to do whatever was required to make Robbie smile again. More than anything, I wanted to see that brilliant grin I loved so much, the grin that had greeted me at the end of the aisle. I reached up, placing my hand on his cheek, my fingers tingling with heat as they brushed his skin. I turned his head toward mine, my eyes boring into his.

"Read my lips, Robbie Maclean. That kiss with Willow meant *nothing*." I brushed my fingers over his skin, enjoying the rough stubble across his chin. Damn, he *was* gorgeous. How come I'd never noticed before? "I'm drunk. I'm horny. She's got that whole innocent waif thing going on and it's just a teeny bit irresistible. I wanted to kiss someone, and you weren't around. It's not going to go anywhere. She's as hetero as they come. And she's not the one I really want."

My head swam as my fingers traced the line of his neck,

brushing the edge of his collarbone. The air between us sizzled. My lips ached to kiss him again.

I've drank so much. I'm not thinking straight. I should go downstairs.

Yet, I couldn't tear my eyes away from him.

"And our kiss?" Robbie's eyes narrowed, his face creased with pain. His skin stiffened under my touch. "What about that? Did that mean nothing, too?"

"No, I—" I struggled to find the words. "It wasn't—"

"Come on, Bianca." A note of anger crept into his voice. "If this fake-marriage is going to work, we have to be completely *honest* with each other, remember? Are you just going to toy with me until you get tired of me, and then toss me away like you do with everyone else in your life?"

"That's not fair." I yanked my hand away.

"It's completely fair. You don't let anyone get close to you. You have hundreds of friends, but not one of them really knows you, not the way I do. Fuck, I'd do *anything* for you. Could you even say the same about *anyone?*"

I balled my hands into fists. This wasn't going the way I expected. "You think you have me pinned down, don't you. Well, we *do* have to be honest, don't we, Robbie? What about being honest about how *you* feel? What about all the times I asked you if you were okay with our arrangement, if there was any reason we shouldn't do it? But oh no, it's all my fault, because I foolishly expected a little honesty from my best friend."

"What do you mean, I haven't been honest?"

I shrugged, leaning back to rest on my ankles. I folded my arms across my chest and adopted the petulant expression that drove my mother crazy. "You like me. Everyone tells me so. You didn't tell me, and so I didn't know that I shouldn't snog girls in front of you—"

"I don't *like* you," he growled.

"Then why—"

"I thought it was obvious. I'm fucking in love with you, Bianca."

The words slammed against me, jolting through my body like an electric current. Robbie's strong hands grabbed my arms, yanking me onto my knees. His eyes blazed as his lips slammed against mine. Heat surged through my body, lighting every part of me on fire. *God, I want you. Touch me, Robbie. Tell me again that you love me.*

Robbie cupped my neck, pushing my head against his as he deepened the kiss. "Robbie, I can't—" I tried to say, but his lips smothered mine, chasing away my protests. I sank into the kiss, savouring every delicious moment, every surge of energy as it coursed through my body.

I fucking love you, Bianca.

The words pounded against my skull. Women and men had told me that before, and it was usually the signal that I had to end things. This time ... the words surged through my body, lighting up something dormant within me, something that desperately wanted to speak the words back.

Robbie's tongue circled mine. His hands stroked my body, looping under my arms and tugging me up. He leaned back against the sheets, and I crawled on top of him, pressing myself hard against his tight body.

This is such a bad idea. The protest seemed flimsy in the face of our passion. My body responded to his touch, synapses firing in all directions. I wanted this. I wanted him. Maybe it was all the absinthe and champagne talking. Maybe it was the fact that only hours ago I'd said marriage vows to him. Maybe it was the way Robbie was staring at me, eyes dancing with glee like he'd just won the lottery ...

I pulled my tight skirt up around my hips and straddled Robbie, pressing myself against his naked skin. My fingers traced the tattoos on his shoulders, trailing over the Lowe pack crest that I'd inked there a month ago. My own Lowe tattoo, on the inside of my palm, rubbed against it. We were already linked, part of the same family.

This is so wrong; why does it feel so right?

Robbie's hands were all over my body, darting over my breasts, squeezing my hips through my skirt. *There's too much material between us.* I rocked back on my heels, wriggling my hips as I unzipped the back of my skirt, and tugged it down over my hips. Underneath, I wore my favourite black lace g-string, and a black garter holding up my stockings.

Robbie's eyes grew wide as he took in the garter. His hands gripped my thighs. "You're amazing," he said. "You're like a dream."

"I've had a lot of champagne. For all I know, this *is* a dream."

"Bianca." Robbie withdrew his hands, slithering out from between my thighs, so he was sitting against the brass bedstand. His cock bounced in the air between us, demanding attention. "We've both been drinking. Are you sure this is a good idea?"

"Not in the slightest." I grinned, leaning over him and wrapping my hand around his cock. Robbie shuddered as I stroked him slowly, alternating with both hands. He started to say something, but all that came out was a low growl.

I bent forward, wrapping my lips around his shaft. He tasted *amazing*. I had no idea he was hiding this enormous, glorious cock. If I'd known, I might not have waited this long.

I stroked as I sucked, flicking my tongue over his balls before taking in his whole length again. I scraped a nail across the sensitive skin between his scrotum and anus, causing another shudder to rock through his body.

"Bianca ... no ... you have to stop ..." Robbie gripped my arms, tearing my mouth off him.

"Damn, I was having fun." I flicked my tongue over my lips.

"I could tell. I ... I was too ... but if you go much longer, I'll be done. And I don't want this to be over yet."

Robbie pulled me against him, kissing me deeply. His mouth tasted warm. I knew he could taste himself on my lips. I loved that he kissed me deeper despite this, as though he couldn't get enough of me.

His hands gripped my thighs, thumbs digging under the garter straps. An ache rose within me, calling for his fingers to move closer, to make me want him even more. As he explored my body, his intense gaze remained trained on me.

"You don't close your eyes," I said, coming up for air. "Most men, when I give head, they just roll their head back and close their eyes."

Robbie shook his head. "I want to remember every moment of this for the rest of my life. Can I take your corset off?"

I gestured down at the blue corset still strapped tight around my torso. "Don't you like it?"

"I love it." His lips danced over my shoulder, as he ran his hands down the laces. "But I've spent many a night imagining what was underneath."

"You can't take any of this back now. I know you were pining for me."

"I don't want to take anything back," he growled, his fingers tightening on my hip. The ache inside me flared.

"You don't have to ask permission, you know. I like the wild wolf side of you."

Robbie moaned, pressing his lips against mine. His fingers hooked through the laces at the back of my corset, tugging them loose. He worked his way slowly down my back, grunting as he tugged at the garment without making much headway. Every time his fingers grazed my skin, desire shot through my body. I grinned despite myself; Robbie clearly didn't have much experience with corsets.

The anticipation shivered through my skin. I wanted his hands all over me. I wanted to melt against him.

"Right, I think I got it. Arms up." I lifted my arms over my head, and Robbie tugged the corset up. He managed to wiggle it up over my arms, only to get it stuck over my shoulders. No matter how hard he tugged, the thing wouldn't budge.

Robbie groaned, as he tugged hopelessly at the strings. "This is ridiculous. I just want to see your tits. Is that too much to ask?"

I collapsed with giggles, falling back against the bed, my arms still flailing above my head, trapped by the corset. I tried to wriggle my way out, but it was stuck tight. "Hold still, will you?" Robbie growled, as he loosened the cords a little bit more, wriggling the garment back and forth as slowly, slowly it started to come loose.

"There we are." He grinned, yanking the boning over my head and tossing the corset to the floor. Beads skittered across the floorboards. "Hello there."

I grabbed my tiny tits and pushed them up and together. "Sorry it's a bit disappointing. This is the only way I actually get any cleavage."

"Don't ever say this body is disappointing." Robbie's fingers stroked my skin. I dropped my hands, and he cupped my breasts, his fingers brushing over my nipples. A shiver of delight raced through my body. I loved having my nipples touched and licked and sucked, a fact most of my female conquests relished. So many guys just gave them a cursory squeeze and then went straight for the grand finale.

Not Robbie. He bent his head down, his tongue darting over the tip of my nipple. I gasped as his warm mouth slid over me, and shivers of fire darted under my skin. I watched his tongue swirling around the tip, driving the ache inside me to new heights.

Robbie licked and sucked until I thrashed my head about

from the sheer pleasure of it. The ache had grown into a full-scale inferno, pounding against my skin, desperate for release. He moved to the other nipple, driving me closer and closer to the edge.

"God, you're good at this," I moaned, my hands cupping his head, forcing him to keep up his ministrations.

"I have spent several nights down at the pub listening to you complain about how girls do this so well and guys suck." Robbie glanced up at me, grinning that beautiful, wicked grin. "I've picked up a few things."

"It's not fair. I'm a talkative drunk. You know all about what I like, but I don't know anything about what you like."

"I like you." Robbie's hand cupped my thigh. "I like you in this garter."

"Oh, yes?" I grinned back.

"Yeah. But I think I'd like it even better if you took it off."

I raised an eyebrow.

"Emphasis on the word *you*. After that corset, I'm not touching any woman's undergarments ever again."

Grinning, I bent down and unclipped the garter clips, rolling my stockings down my legs. I felt like a pin-up model, coquettishly undressing for a photoshoot. First one stocking slid down my leg, then the second. It caught on my toe, so I snapped it back, flinging it onto the floor to join the rest of my clothes.

Next, I unclipped the hooks holding on the garter and slid that over my hips. I reached down to remove my g-string. Robbie's hands closed over mine.

"This one, I've got a handle on." He grinned as he tugged it off, his fingers brushing against my most sensitive skin. I moaned, fire rolling over me, nearly ready to burst.

Completely naked now, I leaned back on the tiny bed, my gaze flicking over the low ceiling. Beneath me, the music from the party boomed, shaking the floor with a steady rhythm.

I can't believe the first shag in my new house is going to be in the attic, with Robbie.

My thoughts might've continued in that vein, had Robbie not bent between my legs and placed his tongue against my clit.

Oh wow oh wow oh wow.

Usually men were so ... probing. They either came in too hard or too soft, tongues like little jackhammers trying to drill out an orgasm in record time. That was why I usually preferred woman – their soft fingers so silky inside you, their wet tongues knowing exactly how you liked it. Maybe I'd just never had good head from a guy before, because it's never been like *this*.

Robbie's stubble brushed against my thigh as his tongue drew down the length of me. I thrust my hips toward him, begging for more. But he held back, taking his time, making slow circles around my clit and driving me crazy with lust. He reached up with one hand and pinched my nipple, the sharp pain only increasing my pleasure.

He slipped one finger inside me, pressing it against me as he increased his pace, licking faster now. The fire rose from my stomach, the pressure building.

Robbie pressed his tongue against me, rolling it ... I don't know. I don't know what he was doing, but it was so sharp and hard and hot and amazing and the fire became an ocean of flames rolling over me in waves and I lost myself in the inferno and the room disappeared and the house disappeared and all there was left was my convulsing body and Robbie's unrelenting tongue.

I think I screamed. I might have sworn. I don't know, because I was gone.

Slowly, the fire dulled, and I came back. I was still lying on my back, the ancient sheets balled up beneath me. Robbie had crawled up beside me, his fingers dancing a line across my chest.

His eyes regarded me with a mixture of awe and unrelenting lust.

"Good?" he whispered against my ear.

"Mmmmmm." As soon as I could move my legs again, I grabbed his shoulders, shoved him back, and climbed on top. My body shook from residual energy of my orgasm, but I managed to balance over him. Robbie's eyes grew wide again as I eased myself down on his cock. It felt so good, thick and long, filling me completely.

Robbie grabbed my shoulder and dragged me against his chest, his tongue fighting against mine as he thrust his hips up, driving himself even deeper inside me. Good. I was done being slow. I wanted the wild passion that danced in his eyes.

I rocked backwards, grinding my hips against Robbie's, driving him as deep inside me as I could get. Robbie gripped my thighs, his eyes narrowing in concentration, pounding against me in a steady rhythm.

"Why so serious?" I gasped through our kiss.

"I don't want to be disappointing."

I snorted. "This has been about as far from disappointing as you can get. Disappointing has left the building. Now, smile, you fool, and fuck me like the animal you are."

Robbie obeyed, his lips drawing back in a wide, gorgeous smile that lit up his whole face as he pounded against me with fresh vigour. I kissed him again, then tossed my head back as I rode him like an animal. He dragged his fingers down my back, drawing lines of fire across my skin.

Everything blurred into a flurry of limbs and fingers and kisses and endless, unrelenting pleasure. At some point, Robbie flipped me over, dragging my hips back against him as he pounded me from behind. I gripped the brass bed end and howled as I came again, contracting around that glorious cock as Robbie's teeth bit down against my neck.

He drove himself deep into me, his muscled torso tightened as he neared his own release. As I felt his cock shudder, the ache inside me grew again, the fire roaring as it threatened to over-whelm me once more.

Robbie's whole body clenched, his teeth clamped down on my neck. The pain seared through my skin, tipping me over the edge. We came together, a whirlwind of limbs and teeth and pleasure, our bodies crashing against each other as the inferno devoured us both.

As the heat subsided, I lay back against Robbie's chest, my head swimming, my body warm with the flush of three incred-ible orgasms. Music shook the floor beneath us. Downstairs, the party of the year was going on without us.

As Robbie draped his arm across my chest, pulling me closer and kissing the top of my head, I realised I didn't care a single bit.

14

ROBBIE

*W*ow.

All the nights I'd lain awake, my dick in my hands, imagining what it would be like being with Bianca ... my wildest dreams were nothing compared with the reality. My body still buzzed from the heat of our mating.

Bianca's head rested on my chest, wisps of her pixie hair trailing across my skin. Her chest rose and fell, a perfect rhythm. Through the grimy attic window, pale moonlight streamed across the bed, illuminating her skin with an eerie glow. I rubbed my finger over the wound on the side of her neck, the mark that said she was mine.

She's mine.

Even though exhaustion clung to my body, and from the sounds of the dying party below it must be the early hours of the morning, I couldn't sleep. I could only count the knots in the wooden planks along the wall, and replay scenes from before. Bianca's lips on mine, Bianca's tiny, pert breasts, her nipples hardening under my touch. Her tongue sliding along my cock ... the way her mouth opened when she came ...

Damn, now I was hard. I'd never be able to sleep.

Bianca let out a tiny snort, her eyelids fluttering before settling still. Her arm weighed down on my chest. I groaned as a cramp seared along my arm.

Bianca wasn't a morning person, especially after a night of partying. She'd sleep for most of the day. Meanwhile, this cramp wouldn't get any better, and my stomach was starting to rumble. I'd been too nervous to eat before the wedding, and too agitated to enjoy all the amazing food at the party.

As gently as I could, I dragged my arm out from under Bianca. She moaned a little, settling back into the pillow as though I'd never been there. I rolled off the tiny bed and grabbed a clean set of clothes from my rucksack in the corner. I backed out of the room, half certain that when I returned she'd disappear, like a mirage.

I padded downstairs, trying to avoid the creaking steps, but pretty much every wooden board in this old house creaked. A Dutch artist collapsed at the foot of the attic stairs lifted his head and glared at me. Half a cupcake was stuck to his forehead.

I picked my way across the first floor landing, trying to avoid disturbing the overturned bottles, glittery costume remnants, streamers, and tangled, collapsed bodies. From the balustrade of the main staircase, Bianca's cat Macavity glared at me, as if to say, "Look at the chaos you have wrought."

"If only you knew, Mac." I patted his head. Macavity shot me a disgusted look, and bounded down the stairs toward the kitchen.

I gripped the balustrade and started down the stairs. My fingers dragged through something sticky. *Fuck, I don't even want to know what that is.* I yanked my hand away, fumbling my way down to the entrance hall and through the sitting room. Moonlight streamed through the tall windows, casting eerie pools of light across the mess.

People slumped in every available chair and corner, bodies twisted in various contortions. Bottles and plates lay strewn across every surface. Several cupcakes were stuck to the wall by crusted icing, forming a giant anarchist's A.

I set about cleaning up, dumping all the empty bottles into the recycling bins, and carrying the glasses and plates into the kitchen to be picked up later by the rental company. In the centre of the ballroom, I found my torn shirt and kilt. There were lipstick marks all over it, and someone had stolen my sporran and boxers. I glanced around at the collapsed party guests, wondering which one of them had nicked them. Artists were *weird*.

I went into the kitchen with arms full of dishes, and turned the coffee machine on. I'd never been much of a coffee drinker – there wasn't exactly a good place to plug in a machine in the Aberdeen woods – but ever since I'd started hanging out with Bianca, she'd been trying to convert me. While the beans roasted, I rummaged around in the fridge to find the milk. Belinda had left some trays of savouries and cheesecake bites in there. *Breakfast of kings.* I stuffed a few in my mouth and gathered up a plate to take up to Bianca.

I picked my way back through the darkened house, resisting the urge to whistle a tune. I'd never been this happy in my entire life. As I stepped onto the first floor landing, a muffled voice called something out to me. I whirled around, but couldn't see anyone conscious. It took me a moment to realise I was hearing a voice coming through one of the bedroom doors. Serenity Jones' room.

I waded through the filth on the floor and stood against the door, trying to keep my breathing shallow so I wouldn't make a sound. I pressed my ear against the door and listened, although I could only pick up a few snatches of conversation.

"... a pretty wild night ... yes, debauchery aplenty, and you wouldn't believe... a werewolf ... don't worry ... going to expose ... much know the truth ... yes, I've got pictures ... emailing them through now."

Great. That's just wonderful. She's already calling in her story. In a matter of hours, photographs of the world's first werewolf would be circulating across the globe.

Should I do something? Now was my chance to make good on the stupid mistake I'd made. I could leap in there, teeth bared, and threaten her into silence. My hand closed around the door handle.

No. That was what my father would have done, solved the problem with intimidation and violence. What if she refused to stop the story? I'd have to hurt her. I stared down at my hand, watching my fingers curl into a fist.

I stepped back, determination setting in. I'd find a way to make this right, *somehow,* and I'd do it my way, without threats or violence or breaking any laws.

Talk to Caleb. He'll already have a solution. Apologise and hope like hell he doesn't kick you out.

I turned away from Serenity's door. A stream of moonlight stretched from the window at the end of the hallway, illuminating a long rectangle, ending on one of the gilded portraits on the opposite wall. I stopped and stared at the image. It was of a young girl – she couldn't have been older than sixteen or seventeen when it was painted. She sat in one of the high-backed chairs in the downstairs library, her hand resting on a closed volume in her lap. The artist had taken great pains to render the folds of fabric and elaborate embroidery of her dress, and the enormous choker and ring that adorned her body.

Moonlight glinted off the girl's eyes. They held me mesmerised – deep pools of icy blue that beckoned me closer, that seemed to follow me as I took a step across the landing. They were Bianca's eyes.

Her face was Bianca's, too – the pointed chin, high cheek-bones, tiny, bow-shaped lips. I knew without a doubt I was looking at one of Bianca's ancestors and—

Holy shit.

The realisation hit me with the force of a freight train, stunning me so much I nearly dropped the tray.

The ring. The girl was wearing the Benedict Ring. It was right there on her hand – the twin snakes coiled around a large, blood-red stone. I couldn't believe it – I'd walked past this portrait dozens of times while heading back and forth from the attic. I'd spent a month trawling through the papers in The Prim's attic, and all the time, evidence of the ring was right in front of my face.

I stared at the calligraphy in the frame's nameplate – Silvia Sinclair, 1835. *It's the same girl who wrote the scrapbook we discovered in the attic.* My heart thundered against my chest. I stepped over a Sicilian acrobat slumped against the wall to peer at the ring, wishing I could reach inside the painting and pluck it from her fingers.

Spurned on by the discovery, I dropped the tray on the sideboard and flicked on the light. "Hey, what gives?" the acrobat grumbled from below my feet. The German by the stairs groaned and pulled the corner of the rug over his head.

I scanned the other portraits in the hall with fresh eyes. I located the ring in five more, all dated before Silvia's. Two women wore the rosary Bianca's dad had shown me as well. In all the paintings dated after Silvia's, the rosary was present in some, but the ring was nowhere to be seen.

For weeks I'd been straining my eyes on old documents, desperately hoping I'd find some clue as to the whereabouts of the ring. Now I had a date for the last true sighting of the ring. Silvia was the last person in the family to wear it.

But where had it gone? If it was such a family heirloom, why had it disappeared? With its tiny rooms filled with nooks and crannies, Primrose House was the perfect place to hide something small, something you didn't want anyone to know you had.

The ring ... it could be somewhere in Bianca's house.

15
___

BIANCA

I awoke to the smell of smoked salmon quiche wafting under my nose, which is a very unnerving smell to wake up to while trying to pull myself into the real world with a pounding headache and quivering stomach.

"Rise and shine," a deep voice said from behind me. "I brought you the perfect hangover cure."

Hangover ... at the sound of the word, the pain in my body registered. My head throbbed, and my stomach churned with nausea. My eyes felt like they were about to pop out of my skull.

I rolled over, my bleary eyelids flickering open, revealing a shaft of blinding light shining directly on my face.

"Uuuurgh." *Who is banging my temples with a mallet? I'll kill them, after I kill myself ...*

A shadow moved in front of the light. My eyes blurred, then started to adjust. Robbie came into view, standing in front of the window, from which that blasted sun was going about its morning torture. He held out a tray upon which balanced a plate piled high with leftover party food: the aforementioned offensive salmon quiche, meatballs with spicy peanut dipping sauce, stuffed peppers with goat's cheese filling, and several cheesecake bites and mini cupcakes. Beside it sat a pot of steaming tea ... the perfect gentleman.

In his other hand, he held a bottle of Powerade.

I took the tray and the Powerade gratefully, my fingers struggling to pull off the plastic cap. As I shuffled into a sitting position, my foot hooked around my corset, which was lying across the end of the bed where we'd tossed it the previous night. Black beads skittered across the sheets as I balanced the tray on my knees. Robbie knelt down to pick up the corset. He placed it on the wooden stool under the window.

Owwwww, my head ...

I sipped the Powerade, clutching my stomach as it squirmed in protest. Robbie stepped back into the doorway, his face sympathetic. "Sorry it's so early. I couldn't sleep. I thought I'd bring you some snacks for when you woke up. I was just gonna drop them and leave—"

I waved a hand as I took another swig of Powerade. My stomach churned. "Stay. Quiche it up with me."

"You sure?" He looked hopefully at the corner of the bed. I patted the spot next to me, and held out the plate.

"Of course. Just beware that I am in no mood for any of the usual morning-after shenanigans."

"No deep conversations or tickle wars. Got it." He slumped down next to me, facing the window.

"In fact, if you could dispose of these salmon quiche for me, it would be very much appreciated."

"Consider it done." Robbie whipped the quiche off the plate and stuffed two into his mouth in one go.

I draped my legs across his, and placed the plate between us. I picked up a piece of chicken and took a tentative bite off the edge. Okay, that stayed down. Good. Maybe I'll be able to enjoy a little more. Beside me, Robbie bit into a stuffed pepper. For a few minutes, we munched in silence, the impact of what we'd done last night hanging over us.

The last thing I wanted to do was talk about the state of our relationship. I wasn't even sure I'd be able to get many words out before I threw up everywhere. But we couldn't risk getting things confused any longer. We needed to make everything plain and clear.

We were married now, and we should be desperately trying to salvage our friendship. But despite my throbbing head and churning stomach, I wanted nothing more than to feel Robbie's cock inside me as soon as possible.

He was still looking out the window, not saying anything. I'd have to make the first move. "That was some party," I ventured, watching his powerful jaw muscles move as he devoured another stuffed pepper. I remembered his wolf form bounding through the ballroom, how his powerful shoulder muscles tensed as his legs moved in a blur.

Robbie nodded. "It sure was. Bianca?"

His hand brushed my thigh. I closed my eyes, willing my stomach to settle. "No shenanigans, remember?"

"I'm so sorry I changed into a werewolf in the middle of the party." Robbie scratched his head. "I was an idiot. I ... I got jealous, and lost control. I think I may have destroyed everything."

"What do you mean, destroyed everything? Did you claw up my new furniture?"

"I mean, for the Lowes, and between you and me. All those reporters were taking pictures—"

I held up my hand. "Don't you dare apologise. Caleb will sort it out. He always does. And as for us ... I was just thinking about how hot it was, watching you change."

"You think it's sexy that I'm a werewolf?"

"Hell yeah. Plus," I sipped my Powerade, "it falls well within the 'would my parents disapprove of this?' filter I apply to everyone I shag. I've been the hedonistic bisexual sinner for years. If my mother knew her son-in-law was a werewolf ..."

Robbie laughed. "I wish Caleb would see things your way."

"You wish Caleb thought you were sexy?"

"No ... I mean ..." Robbie looked away. "Caleb and Irvine have this big plan about revealing the existence of shifters to the world. My little stunt has probably put paid to that."

"Do you know that for a fact?"

"I overheard your friend from *London Underground* on the phone in her room. She's already talking about 'werewolves' and 'exposing the truth.' Caleb is going to *kill* me."

Serenity. Great. I thought of her camera in my face while I was snogging Willow. Completely aside from the werewolf problem, I didn't exactly want that plastered all over the papers for Robbie to see. And judging by Caleb's angry face last night, Robbie wasn't wrong about that, either. "Don't worry, I'll talk to her. Just as soon as the idea of going downstairs doesn't make me want to puke."

"Okay, thanks." He paused for a moment to divide the last cheesecake bite into two, and handed one half to me. "Bianca?"

"Yeah?" I set the cheesecake back on the plate. No way could I handle that in my current condition.

"It's okay if you want to forget last night."

I rubbed my temple. "Forget it?" The details from last night were still pretty hazy, but one thing was absolutely certain in my mind: I didn't want to forget that kiss.

"Yeah, I mean, the two of us ... we have to pull off this fake marriage thing if we want The Prim to be a success. You've worked so hard on it, I dinnae want to complicate things and risk that."

"Oh." Disappointment surged through me. "Do you want to forget it?"

He sighed. "I think we're veering dangerously close to a serious conversation."

"Robbie. We're friends, and now we're married. We've got to be honest with each other if this thing is going to work. I remember you saying something pretty intense last night, something that very much implied you don't want to forget jack shit. Does that statement still stand?"

"You mean the one where I said I loved you?" Robbie's face grew pale. "Aye ... it ... it stands."

"Good."

"You mean—?" His whole face lit up.

"Don't get ahead of yourself. I'm not sure those words will ever come out of my mouth. But last night was pretty incredible, and I don't want to ignore it. I want more."

Robbie bent toward me with a filthy grin, but I waved my hand. "Don't kiss me. My mouth tastes like cardboard."

"Take it easy today." He patted my knee as he stood up to leave. "When you're feeling better, we'll see about having a repeat."

"I'm totally down with that. How hungover are you?"

"Just a little fuzzy, nothing too horrible. I'll help with the cleanup."

"Is it in a bad state down there?"

Robbie grinned. "It's better you dinnae see it. You've also acquired several stragglers." He told me about all the people he'd encountered on his journey down to the kitchen.

"What's an art house for if not for eccentric Dutch tattoo artists to fall asleep in a pile of their own urine?"

Robbie laughed, the sound searing my ears. "Aye. If it's okay by you, I'm going to have a hunt around some of your aunt's old stuff. I might have to go into your bedroom."

"Sure. Why?"

Robbie explained about the discovery of the ring in Silvia

Sinclair's portrait. I squeezed his hand. I couldn't believe it. All along, Silvia was the key to solving the mystery of the ring. I rubbed my fingers along Robbie's knuckles, pleased to hear the excitement in his voice. I'd watched him struggle with his task over the last couple of weeks, and I knew he worried that Caleb was getting impatient with him.

"I'll come help you look for it once I can move again. Silvie's scrapbook is on my bedside table, as well. There might be some clue in there I've overlooked."

"Thanks so much, Bianca. You take it easy. Listen, one other thing – all the stuff we have downstairs for the charity shop. Do you mind if I use it?"

"Use it? What for?"

Robbie shrugged. "Maybe ... I've been a little inspired by all the artwork in the house and all the creative people you know. That crown Alex made for you gave me an idea. I was thinking it would be dead pure brilliant to make some garden sculptures out of some of the old junk to line the path up to the door. It would really give visitors a taste of what they could expect inside, and it would be brilliant if they were made from things that actually came from the house, you know, repurposing – the way you're repurposed The Prim itself. I was going to have a go at making something."

"You? Make some art?"

Robbie shrugged again. "Why not? I can nail some shite together. It can't be that hard."

I laughed. "No, it's not hard at all. Art is totally just nailing shite together. Knock yourself out. I reserve the right to laugh at you if your piece is horrible, though."

"Fine." He shuffled his feet. "So ... seeya then."

"Bye—" I started to say, but he'd already left.

As I SLIPPED in and out of sleep in Robbie's tiny attic bed, interrupted by thuds and bangs from the house below, I dreamed about the girl Hattie, who used to sleep in this same room. I imagined a maid's uniform hanging from the rusty nail behind the door, and Silvia sneaking up the stairs in her lacy nightgown to share her first fumbling sexual explorations right here in this bed ...

And now Robbie and I had sullied the place all over again. I grinned as I drifted back to sleep again. *And didn't we do you proud, Hattie? I think you and I would've got on very well if we'd ever met ...*

My eyes fluttered open again. I fumbled for Robbie's phone, which he'd left beside the bed. I clicked past the screen that blinked 72 missed calls from Caleb, and pulled up the time. It read 2:43 p.m. when I finally dragged my body out of bed. I scrambled around on the floor for the remnants of my wedding dress, before discovering Robbie had left my dressing gown, a pair of jeans and my favourite Ramones shirt folded up on the small chair beside the door. Beaming, I pulled the dressing gown on, tucked the clothes under my arm, and headed for the stairs.

Robbie was on the first floor landing, trying to roll Hans over so he could vacuum underneath him. He waved at me as I headed to the bathroom. Behind his head, I caught a glimpse of Silvie's portrait, and noticed for the first time the ring on her finger. The Benedict Ring. The treasure the whole pack was hunting for, right here in my own home.

As the hot water cascaded over my body, the fogginess in my head started to abate. I stared down at my tiny breasts, remembering Robbie's hands cupping them reverently, his lips closing over the tiny buds. Despite the heat of the water, my nipples grew hard.

Robbie. I still couldn't believe we'd fallen into the sack together, and on the night of our fake wedding. And yet, it felt so, so right. I couldn't wait to climb back into bed with him again and see if last night was a fluke or not.

I switched the water off and towelled myself dry, then slipped on my clothes. I was applying makeup when I heard the front door slam and a familiar voice calling up the stairs.

"Hello, Bianca! Are you sober yet?"

I patted into the hall and peered over the balustrade. Elinor stood in the entrance hall, wearing jeans and an old dress shirt of Eric's, and carrying her laptop, sketchbook, and a bucket of cleaning supplies under her arm.

"Where's Eric?" I asked.

"The band had to head back down to London for a show," she said. "I thought I'd come and help you clean up, but I see you've already been at it for hours."

I noticed that the entrance hall had been cleared of rubbish and passed-out drunks. The rug was rolled up against the wall, and the floor shone from a recent scrub. Several rubbish bags and recycling bins had been stacked beside the front door. *Robbie.* I grinned wider. *I sure know how to pick a fake husband.* "Something like that. Go put the coffee on. I'll be right down."

As I stumbled my way through the front rooms, bleary-eyed guests rose from their stupor to greet me. Robbie hadn't done much work in these rooms. I figured he was probably too afraid to face anyone after his accidental transformation. I smiled as I saw the remains of the cupcake tossing game I'd been playing with my German friends still clinging to the wall.

I love The Prim so hard. This place was exactly what I wanted it to be.

I entered the kitchen. Elinor was already at the table, tapping away on her computer. The coffee machine beeped. I frothed some milk and served us both an espresso.

"You're a hit." Elinor swirled around her computer as I

slumped down in the chair opposite. I grimaced at the headline. "WEREWOLVES, LESBIANS, DEBAUCHERY AT ART HOUSE OPENING." It was the blog post on *London Underground*. The hero image was me and Willow, lips locked in a passionate kiss. Right underneath was Robbie, his face frozen halfway through his shift, tufts of hair sprouting from his cheeks and his lips pulled back in a terrifying howl.

Shit. That Serenity sure worked fast. With shaking hands, I pulled the laptop toward me. *Please don't let this reveal too much about shifters. Please let Robbie not have ruined Caleb's plan.*

I skimmed the article, words and phrases jumping out at me *... The hit new spot on the alternative arts scene ... hottest party of the year ... only Victorian manor to have its very own werewolf ... performance art like no other ... lesbian feminist icon Bianca Sinclair's finest hour—*

I couldn't believe it. One killer party, and I was a "lesbian feminist icon"? Yikes. But at least Serenity had written about Robbie's shift as though it was a performance piece. Robbie was safe, for now. But I thought back to what Robbie had said she was saying on the phone, about "exposing the truth"? Was Serenity keeping the real story of shifters back, saving it for a different publication, or until she had something more to show?

My eyes met Elinor's. "Do me a favour, and don't let Robbie see this."

"Deal."

I skimmed through the comments. There were several people who'd attended the party talking about Robbie's shift, claiming it couldn't possibly have been a performance. One person said he'd thrown a bulb of garlic at the wolf to destroy it. Someone else said they saw a wolf roaming around the manor garden. The hashtag #crookshollowwerewolf was even trending on Twitter. I rubbed my temple, my headache starting to return. "Has Caleb seen this yet?"

Elinor nodded. "Oh yeah. He's doing damage control, getting the word out that it was an elaborate stunt. He's got Eric to do a TV interview about the party today down in London, which is why he went down early. Eric will say it was a publicity stunt. Cole's down there too – he's pretending to be an SFX artist who created the piece. Apparently, he's already got two commissions."

"That's hilarious."

Elinor glared at me. "It's really not. Caleb will be over later to talk to Robbie. He's not happy, Bianca. If this gets worse, it could throw all their plans off. You and Robbie have to be more careful. You don't know what kind of attention this might attract."

"You think other wolves might take offence to this?"

"You bet I do. So does Caleb. And it's not just wolves." Elinor flipped to another tab, and jabbed a perfectly-manicured finger at an article. "Not everyone is so enthusiastic about your kiss."

I squinted at the screen. It was a conservative Christian website reporting on events in the Loamshire county. They had reprinted the same image of me, lips locked with Willow's, underneath a heading that read, "MEET THE JEZEBEL OF CROOKSHOLLOW." The article declared the Crookshollow art scene a hedonistic cesspool of debauchery, and I its demonic conductor.

I rubbed my throbbing temple. This was too much to take in after a hard night. "My mother will just *love* this."

"Your mother was singing *I Will Survive* with Eric's band last night. Don't you remember?"

"No. How on earth did I miss that?"

"I don't know. I didn't see you after Robbie's shift. Come to think of it, I didn't see him, either. Did something happen?"

I gulped down a mouthful of piping hot coffee, scalding my tongue "Um ... no, nothing happened."

"Bianca." Elinor had on her stern voice, the one she used when she knew someone was lying.

Damn, nothing gets past Elinor. Sometimes, I really hated having an ex-lawyer for a friend.

I shrugged, trying to hide behind my coffee mug, but I couldn't stop the smile that crept across my face.

"If you did *anything* to lead him on, I'm going to kill you, that is if Caleb or Marcus doesn't get to you first. The whole day must've been painful for him, and then having to see that kiss ... no wonder he got agitated and shifted by accident. A lot of people care about Robbie, and you can't just—"

"Oi, relax, would you?" I held up my hands. "The truth is, something did happen, but—"

"I knew it!" Elinor slammed her cup on the table so hard, she splashed coffee across my grandmother's lace tablecloth. "I knew eventually you'd end up shagging him. You can't help it. You can't resist anyone who's crazy about you. I just can't believe you'd play with him like that. You *know* how Robbie feels about you."

"Relax, would you? It turns out, I think I feel the same way."

"You ... what?" Elinor's stern expression faltered.

"Robbie's great. He's amazing, actually. I think ... we're going to try and give it a serious go."

"You mean, like a relationship?"

"I don't mean *exactly* a relationship." I shrugged. "I mean, slightly more serious than my last fling. We'll just see how it goes."

"But ... you've never liked Robbie like that."

"I changed my mind. Am I not allowed to do that?"

"No, no, of course you are." Elinor cleared her throat. "I think that's great, really I do. I just ... be careful, Bianca. If this goes tits up, Robbie won't just recover like you do."

"What's that supposed to mean?" *I get it. You're worried about*

Robbie. But he's a big, strong, sexy shifter. He can look after himself. And just because I've had a lot of partners doesn't mean I don't know how to commit or that I can't get my heart broken.

Well, that last part's true, anyway.

"Nothing. Forget I said anything." Elinor dug her phone out of her pocket. "I got some pictures of your mum with the band. Want to see?"

"Oh, god yes." Conversation forgotten, I leaned over as Elinor scrolled through her images, giggling at the images of my prim and proper mother letting her hair down for once.

Elinor's just trying to be my friend, but she doesn't have anything to worry about, and neither does Robbie. I care about him. I'm not going to hurt him. And even if I did, he's a big, tough shifter. He used to be in a gang, for fuck's sake. He can survive anything, even heartbreak.

Can't he?

16

ROBBIE

Elinor, Bianca and I spent most of the afternoon cleaning up The Prim. Hans tried to help, but after he used bleach on a silver candelabra, Bianca made him go back to bed. He did so gleefully, followed by a long line of scantily-clad German artists of both sexes.

That Serenity chick didn't leave her room until just after five. Every time I went past, I could hear the *clack clack clack* of her laptop's keys. Bianca told me that her article had already been published, and that it only showed my shift as a piece of performance art. Even so, my stomach tied itself up in knots, wondering what else she might be writing, and for whom. It must be obvious from her pictures that I wasn't just wearing stage makeup.

When Serenity came downstairs, she asked Bianca if she could stay a few extra days. "I can't get enough of this place. It's so nice to get away from the London traffic for a few days. Plus, I'd still really like to get a tattoo from you, if you can fit me in." I was shaking my head no, but Bianca must not have seen me, because she told Serenity she could stay.

After Elinor and the guests who weren't staying left, and everyone else retired to their rooms, I ordered some takeaway curries, and Bianca and I settled down in the library for our very first dinner as husband and wife.

We hadn't been alone in the house all day, so we hadn't really talked about what happened since this morning. I tried to act cool as I set down two containers of hot curry and rice and unwrapped the *naan* bread, but my hands trembled so much, I dropped the forks.

"Aw, Robbo." Bianca picked up her fork and rubbed it against her jeans to clean it. "You're like an awkward schoolboy."

I didn't answer. I felt like an awkward schoolboy around her.

Bianca waved her fork in the air, then pierced a piece of butter chicken. "We've been friends for ages now. We shouldn't be nervous around each other."

"This is different," I mumbled, as I picked up my own food.

Bianca slid out of her chair. I heard the clatter of her fork landing on the table, and the slide of her knees crawling across the floor. She knelt in front of me. Her hands gripped mine, sending the sizzling energy cascading down my arms.

Bianca's lips found mine, devouring me with a hunger that made my chest ache with need. I reached up and wrapped my arms around her, pulling her closer, tangling my fingers through her hair.

She pulled back, her forehead touching mine. "If there's anything I can do," she whispered, "to help make you less nervous, I'm willing to try it."

I opened my mouth, but I couldn't find any words.

Bianca blinked, her eyelashes tangling together. Her hand found its way between my legs. She unzipped my fly with one hand, the other gripping my shoulder for balance. She drew out my hard cock, a tiny moan escaping her throat. Her hand wrapped around the shaft, and she moved her hand slowly, drawing along my full length.

I moaned against her lips as her hand moved faster, squeezing me tight. Her tongue slid over mine as she worked me harder, quickly bringing me close. I pressed my mouth against hers, savouring the scent of her, the feel of her fingers wrapped around me as—

Knock knock knock.

We sprang apart like two naughty children. Bianca was breathing hard, her hair sticking out at odd angles. The knocks kept coming, louder and more urgent. "I'll get it," she said, wiping the edge of her mouth. "It's probably my mother."

I grabbed my stiff cock and shoved it back into my pants, untucking my shirt and pulling it down to hide the bulge. I had a feeling it wasn't going to stay hard much longer.

I followed Bianca into the sitting room, my stomach flipping. I was pretty sure I knew who was on the other side of that door—

"Where is he?" Caleb's unmistakable growl boomed through the entrance hall. He tried to shove his way past Bianca, but she pressed her foot against the door, jamming it open only a crack.

"You need to calm the fuck down before you can come in," she said. "Robbie didn't mean to—"

"Didn't fucking *mean* to? That bastard destroyed the one shot we had of gaining control over the shifter reveal. He knew we weren't ready for this to come out ... he had to know, because it's his damn fault we're still waiting. He's landed us in a huge fucking mess and it's my job to figure out how to get us out of it."

"I know, but storming in here like this isn't going to—"

"I'm Robbie's alpha, not you, and I need to talk to him, *now.*"

My face stung. When Caleb roared like that, he sounded exactly like our dad. I shrunk back against the wall, my breath coming out in short gasps. This was it. He was kicking me out of the pack.

My inner wolf flared up, pressing against my skin. The fear fled my body, replaced by a seething confidence. I glanced over at Bianca, at the way she held her body, proud and tall and in charge, and I remembered what I was – a man with the heart of a wolf, tough and loyal and fierce when attacked. I didn't have to be afraid of Caleb. I needed to own my mistake and whatever happened, I would survive. I always did.

"Bianca, it's fine. Let him in."

"Don't be an idiot, Robbie," Bianca said, shoving Caleb back with both hands. "He doesn't have the right to come over here and yell at you."

"He's my alpha. He has every right, especially when I fuck up the way I did last night. Let him in."

Bianca gave me a weird look, but she removed her foot from the door. Caleb shoved his way through, his eyes blazing.

"Of all the stupid things you could've possibly done, that was the absolute worst!"

"Aye, I ken. I'm sorry."

"You're sorry? You're *sorry*." Caleb grabbed my collar, dragging my face to within inches of his. His hot breath landed on my face. I wanted to turn away, but I held my ground. "Give me one good reason why I shouldn't drop you from the pack *right now*."

Panic rose in my throat. I'd given up everything to join Caleb. If he kicked me from the pack—

You can't let him do this, I told myself, forcing down the panic. *For once in your life, Robbie, you have to stand up for yourself.*

"Because I devoted my life to helping you achieve this goal, *brother*," I shot back, drawing from some deep inner resource of strength. My words came out clear, cutting through Caleb's so completely that he stood dumbfounded while I continued.

"Because we're so close to achieving what our mother envisioned. Because sometimes people fuck up, and you just have to roll with it." I grabbed my sleeve and rolled it up, shoving my Lowe tattoo in his face. "But most of all, because we're supposed to be family. I thought when I joined with you, that I wouldn't have to live in fear any longer that I was just one mistake away from death."

"That's not an excuse—"

"You've spent months proselytising over how the Lowe pack was going to be different. You said you didn't want to rule with fear, the way Angus and Colin did. You *said* that this pack was a family. Well, you don't just kick out a family member because they fuck up, unless you're my dad, that is. That's not how real families work. Families forgive each other, and they band together to find a way through their troubles. Well, at least that's what I'm told they're supposed to be like."

Caleb's jaw clenched, but I could tell from the look in his eyes that he was wavering. Caleb had just as difficult a life as I had, facing my father's constant disapproval because he wasn't his son. He knew all about longing for a family that accepted him. I had him. I opened my mouth to continue, but Bianca's voice cut through.

"Robbie's right." Bianca folded her arms. "You can't kick him out for this."

"I'm the alpha, Bianca. I have complete control over who remains in the pack. This doesn't have anything to do with you."

"It has everything to do with me." Bianca pulled up her cuff to reveal her own tattoo. "I've already survived one family that kicked me out just because I happened to fancy women. If this is the same kind of family – the kind that disowns someone just because they disappoint you in some way – then you can count me out, too. Because I've already got one family like that, and I don't need another."

Caleb glared at Bianca. For a long, painful moment, I thought he might kick us both out of the pack. Instead, his shoulders sagged, and he dropped my collar. As his eyes met mine, something like pain flashed in his gaze. It was there for a moment, but then it was gone again.

Caleb held out his hand to me. "I don't say this often, but I'm the one who's sorry, mate. Everyone makes mistakes. Fuck knows, I've made a few in my lifetime. It's just been a long day, and I could have done with your help. I'm worried we might be running out of time to turn this in our favour."

"I'm sorry I didn't come talk to you immediately. I guess ... I didn't want to face it. Elinor said you had Eric convince the press that it was just a publicity stunt – special effects and stuff," I said, heading over to the table and picking up my curry.

Caleb nodded, settling himself down on the chair opposite me. He grabbed a *poppadom* from our stack and bit into it. "I think they bought it. That London Underground article really helped, as it backs up Eric's claim that it was just a stunt. The alternative is that there are really werewolves, and the world isn't quite ready for that. The problem is that the shifter community saw the article, and now all eyes are on us. They think we're being reckless, that maybe we did this on purpose to reveal the existence of shifters to the world."

"But isn't that exactly what you're going to do?" Bianca asked, scooping up a big mouthful of curry with her *naan*.

"Of course, but not *yet*. We're not ready yet. We don't have the ring, and we can't keep hiding behind this fake ring forever. Without the ring, we'll never get the other packs behind us, which means we won't be able to control the new shifter government. We'll be at the mercy of power-hungry maniacs like Isengrim and your dad." He jabbed me in the chest.

"I made some progress on the ring," I said.

Caleb turned to me, his eyes shining. "You found it? Why didn't you say something—"

"You were too busy yelling at him," Bianca said, her mouth full of curry.

"I didn't find it, but I definitely found something." I slumped back in my chair. Caleb reached across the coffee table and tore off half my *naan* bread, dunking it into my curry before stuffing it into his mouth. He chewed while I described the paintings and dates.

"Have you started looking?" Caleb glanced around the room, as if he might somehow be able to see the ring hidden in a dark corner.

I nodded. "Unfortunately, there's a *lot* of old junk in the house I have to go through. Of course, it might not even be here, but it seems likely. Silvia was young in the painting where she's wearing the ring – there's a good chance she lost or hid it here before she went off to live with her husband, which corroborates what Bianca's mother told me. Of course, the other possibility is that it's at her husband's estate in Yorkshire, but I haven't seen any evidence of it in the portraits on the castle website." I was quite proud of the research I'd managed to do that day, once it occurred to me that the portraits were the key to dating sightings of the ring.

"I've been meaning to get onto that. I'll send someone up there to look first thing tomorrow," Caleb said.

"I can do it—"

"No, Robbie. I agree with you. I think the ring's probably here. That's why I want you to stay." Caleb stood up. "I have complete confidence in you. Now find that ring. And next time you guys have curry, invite Rosa and I over. That was delicious."

Caleb left. Bianca hung over the chair arm, draping herself across me. "I've never seen you stick up for yourself before."

I snorted. "You didn't know me before. Angus and I always

gave Caleb hell. I think he enjoys being the alpha and pushing me around now."

"Why do you let him?"

"Because," I sighed, "Caleb was always a decent guy, and I treated him like shite. I wanted to show my father I was tough, like him and Angus. What I actually was, was a coward, and I don't want to be that guy anymore."

"I think you're pretty damn tough, Robbie."

"Because I'm so strong and manly?" I flexed my bicep, and Bianca giggled.

"Because you survived, Robbie. Because you walked away. You made the right choice. Sometimes, choosing is the toughest thing you can do."

Bianca leaned against me, and I fell into her spicy scent and warm body, never wanting to move again. We lay like that, our cheeks pressed against each other. After some time, Bianca's stomach rumbled loudly. I noticed our food sitting half eaten on the table. Extracting myself, I went to the kitchen to reheat our curries. I was just pulling mine out of the microwave when Bianca crept up behind me.

She placed her hands under my shirt, her nails scraping against my skin. She pressed her lips against my neck.

"I love a man who knows his way around the kitchen," Bianca murmured against my neck.

I whirled around, wrapping my arms around her and drawing her close. Her lips found mine, her kiss leading me right back to where we'd been before Caleb showed up. I skimmed my hands down her body, feeling her nipples hard through her shirt.

My cock sprung to life again. Bianca's hands explored my crotch, rubbing me through the fabric of my jeans until I moaned against her lips. I tried to pull off her shirt, but she grabbed my wrists and started dragging me toward the door.

"But the curries ... I thought you were hungry?"

"I am damn hungry," Bianca purred as she led me up the stairs. "This time, Robbie Maclean, we're going to use a real, proper bed."

I grinned, and followed her gorgeous arse up the steep stairs of the turret to the Rose Room. As we sank against Bianca's rose-covered sheets, Caleb and the Benedict Ring fell completely from my thoughts.

17

BIANCA

The next morning, I woke up around ten to find Robbie had once again left me alone in bed with a breakfast of leftovers and fresh coffee. *Bless him.* I picked up the cup and sniffed the brew.

Gross. I set it down in disgust. Robbie grew up without the life-giving joy of coffee. I'd have to teach him how to use the espresso machine. Not now, though. I was late as it was.

I fumbled my way into the nearest mostly-clean clothes, hastily applied some makeup, grabbed my wallet and bike key, and raced for the stairs. When I trudged out the door to head to the shop, Robbie was in the entrance hall, pawing through a cabinet. Delicate crystal goblets and creepy toby jugs covered every inch of the floor around him.

"No luck?"

He shook his head, setting down a porcelain pipe. "Not so far, but I've only just started looking. What time will you be home tonight?"

"About quarter-past-five, unless we get a sudden rush of new clients. What shall we do about dinner?"

"I thought we could try that Chinese place down the road."

I grabbed my stomach, pinching the skin between my fingers. "All this fast food is going to destroy this slim figure you love so much."

He grinned at me. "I'll love you whatever you look like. Besides, you're a married woman now. You're allowed to let yourself go."

Usually, I'd hit someone for a stupid comment like that, but Robbie's grin was too infectious, and his words too sweet. I settled for a slap on the shoulder. I shut the door behind me, unlocked my bike, and headed off to work.

Elinor sighed and pointed to her wrist as I walked in. "You can't make that face at me," I said as I started prepping my inks. "You don't even have a watch."

"I don't even need a watch to know you're late," Elinor grumbled, pointing into the waiting area, where my first client was already seated.

We had a busy day in the shop – my friend Iris from Holland stayed on after the party to do a residency, which meant she'd booked out one of our chairs for the whole day. Elinor and I had a booking each in the morning, and then a couple of walk-ins – eighteen-year-old girls getting butterflies on their lower backs. I had to resist cringing as I drew them up some generic butterfly stencils. I've drawn so many butterflies in my career I could practically be a butterfly botanist.

After the girls left, Iris got to work on her next client. Elinor took out her sketchbook and made another flash art page – this one was all themed around skulls and roses. Flash art is the sheets of drawings we display on the studio's walls and in folders in the waiting area. Walk-ins (like the butterfly girls) will often pick something direct from the tattoo books, which we just copy onto their skin. We deliberately design flash to be quick to tattoo. It's fun to create, and a way to show off our individual styles, but flash also kind of represents everything I hate about the tattoo industry. I've tattooed the exact same skull I drew five years ago nineteen times now.

While Elinor worked on her drawings, I made some updates to The Prim website and social media. Serenity had sent me some of the pictures she took from the party, and I was uploading them all to Facebook when I came across one of Robbie and me at the altar, sharing our first kiss.

My fingers tingled as I gripped the mouse. An ache rose in my chest as I remembered the feeling of his lips against mine, the way my whole body surged with heat. It wasn't just a good kiss, it was an *incredible* kiss.

Look at us, just like a real married couple.

My mind flashed to a photograph that hung in my parents front hall. My mother and father, standing outside the church where they were married, their hands clasped together. They stared straight ahead, eyes glazed, bodies so far apart you could fit another person between them.

I made the mistake of pointing that out to my mother when I was seven. "Of course," she said, stiffening her spine the way she did when she was going to teach me a moral lesson. "We must always leave enough space for the Holy Spirit."

That photograph haunted me, overshadowing every "happily ever after" fairytale I'd ever heard. My parents, always stiff, always drifting in different directions, never meeting anywhere in the middle. *That's what real marriage is — suffering and misery and oppression. It's not the fairy-tales.*

I stared at the picture of me and Robbie. Would that happen to us? Would we fall victim to the marriage curse, to the space that engulfed my parents? Would our friendship survive us?

Damn. Trust a kiss to ruin a perfectly decent fake marriage.

"Bianca." Elinor waved her hand in front of my face. "Can you hear me?"

"What? Oh, yeah, sorry." I quickly clicked away from the picture.

"Caleb's here to see you."

I waved to Caleb, who was waiting on the leather sofa under the window. He came over and leaned across the waist-high partition separating the working area of the shop from the waiting space. "Good news," he said. "It took some doing, especially after Robbie's accident the other night, but Irvine and I have secured our first major alliance, with the Wulfric pack of Germany."

"That's great news." From what Robbie had told me, the Wulfrics were one of the biggest lycanthrope packs in Europe. If we had the Wulfrics on our side, we'd soon notice a domino effect where more packs would align with Caleb, and he'd be able to become a real force for change. Of course, Robbie also hated the Wulfric pack, but I got the impression most shifter packs were pretty antagonistic toward each other, so I didn't think that really mattered much.

"It is." Caleb narrowed his eyes. "The only thing is, as part of their alliance, they want their representative Rolf to remain with us in Crookshollow, and work with us on forging additional alliances and establishing the shifter government. Effectively, he'll become part of our pack."

"You're okay with that?"

Caleb shrugged. "I don't like it, having some shifter lording it over us, insisting on being in on all our secrets. But that's the only way we'll get these guys on our side. Hence, why I'm here. I was wondering if you could put him up at the art house? I'd ask Ryan to, but I think having him stay at Raynard Hall sends the wrong message. Your place is a bit less ... intimidating."

"I agree." Ryan's palatial manor was certainly majestic, but if the Wulfric pack was anything like how Robbie described them, they would see accommodation there as us trying to show off our superiority. The last thing we need is the Germans thinking we were trying to show we're better than them.

"Plus, Rolf kind of took a shine to the place when we were there for the wedding. He specifically asked to be put up there if possible. Practically begged, in fact."

"Well, if he begged ..." I grinned.

"As much as a shifter can ever beg. So it's okay, then?"

"Yeah, sure. Hopefully, he'll give me a five-star review on TripAdvisor. It'll be a win-win."

"I'm sure we can figure out some kind of arrangement." Caleb glanced at his phone. "I've got to get back. We've still got a lot of negotiating to do to figure out exactly what this alliance looks like, and Rolf isn't always an easy guy to talk to. I'll bring Rolf by The Prim when we're done – maybe around six?"

"Perfect. I'll see you both then."

I sat back down at the computer, my mind whirring. I knew Robbie hated this guy, but if the pack's plan was going to work, all those old shifter grudges were going to have to be settled, sooner or later. Seeing Robbie stand up for himself against Caleb yesterday gave me an idea – if I forced Robbie to face Rolf, then that would help him feel as though he'd made the right decision in coming here. Robbie would get the ego boost he needed, and Rolf would be put in his place so he wouldn't bother Robbie anymore. If I could make it go down the way I envisioned, it would be awesome for everyone.

Things were about to get *really* interesting at The Prim.

18

ROBBIE

I grabbed the next crumbling wooden trunk from the stack, and prised the lid open. A great dust cloud rose from inside and hit me in the face. I staggered back, holding my mouth as another coughing fit took hold.

My throat was already raw from inhaling all the dust I'd disturbed in the attic, and so far, it was all in vain. I'd already torn the three servants bedrooms apart, in case Hattie had squirrelled away the ring along with the rest of her horde, but no such luck. Now, I was finishing the search of the attic – I found an ancient camera, several moth-eaten trunks of clothing, boxes and boxes of glass preserving jars, and a creepy porcelain doll I'd had to turn to face the wall because her eyes kept following me around the room. All this, but no Benedict ring, and no other clue where it might be.

Caleb's angry face flashed before my eyes. I rubbed the back of my head, raw and aching from all the times I'd stood up straight and banged it on the ceiling.

Downstairs, the front door slammed. I leapt up, banging my head on the rafters. Again.

"Honey, I'm home!"

It was Bianca. I grabbed my phone from my pocket and checked the time. 4:15. She was early. I dusted off my clothes as quick as I could, and scrambled down the steep staircase.

Bianca grinned up at me from the entrance hall, her arms laden with a heavy box of groceries. "The shop was empty except for Iris' clients, so Elinor and I decided to call it quits for the day. I even stopped by the supermarket and got us some real food. Why are you so dusty?"

"Oh, just hunting around in the attic," I said, meeting her at the bottom of the stairs and following her into the kitchen. "You'd love it up there. There's all sorts of crazy old things. I'm thinking of using some for my art project."

"You still doing that?" She stacked boxes and tins on the bench in the kitchen.

"Of course. I want to contribute something to the house."

"You're already contributing, Robbie. You've fixed up so much already. Without you, there wouldn't even *be* a house. The Prim wouldn't exist." She flashed me that beautiful Bianca smile. "I am seriously so grateful."

"Grateful enough to make spaghetti and meatballs for dinner?" It was my favourite. Bianca made her meatballs extra spicy.

She held up a packet of mincemeat. "Already started, my friend."

"Can I help?"

"Not covered in dust, you can't." She shoved me toward the door. Her hand against my chest sent a shiver through my body. "You'd better get cleaned up before Rolf gets here."

"Rolf?" My heart plummeted to my chest. *Did she just say that Rolf was coming here?*

"Yeah. Sorry, I thought Caleb would have told you. He came to chat with me at the shop today. Apparently, the Wulfric pack are going to become our allies, but only if they can keep someone here to represent them in all our decisions."

"Caleb would've loved that."

"Oh yeah, he looked *real* thrilled. But it was either agree or lose the Wulfrics. So he's agreed that Rolf will stay here and work closely with the pack until the time we are ready to make a bid for a new parliament. And apparently, he wants to stay here."

I shook my head. This can't be happening. That bastard can't be moving in with Bianca and I. "That's crazy. Caleb can't do that. Does he even *know* what the Wulfrics have done over the years? They've assassinated major German politicians in order to get their own alphas inside parliament. They're *ruthless*. They're not going to let Caleb tell them what to do."

"I'm sure Caleb knows what he's doing. Anyway, he and Luke are bringing Rolf over soon and—" There was a sharp knock at the door. Bianca dropped the meat on the bench. "That must be them now."

My heart sank as I followed Bianca into the hall.

She flung open the door. Caleb and Luke stood on the step, their arms folded across their chests. Rolf stood behind him, his arms folded and feet spread – his body language exuding dominance. I spread my own legs and folded my own arms, resisting the urge to bare my teeth. My inner wolf scratched against my skin, desperate to chase this interloper off my territory. But one look from Caleb and I knew that wasn't going to be how this went down.

Bianca outstretched her hand. "Rolf, hello. It's great to meet you."

Rolf stared Bianca up and down, licking his lips like she was a rare steak fresh off the grill. He turned to Caleb, and slapped him on the shoulder. "You didn't tell me you'd organised a mate for me. Thank you for your consideration. She's perfect. She's *exactly* my taste."

Back the fuck up, Rolf. My hands balled into fists.

Bianca's face froze. "Excuse me?"

Caleb shot me a pained look. I bared my teeth, making for the door, but he held up his hand. He turned to Rolf. "Bianca's not for you. Remember, you saw her get married just the other night. She's just the owner of The Prim. She'll look after you while you're here, make sure you have everything you need."

Rolf leaned forward, grabbing Bianca under the chin, tilting her head up so his eyes bore into hers. "Oh, I think I'll get everything I need from you, and more."

My blood boiled in my veins. Of course he thought he had a right to Bianca. But she was mine.

I growled, low in my throat. Rolf turned, noticing me for the first time. He tossed his head back and laughed. "Oh, didn't see you there, little Robbo. Don't worry, I won't hurt your friend ... *much.* From the looks of her, I bet she likes it rough—"

I expected Bianca to flare up, but instead she gave the wolf a salacious smile. "Wouldn't you like to know," she purred, holding the door open and ushering Rolf inside. As he whipped past her, he leaned in close, his hand groping for her arse, his long nose sniffing her face. She giggled.

Anger flared inside me. *How dare he come here, to my home, and speak to my mate like that?*

And why was Bianca allowing it?

As Rolf and Bianca stood in the sitting room, pointing to one of the paintings and laughing at some joke, I took a long, hard look at Rolf, trying to see him through Bianca's eyes. I hated to admit that I liked what I saw. At well over six foot, Rolf towered over Caleb and I, his long legs striding through the house with the utmost confidence. His chiseled features and broad shoulders belonged on a men's swimwear commercial.

Most importantly, he *oozed* confidence. His power practically sizzled against his skin. His presence filled the room, leaving no space for me.

This can't be happening. He can't be staying here. But he was. Bianca was hauling Rolf's backpack up the stairs, explaining in breathless tones that he'd have the Hummingbird Room, the first in the hallway leading up to hers.

Rolf glanced over to me, grinning like the cat that had just found the cream. He must have read something of my anger in my face, because he elbowed me in the ribs and said, "She's a fine woman. She'll make a great mate."

"She's mine," I growled. "She's *my* mate."

"Ah, yes. I can smell your claim on her. But I know something you don't know, little Robbo. You're on shaky ground with your pack."

"What are you going on about?"

"Your fearless leader Caleb is getting very impatient that you haven't located a certain artefact." Rolf laughed at my stricken face. "Yes, the secret is out. He was a fool to think a fake ring would fool me for this long. Without that ring, he can't move forward with his grand plan, a grand plan that now includes me and the Wulfric pack on a high level. The thing is," he rubbed his chin, like he was deep in thought, "I am a handsome wolf with high status in my pack, who will have a vital role in reshaping the world. You are a piece-of-scum criminal who can't even read—"

"You don't know what you're talking about," I growled.

"Oh, yes? You mean, I do not know that when you were at the library, you were writing out the text in big, loopy, childish handwriting? I do not know that you took an entire day to read three pages of a medieval document?"

I grabbed for his throat, but Rolf was too quick. His fingers tightened around my wrist, and he yanked my arm down, drawing our faces so close, I could see a tiny vein on the edge of his eye pulse as he spoke.

He tsked. "Now, now, we are not animals here. At least, not at this moment."

"Get out of this house," I growled.

"I cannot do that, and if you force me out, your alpha will drop you for certain."

"He wonnae dare if he knows you are trying to take my mate."

"Ah, but is that the truth? Remember that only a few months ago, you did the exact same thing to him. You kidnapped his precious Rosa and took her back to your scumbag father. You tried to manipulate him into doing what you wanted."

I glared at him, boiling rage coursing through my veins. How did he know about this? Did Caleb tell him? Caleb knows that I was only acting under Angus' orders, and I helped set Rosa free and stood up to Dad in the end. But Rolf wasn't anywhere near Aberdeen at the time, and no one in the Maclean pack would have told him a thing. The only way he could know about Rosa was if Caleb told him. Why would he speak about me like that to someone outside the pack?

Unless, the thought turned my veins to ice, *unless he doesn't really trust you after all. Unless he's getting ready to cut you out completely. He waited until you had given up everything, so that when he cast you out, you'd have nowhere to go. Maybe it's his way of punishing you for what you did to Rosa.*

Rolf grinned. "I see that you are starting to understand. Allow me to be clear and simple, because I know that big words confuse you. I control you, Robbie Maclean. You back off from Bianca, and do everything I say, and I won't destroy your precious second chance. But if you don't do as I ask, I'll make sure you're cast out quicker than you can say 'dead pure brilliant.'"

"Bianca's not some piece of meat we're fighting over," I growled. "You may be able to control me, but you can't tell her what to do. She'll make up her own mind."

"Indeed she will." Rolf's grin grew wider. "And who do you think she will choose? Bianca may be with you for now, but she didn't have any other options then. I am a powerful alpha who will be one of the world's shifter leaders, and you are an illiterate criminal who will soon be without a pack. You can offer her nothing. It's just the truth, I'm sorry to say. A girl like that, she'll never stay mated with a pussy like you."

I wanted to protest, to haul him out of the house by the scruff of his neck. My inner wolf pressed against my skin, desperate to come out and tear his throat out. But I gulped back the rage. Because I knew he was right.

I'd had Bianca for one incredible night, but I'd been a fool to think I could keep her. She deserved a man like Rolf, and as soon as she realised that, I'd be cast aside, just like always.

19

BIANCA

I cooked spaghetti and meatballs for dinner. Usually, Robbie would hang around to help with the prep, but tonight it was Rolf who entertained me in the kitchen. He was quite a funny guy, really.

Robbie skulked away to the sitting room, his nose buried deep in another box of old documents. Every ten minutes, I heard him sigh or mumble loudly, sometimes even growling low in his throat.

Something was definitely up with him. Probably it was a wolf territory thing – after all, Rolf had been a rival pack for most of Robbie's life, and after what Robbie had gone through because of Rolf, I could understand him being less than hospitable. It's hard to just shut off that programming.

Let him sulk. I'll talk to him later. I tried to tune Robbie out and focus on making sure our guest was well taken care of.

That was an easy job. Rolf was a cool guy. He knew his way around a kitchen, helping me to crush garlic and chop basil like a pro. Robbie could barely boil water, which is probably what happened when you lived most of your life as a wolf in the forest.

While I prepared the meatballs, Rolf found a bunch of half-open bottles leftover from the party and made us a pitcher of sangria, all the while regaling me with hilarious stories about his pack's overly-protective top alpha. I loved hearing about his life as part of the pack. Robbie almost never talked about his time before he joined with Caleb, and I knew enough to understand that the Lowe pack wasn't your typical werewolf horde.

Delicious, garlicky smells wafted up from the stove. I sent Rolf upstairs to tell the others dinner was ready, while I heaped meatballs and sauce onto beds of pasta, and brought the plates out to the dining room. Rolf followed with the sangria and a plate of parmesan.

"This looks *köstlich*." Hans rubbed his hands together as I set his plate down in front of him. On either side of him, two stick-thin German supermodels stared at the heaped plates of pasta with thinly-veiled expressions of disgust. Serenity accepted hers with a smile and a nod. An empty seat next to me alerted me to Robbie's absence. Odd, usually he was clamouring at the bit for food.

I poked my head through the hallway door and yelled, "Robbie, dinner!"

"Robbie, dinner! Don't forget to wash behind your ears," Rolf mimicked in a high-pitched squeal, sounding eerily like my mother. I burst out laughing.

My laughter died on my lips as soon as Robbie entered the room. He looked miserable, his face long, his eyes flashing. He slumped down in his seat and started shovelling his food into his mouth like he couldn't wait to get out of there.

I knew he didn't like Rolf, but this was intense. *What's wrong with him? It's not me, is it? He's not having regrets about the other night?*

"Rolf made sangria. It's delicious." I held up the pitcher. "Do you want some?"

Robbie shook his head, his eyes not moving from his plate as he gulped down the food, seemingly without chewing.

"Robbo isn't really a cocktail kind of guy," Rolf said. "He's more a beer-and-pizza kind of guy."

"That's true." I nodded, thinking about all the pizza and beer we'd consumed while we were cleaning up this place.

"I could relate to that," Hans said, waving a fork in the air, "if it were not for the fact your English beer tastes of squirrel piss."

The German supermodels sniggered.

"Well, maybe we'll do pizza tomorrow night. I know you've brought a case of your own beer over, Hans, so the rest of us will indulge in an inferior English brew." Hans made a face at me across the table. "There's actually a surprising number of decent takeaway in Crookshollow. We can try them all."

"We sure can," Rolf said, chomping into a meatball. He grinned across at me. "I'm not going anywhere in a hurry."

"I'm done." Robbie pushed his chair back and picked up his plate. "That was great, thanks."

"Okay, but there's some leftover heaven and hell cake, too—"

"No, thanks." Robbie disappeared into the kitchen with his plate. I heard the clatter of it on the bench. When he didn't emerge again, I realised he must have taken the secret staircase up to his bedroom.

I guess that talk is going to have to happen now.

"If he doesn't want the cake," Hans said, pushing his plate away, "send it my way."

I stood up. "I should go talk to him."

"Why?" Rolf grabbed my hand.

"Because ... you're staying here and I think that upsets him. Apparently some stuff happened before ..."

Rolf stroked my knuckles with his finger. "That was ages ago. Yes, I showed him up a couple of times, but it was his ego I bruised more than his body. We *were* part of warring packs, it is the nature of the game. We are both on the same side now, and he may need some time to realise that. If I were you, I would just leave him be. It seems like he really wants to be alone."

"I don't know ..." I stared into the entrance hall, listening for Robbie somewhere in the house, but all that met my ears was the ticking of that obnoxious grandfather clock.

Rolf leaned over and filled my glass again. "*I* was thinking you could give me a tour of the house. It's such a fascinating building, and I want to see what you've done. I didn't get to see much of it during the party."

Maybe he's right. Robbie will come around if I just give him some time.

"Oh, yes." Hans jumped up. "I too would like to join this tour. Last time you gave one I was far too drunk to remember anything."

I picked up my glass, and headed toward the entrance hall. "Sure. Let's go."

For the next hour, I led the whole group through the rooms, pointing to the new touches Robbie and I had added, and all the crazy artwork my friends had sent in. There were already a few empty spots on the walls from pieces purchased from wedding guests. Rolf asked lots of intelligent questions, and admired all the paintings I'd chosen as my favourites. We spent a long time in front of the wall of portraits on the first floor landing. As allies, Caleb had obviously told him about the ring, and after Serenity, Hans, and the models had wandered off to their rooms, Rolf asked lots of questions about Silvia Sinclair and how our search was going.

I shrugged. "Honestly, I've been so busy with the house and the shop, I haven't been much help. You should talk to Robbie. He's the one heading up the research."

Rolf snorted. "It seems ridiculous that Caleb has placed him in charge. You know he can barely read, right?"

"That's not true." Robbie was a bit slow, sure, but some people didn't read fast. I'd seen him read plenty of times, hadn't I?

"Are you certain? From what I know, little Robbo never even finished his O levels. His father, Angus, didn't see the point in his boys getting an education. They just lived in the forest like animals, too busy running the world's most incompetent werewolf drug ring to even bother to open a book." Rolf patted his chest. "I was fortunate that my father believed in his cubs getting an education. For this reason, the Wulfrics have pulled ourselves out of the gutter, and we now command the respect of all of Europe."

Robbie can't be that uneducated ... it's impossible ... he's just not ... "But he's so ... so polite."

"That's his mother's influence. She's a librarian."

I jumped as a floorboard at the end of the hall creaked. Out of the corner of my eye, I noticed the bathroom door was open a crack. *One of the others could be in there, listening to us talk about werewolves. Or, it could be Robbie ...* "I don't think we should talk about him anymore."

"As you wish." Rolf took my hand and raised it to his lips, brushing them over my fingers. "Goodnight, m'lady."

I rolled my eyes. Rolf was a bit silly. He seemed harmless, though. And he'd just told me something unbelievably useful about Robbie, if it was true.

My mind whirring, I said goodnight to Rolf, fielding his flirtatious invitations with polite mirth. As I shut the door to my own room, and started undressing, my mind turned back to what he'd said about Robbie.

I knew so little about him, really. Imagine not going to school, not reading books or learning sums or getting into fights on the playground. How could someone grow up without any contact with other kids ... and be so kind and courageous about it all? No wonder Robbie had chosen that tiny attic room. I've lived my whole childhood in a house like this, surrounded by fancy objects. But he ... he didn't even have a house. He must feel so profoundly uncomfortable with all this *privilege* around him.

I stood naked in front of my mirror, feeling like a complete selfish bitch for not figuring this out earlier. Robbie was upstairs in that tiny room ... what was he thinking about?

I touched the edge of my breast, my nipples hardening as I remembered how Robbie's tongue had worshipped them. He may not be able to read, but Robbie Maclean definitely had talents.

I think now he might need a little reminding of that.

Grinning to myself, I pulled on a set of black Agent Provocateur lingerie, wrapped myself in a shimmering kimono, and crept up the attic steps. I knocked on Robbie's door.

"I'm asleep," a muffled voice came from within.

"This is worth waking up for." I grinned, pushing open the door.

Robbie sat on the side of the bed, the blanket wrapped around his naked torso as he stared out the open attic window. As he turned toward me, the shaft of pale moonlight lit up his upper body, highlighting his sharp jaw and the sexy curve of his biceps.

A cool breeze fluttered the curtains. I dropped the belt of the kimono and it billowed open, revealing my two-piece g-string and longline bra criss-crossed with black straps. Robbie's eyes bugged out of his head.

Good. That's a good reaction.

Holding my finger to my lips, I climbed in bed beside him. My hands cupped his cheeks, pulling him against me. My lips sought his, burning with heat as they connected with their target. The shiver of energy passed between us as our bodies slammed, our limbs entwining together on the tiny bed.

Robbie pulled away, his hand stroking my cheek. "I ... I thought you wouldn't come back," he breathed.

"Why on earth would you think that?"

He didn't answer, just mashed his lips against mine, devouring me with need.

My own need rose within me, and I fell against him, tearing at the sheets, discarding everything that lay between us until we were skin on skin. His fingers slid behind my back and unhooked the bra, and after some struggling with the straps, he managed to toss it away. Our bodies sizzled with heat. He pulled my g-string to one side, not able to wait even to take it off completely, and entered me. I sighed with pleasure as his immense length slid inside me. Robbie moved slowly, languidly, letting me feel every tiny movement. I lost myself in the sensation of him – his fingers tracing my skin, his scent enveloping mine, the tickle of his stubble on my cheek.

Our bodies pulsed against each other as the strange energy that consumed us every time we were together cocooned us in erotic heat. Time and space ceased to exist. All that I was lived in his touch, in the rise and fall of our bodies.

We came together again. The heat exploded through my chest in a supernova of pleasure. The attic room faded away, the peeling paint and rickety brass bed frame disappearing into a deep void into which all my pleasure flowed.

I emerged from the void, moments or maybe hours later, my body rocked with tremors. Robbie held me in his arms, his body fitting so neatly against mine, like two puzzle pieces slotted together.

I held his arms against me, ready to fall into him once more. Robbie was so different from every other guy I'd been with. He was ... like the best parts of all the kinds of people I loved. Gentle and sweet like a poet, but hard and tough like a warrior.

He was also a complete mystery. Past conversations of ours run through my head. I thought of all the times I'd watched him read a menu at a restaurant, then order the exact same thing as me. I thought back to the day at the pub when I'd shown him June's letter and he'd frowned as he read it ... or pretended to read it. How he'd been so slow to get through all the archive material for the Benedict Ring search ... why did he volunteer if he couldn't read?

Why did you hide it from me? Why did you lie? I would have understood.

I opened my mouth to confront him, but I couldn't form the words. Moonlight from the waxing moon shone across the tiny bed. What we had here, now, was so perfect, I didn't want to ruin it.

Robbie was the one who broke the spell of the moonlight. "Bianca?" His voice, husky and heavy with exhaustion, brushed my ear.

"Yeah?"

"What are we?"

"What do you mean? We're human, I guess, although the jury's still out on you—"

"No, I mean ... us, together. *This.*" He squeezed me, indicating our naked bodies tangled together.

"Do we have to give it a name? Does it really matter? Can't we just be two people enjoying each other's company."

"Can you really live with that? The uncertainty ..."

"That's the way I do things. I don't do relationships, Robbie. I never have. Relationships end in marriage, and married people become my parents. I don't want that. I don't want stale and stodgy and sleeping in separate beds. I don't want to be two ships passing in the night. I want excitement and adventure and loud sex and rock'n'roll—"

"But cannae all that stuff be *part* of a relationship? The others seem pretty happy ... Caleb and Rosa and Elinor and Eric. Hell no one's more rock'n'roll than Eric. And I've lived with Ryan and Alex. Trust me, they're loud enough to hear even on the other side of Raynard Hall."

I giggled. "I don't doubt it. I'm sure it works for some people. It just isn't me. You know that, you've seen the way I go through partners. I don't do relationships, period. What's brought this up?"

Robbie sighed. "I wish it were that easy for me. I think I need ... a label for us, for what this is. I need to know where I stand."

"Why? Why is that so important?"

"It's important because I ... I've wanted this for a long time. Since we first met, actually. I never said anything because ... well, because I was afraid. Because I never thought you could possibly want me the way I want you. I still don't."

His voice sounded so sad. I hugged his arms tighter to me. "Well, you thought wrong."

"Did I?"

"It took me a while, but I'm totally in this, Robbo."

"But you're not. Not 100%. Be honest, you still want to be able to act like you're single. You'd still jump Willow in a second if she showed any interest. That's why you're flirting with Rolf."

"I'm not flirting with Rolf. You're being ridiculous. Don't let him get to you."

"I want *you*. I want all of you, Bianca, and I want you to have all of me. I want us to be *together*."

I snorted. "You mean marriage, a house, kids ... the whole stupid package."

"No, I mean ... I want those things too, eventually, in the future. But I never in my wildest dreams imagined they'd be mine. They're just stories in the few picture books my mother read to me in secret." Robbie closed his eyes. "You're not the only one who came from a messed-up family."

"Robbie, about your dad—"

"I dinnae want to talk about him. I dinnae want to think about him, not while we're here like this."

"Okay, but—"

"Aye, right, you don't want to end up like your parents. Join the club. But they're not the only example of marriage out there. Think about Caleb and Rosa, and Luke and Anna, and all the others. We could be just like them. It's possible we could have our own happy ending."

"No," I whispered. "No, I don't think it is."

The coldness clamped around my heart, those old pains gnawing in my chest. Robbie dropped his arms, rolling over. The tiny space between us became a gaping chasm.

"Have you heard of fated mates?" he said to the ceiling.

I didn't answer. I couldn't. Tension crackled between us.

"In order for a shifter male to produce a child who can also shift, he has to mate with a human woman who carries the shifter genes. It's relatively rare, and so somewhere in shifter history, we came up with a way to pick these woman out. We're drawn to people who are our perfect genetic match." Robbie sighed. "You and I are fated mates, Bianca."

The coldness crept down my arms, my legs. I opened my mouth to speak, but my throat closed.

"I felt it as soon as we met – the energy between us. I think you dinnae notice it because ... because you have such an energy about you. I think you're attracted to everyone." There was a tiny hint of a smile in his voice, but as quickly as it appeared, it was gone. "I didn't tell you because ... I dinnae want to scare you. But I can't keep quiet about it anymore. That's what the bite on your neck means. It's my mark, claiming you as mine. It's what Rolf is responding to, why he's trying to take you away from me."

"You *claimed* me?" I rubbed the wound.

"I couldnae help it. When we came together, it overwhelmed me. Instinct took over. The connection was too powerful to resist." He turned his head, his eyes burning into mine. "You're it for me, Bianca. And I just think, we're already married, and we live together, and we've got the sex part down. So what difference does it make if we call this a relationship?"

He sounded so hopeful. My throat itched, the words fighting against the ice in my veins. I wanted so badly to make him happy, especially now that I knew he'd had so little happiness in his life. But every word he spoke stabbed into me, wounding my pride, my independence, my very core.

He doesn't want me. It's just biology. He thinks he's in love with me but he's no different than my parents … it's all about keeping the bloodlines pure. He claimed me without even telling me what he was doing …

"I can't give you what you want, Robbie." I blinked, forcing the tears from my eyes as I rolled out of bed, and raced from the room, slamming the door behind me.

Naked and chilly, I fled down the stairs, holding back my sobs until I was safely behind my own door. I sunk to the floor, glaring up at the roses on the walls – staring at me, mocking me. The tears fell thick and fast. I cried for Robbie, because I knew now more than ever that no matter how much I cared about him, I couldn't be the person he wanted so much.

20

ROBBIE

I stared out the window at the waxing moon. Only a thin sliver remained dark on one side, and within the next week that sliver would disappear and my inner wolf would be unleashed.

Even now, he clawed against my skin, already relishing his chance to be free. Soon, I'd become the prisoner as the wolf took over my body. Luckily, there was a forest right outside where I could retreat. Although, Rolf would be heading for the forest as well, and if he crossed my path, I wouldn't be responsible for what happened.

Bianca's words replayed over and over in my head. *I can't give you what you want.* How could that be true, when all I wanted was her? How could she not see that I didn't want to destroy her independence, or quell her strength? Didn't she believe we could be stronger together?

You should never have told her about being fated mates. Now it's too late. You've lost her.

I leaned over and popped the spring on the hidden door, revealing the three shelves that housed Hattie's collection. I'd been looking at it a lot recently, trying to imagine the girl that had slept in this same bed, every night staring out at the same cold moonlight glinting off her assembled objects, waiting for her opportunity to escape.

Hattie wouldn't give up, and neither should I.

It took many long hours for the glow of the moon to become visible over the dark trees at the edge of the forest. I couldn't stand remaining in bed any longer. The sheets smelt of Bianca's spicy scent, the whole room saturated with the memories of her. I needed a distraction.

I crept down the stairs, thinking that I'd go for a run in the forest. If I embraced the wolf and let him have a few hours of joyful roaming, the agitation of his confinement might be easier to bear. As I passed by Bianca's room on the way to the main staircase, I couldn't help pressing my ear to her door. My superior wolf hearing caught the faintest sound – a sob? Yes, there was another one.

Bianca was crying.

Bianca *never* cried.

I longed to push open the door, wrap her in my arms, and make her pain go away. But I couldn't. I was the cause of her tears.

You pushed her. You knew what she's like about commitment, but still you pushed. And now she's crying and it's your fault and you've lost her ... you had your chance and you lost her ...

I tore myself away, and headed for the stairs. Something creaked in the hall, but when I turned around, I couldn't see anything. I sprinted down the stairs and whipped open the front door, the cool night air brushing against my naked skin. I glanced toward the forest at the foot of the garden. The trees leaned in toward the house, cocooning it in shadows. I dropped to my knees, and set my inner wolf free.

I gritted my teeth as the change coursed through my body. My bones snapped and reshaped, forming my new body.

Searing pain tore up my thighs as my knees turned inward. My fingers and toes dug into the wooden porch as they became paws and claws. Prickles erupted along my skin as the thick hairs of my pelt grew through my skin.

Behind me, another loud creak sounded from the hall above, but I was too far into my shift to attempt to investigate.

My nose stung. I watched through the corner of my eye as it elongated, becoming a snout. My eyes shifted to the sides of my face, and my view of the world changed – becoming wide-framed, the colours drab and muted, shades of grey, unremarkable and indistinguishable.

I squeezed the muscles of my legs and back, once again getting used to being in this strange body. The first few moments of the shift were always unnerving, as I remembered what it is to be a wolf. My tail lolled to one side, before I remembered how to engage the muscles to move it.

I raised my nose, and sniffed the air. Rolf's scent drenched the porch, the powerful stench nearly completely obscuring the fading scents of the people who passed over the threshold on our wedding night. The night air hung fresh and crisp, beckoning me. The forest called me, the trees rustling in the wind, a hundred crisscrossed animal paths weaving a technicolour-scented net through the tall trunks.

I ran, allowing the scents to consume me. I darted between the flower beds, leapt over the low garden wall, and bounded into the trees.

21

BIANCA

*K*nock knock.

I threw a pillow across the room, hitting the door with a dull thud. Cruel sunlight streamed in the open curtains, making my eyes water. I yanked the covers over my head and tried to ignore the knocks.

Knock knock.

Dammit, Elinor. I know I'm ridiculously late. My phone alarm has already rung seven times before I took the battery out. I just can't face the shop today. Can't you just take care of it all yourself, and let me wallow in my pain?

Just thinking about picking up a gun and making small talk with strangers made me feel sick.

"Bianca?" A timid voice called through the door. "It's me. Can I come in?"

I bolted up in bed. *Robbie? Why does he want to see me? He should never want to speak to me again.* I rubbed my face, feeling the puffiness under my eyes.

"Just a second," I called, dashing into my ensuite. I grabbed compacts and brushes at random, applying makeup as quickly as I could to hide my splotchy face. I still looked like shit, but at least I could pass for human. I fluffed up my hair, undid the top button on my fleece pyjamas, and climbed back into bed.

Experience had taught me it was always prudent after a fight to not let the other person see how much they got to you. This was even more true when it was someone I really cared about.

"Okay. Come in."

Robbie pushed open the door, and stepped inside, closing it behind him. I expected him to look the way I felt – i.e. shit – but he stood tall, his shoulders back, his jaw set. His skin glowed with colour, like he'd just been for a long run. I caught a whiff of something in the air – a fresh, dewy scent, like the forest after a light rain.

"I'm sorry," he said.

The words took a few seconds to register. He's ... *what?* "Why are you apologising?"

Robbie looked at me like I was mad. "We've been friends for long enough that I feel I ken you pretty well. I *ken* how much you hate commitment. I *ken* that's not how you do things. But I pushed you, and I'm sorry for that. I won't ever do that again. If you'll take me back, if you'll give me a second chance, I promise I wonnae bring it up again. I'm happy to go on with however you want things. If you want to do the open thing ... I mean, I wonnae be with anyone but you, but if you have to do that then I'll ... I mean ... I'll try to—" He gulped. "Just please, donnae let us be over."

I shook my head. "You have it all wrong, Robbie. Don't ever apologise to me for telling the truth."

"But—"

"No buts. You're not living with your father anymore. You don't have to fall about trying to please me. Not everything is your fault. You did everything right." I took a deep, shuddering breath. Tears brimmed in the corner of my eyes, threatening to destroy my slapdash makeup job. "It's me. I can't ... I just can't give you what you want. I wish I could, but it's like every time I think I can, my mother sits on my chest, and her weight starts to choke me, and I just can't ..."

Robbie perched on the end of the bed, his hands resting awkwardly on his lap. "I cannae understand. I met your parents. They dinnae seem so bad."

I tried to speak, but the words caught in my throat. I coughed, shoved my fists into my eyes as if I could push the spilling tears back inside, and tried again. "My father and mother are cousins."

I kept my eyes closed, not wanting to see the disgust on Robbie's face. I'd seen it too often before, on men I'd trusted, girlfriends I'd confided in, all of whom left me soon after finding out. I couldn't bear to see it on Robbie's face.

"Cousins?" he said finally, his voice quiet.

"They did it because in this family, 'preserving the bloodline' is more important than anything, even the rules of common decency. It is legal, but not ... not exactly something you throw around. It used to be quite common in Europe, but most of the prominent families gave up the practice in the last century. Not the Sinclairs. Oh no, we were too proud to be swayed by all that feminist claptrap and birth defect research."

I sucked in another shuddering breath and continued. "From the time I could talk, I was taught to talk down to anyone who wasn't what my parents considered a 'proper' sort of person. Basically, anyone without a title. I just couldn't under-stand why I was supposed to treat the African girl in my class differently from the prissy white girls who treated her like shit. My mother told me it was because she had inferior blood. Even then, I couldn't stand bullies, but my parents, they were the biggest bullies of them all, and I was trapped with them.

"They were the worst to each other. Father had no patience for any of us, especially Mother. He wasn't happy in the company of people, especially women. He got into trouble in The House of Lords for all his racist, sexist, 19th-century bullshit – and that was from the Tories! – and eventually he was asked to step down. Mother was cruel to him. She always wanted him to be more than he was. She hated the fact that he gave up his political career to teach and study history. He was a disappointment to her. Everyone was a disappointment to her, especially me."

"I cannae believe that."

I sniffed. "For years I tried so hard ... to be the girl they wanted me to be. All I wanted was for them to tell me they were proud. I did the ballet lessons, learned to play boring old songs on the piano, tried to get top marks at the stuffy public school they sent me to ... all the activities that proper ladies did with their proper white lady friends. I hated every minute of it, and they hated everything I *was* interested in. I'd bring home art projects covered with my teacher's praise, and Father would yell at me that art was pointless. I was elected the captain of the school cricket team and Mother made me quit because it wasn't ladylike."

"Whoah."

"I always *felt* different, like I didn't belong. And then, I hit puberty, and I started to articulate my attraction to women, and act on those feelings. The first time, my boarding school matron caught me in bed with a Muslim girl from my class. I didn't understand ... I didn't see how something that felt so good could be wrong. I always remember her soft, buttery skin, the way every movement she made hypnotised me, like a trance. Mother had the girl expelled, and she gave me a thrashing and sent me to a camp for wayward girls for the entire summer."

Flashes of the camp passed before my eyes. It had been in an old nun's cloister from the 14th century, the walls bare white-washed stone, the doorways framed with gothic arches. We girls slept in cots in a dorm room, with no technology, no colour, no gossip, no books to read apart from the Bible. I remembered the cruelty of the nuns as they tried to break us with hours on our knees in the lofty church, their punishments, the harsh lectures of the Mother Superior on our moral shortcomings.

"At that camp, I met other girls like me – girls who liked other girls, girls who wanted to be artists or writers instead of housewives, girls who fell in love with black men, defiant girls who wanted to do their own thing in life, but that independence made them dangerous somehow. We spent every day being told these thoughts and actions were the devil whispering in our ears. We prayed for hours on our knees, until our skin split and big sores opened up. We had to memorise Bible passages and listen to each other confess all sorts of sins. So many of the girls fell victim to the brainwashing, but everything they tried to shove down my throat made me determined that I'd never deny my true self any longer. I went back to school and snogged as many girls as possible. I stopped caring about any of my classes except art. I got my first tattoo. But no matter how hard I fought, I was trapped. Always Mother dragged me back there, to that house. Always she punished me for nothing more than being who I was."

"But, Bianca, you're not your mother. You'd never do these things to another person, so why would you be afraid of—"

"Don't you see? I got out, Robbie. They nearly took everything from me, but in the end, I won. I got out, with my humanity intact. They couldn't break me. But if I tied myself to someone else ... it could happen again. Just because someone is supposed to love you, doesn't mean they won't try to control you. I won't ever risk my freedom on the slim chance of love everlasting. It's not worth it."

A hand reached out and circled my wrists, the fingers closing around mine. Robbie tugged, drawing my hand from my eyes. "Bianca, look at me."

So soft. His voice warm and kind, like my favourite sweater on a cold day. I opened my eyes.

"I ken a little about what you went through," he said. "I was trapped, too. My old pack ... it wasnae anything like what Caleb has created here. We were a gang of thugs, of men who lived outside the law. My father didnae care about anything except that Angus and I should take over the family business once he was gone. That business being the running of drugs through Aberdeen and beyond.

"I've done horrible things, Bianca ... things that haunt my dreams, all because I was afeard of him. He was so fierce when he was angry, and he made me believe that the only future I could possibly have was with him and the pack. He dinnae even allow Angus and I to go to school ... I always thought it was because he dinnae believe in it, but now I believe it was because it was just another way to control us." He gulped. "I can barely read or write. I cannae do maths. I dinnae know anything about world history I haven't seen in a movie. There's no job I can do with the skills I have except for beating people up."

"That's not true, Robbie. You've done an amazing job on the house. And for someone who can't read, you've got closer than anyone to finding the ring—"

His grip on my wrist tightened. He squeezed his eyes shut as painful memories flooded over him. My heart broke for him, for everything he'd endured.

Robbie's eyes fluttered open, and met mine with an intense gaze. "My mother used to bring home books from the library and read me stories when Dad was gone. She'd show me these beautiful books with bright pictures about kids who slayed dragons and families who worked together to solve mysteries and brave princes who saved princesses from evil witches. I wished so hard that I'd wake up inside one of those stories, that I'd get to live in a family like that. I came with Caleb because when he showed up again, I realised there was hope, that maybe families like the ones in storybooks actually exist, but you had to make them yourself. I thought ... I could find the brothers I'd never had in the pack. And then I met you, and I knew it was true. You inspire me, Bianca, because the life you've made for yourself is so remarkable, and I just want to be a part of it, even if it's only a tiny part."

I laced my fingers in his. Tears spilled down my cheeks. "I've realised we're just as fucked up as each other."

He laughed as he squeezed my hand. "Aye."

"Robbie, I can't go from nothing to a serious relationship right now, but ... I really do care about you so much, and I want us to work. I want to try ... this exclusive commitment thing, see if I like it."

"But you cannae do it, Bianca. You said so."

"I haven't tried it before, so I guess we'll find out. But I want to do it, and I usually get what I want."

He kissed me, long and deep, the kiss sinking right through my body like a deep tissue massage.

"Just don't call me your girlfriend, or partner, or significant other," I said as I pulled away. "I can't handle any of those things right now. Give me some time to ease into this slowly."

"What about if I call you my wife?" Robbie grinned.

"Don't push your luck." I wrapped my arms around him, drawing him back for another kiss.

AFTER A GLORIOUS BOUT OF LOVEMAKING, Robbie left to get dressed. I got out of bed, showered, scrubbed my makeup off and reapplied it, and headed downstairs to get breakfast.

Rolf was in the kitchen, washing dishes, one of June's old frilly aprons tied around his waist. He looked so ridiculous, I had to laugh.

"Good morning." He grinned at me as I hovered in the doorway. "I was going to bring you some breakfast, but Robbie said I shouldn't disturb you. He was quite rude about it, actually."

"He just knows me well," I said, slumping over to turn on the coffee machine. "I'm really not a morning person. I'm running late for work anyway, so I'll just grab something from a bakery on the way."

"What do you do, Bianca? It must pay well if you've got a house like this and you can roll in at ten o'clock."

I grinned. "I wish. This house was inherited, so I don't pay a mortgage. I'm a tattoo artist. I run my own tattoo studio so I can basically show up whenever I want. My boss is pretty relaxed about it."

Rolf gazed down at the ink running along my arms. "I should have guessed. Is your place in Crookshollow?"

"Yeah. It's called *Resurrection Ink*. There are dancing skeletons in the window. You can't miss it."

"Cool. I was thinking of having a look around the town before I met up with Caleb today. Do you have many appointments?" He rubbed his own impressive sleeve. "I'd love to get some of the colours retouched."

"I'm busy until one, but after that, you're welcome to come in."

"It's a date. I'll even bring you a late breakfast."

"Deal." I poured my coffee into a thermos, strapped it over my shoulders, and headed for the door. Robbie met me in the hall, a strange expression on his face.

"You're going to tattoo Rolf?"

I shrugged. "Yeah, why?"

"I don't trust that guy," he mumbled to me, as he draped my coat over my arm.

"Caleb and Irvine trust him. Shouldn't that count for something?"

"I don't exactly trust Irvine either, but I know that's because of our history." Robbie jabbed a finger toward the kitchen. "The Wulfrics ... they're the biggest pack in Europe. But they got that way by attacking and overpowering other packs and integrating them. You have to be pretty ruthless to cut that kind of path to power."

"I get it, but I don't think Rolf did that *personally,* and he's got no path to power to cut in my shop, so I'll be fine." I rubbed his cheek. "It's you I'm worried about. Are you going to be okay alone in the house with him, especially this close to the full moon? If I come home and this place has been trashed and there are claw marks through the ottoman—"

"I'll be fine." He kissed me, long and deep. "Have fun sticking needles in people. I'll see you this evening."

As I turned to the door, an odd shiver ran down my back, and I had the oddest feeling that a pair of eyes were following my every move. I whirled around, but apart from Robbie, I couldn't see anyone else.

Where had that feeling come from?

22

———

ROBBIE

$\mathcal{B}$ ianca waved to me as she headed out the door, her smile lighting me up. The door slammed shut behind her, leaving me alone in the house with *him*.

I hated Rolf being here, touching our stuff, leaving his disgusting Wulfric scent all over the house. It would take weeks after he was gone for that stench to fade. And now that he was threatening me and trying to take Bianca away, it was even worse, and I was powerless to stop him.

Trapped again.

As if reading my thoughts, Rolf wandered into the hallway, shining an apple against his bare chest. "Hi Robbie." He bit into the apple, chewing loudly. "Any luck with the ring yet?"

I balled my hands into fists. As if my failure to locate the ring wasn't frustrating enough, now Rolf knew about it. "It's going fine."

"If it was going fine, you'd have found it by now." Rolf grinned, taking another huge bite. "Don't worry, I'm here to help now, so we'll find it in no time."

"You're not getting anywhere near the ring," I growled.

"*Au contraire.*" He paused. "That's 'You're wrong,' in French, in case you didn't know. It's part of the agreement my pack made with Caleb. I'd have thought your alpha would've explained this to you. I am here to assist with the hunt for the ring."

"I dinnae need your help."

"You do, Robbo, you do." He clapped me on the shoulder, his own shoulders shaking in silent laughter. "You see, unlike you, my father actually taught me to read. And, also unlike you, I have the trust of your alpha. If you don't find that ring soon, Caleb is going to get rid of you, so if I were you, I'd be taking any help you can get."

"Fine." I thought quickly. *I need to give him a job to do that will be least likely to result in him finding the ring.*

"We think the ring is located somewhere in this house, but there's a lot of stuff that needs going through. I'm working in the drawing room. You could take the kitchen. Take all the stuff out of the cupboards, search them thoroughly, and put it all back. Give them a good clean while you're at it. I see you already have the apron for that."

"What about Bianca's room? I'll take that instead." Rolf licked his lips. "I bet it smells absolutely *intoxicating.*"

"Don't you touch any of her stuff," I growled. "Just go into the kitchen and search and don't talk to me or Bianca."

"There, now, that's not very neighbourly. If you don't start acting more accommodating, I might have to tell your alpha how recalcitrant you are." He paused to give me one of his slow smiles. "Do you know what recalcitrant means? Do I need to spell it for you?"

My fists ached from clenching them so hard. Every muscle in my body tensed, ready to leap forward and smash Rolf's face open. But he was right – his pack was an important alliance, and he knew many things about me I didn't want my pack to know. If I did anything that jeopardised the alliance, Caleb would throw me out, and then I'd truly be alone.

I let out a frustrated cry, spun around, and stomped away. Rolf's laughter followed me down the hall to the dining room. I slammed the door shut behind me, rattling the frame and disturbing the crystal in the cabinet.

Why did he have to stay here, with us? I knew why, because Rolf wanted to torture me. It wasn't enough that he'd beat me before, he had to do it all over again, here in my home. And of course Caleb would bend over backward to agree with him, especially since Bianca and I were the only people who weren't part of a couple. If Bianca weren't such a commitment phobe and had told everyone we were getting married for real, then Caleb would have got Rolf a hotel, and everything would be fine.

That's not fair, Robbie, and you ken it. You're just feeling like shite because he's here. Don't take it out on Bianca.

My frustration lasted for the rest of the day, as I pawed through every crystal goblet, looked under every Toby jug, and checked the edges of every drawer and surface for a fake back or bottom. Nothing. The ring wasn't anywhere in this room.

This is ridiculous. More than 150 years have passed since the ring was lost. Bianca's grandmother knew every corner of this house. If it had been in an obvious place, she would have found it already, and restored it to its rightful place as a Sinclair family heirloom.

I slumped to the floor, knees pulled to my chest. My temples throbbed. There had to be something I was missing. Some clue hidden amongst all the other clues. A cleverer person would have already found it. But I wasn't clever, and my time was running out.

You can't let this get to you, Robbie. Everyone is counting on you, and now you've got some extra motivation, as you have to figure this out before Rolf does. Check the diary again; it's the only direct link to Silvia you have. If there's some clue you missed, it's in there.

But what's the point? I argued with myself. *You can't even read the diary. You should just bring it to Rolf, so he can find the clue and take the credit.*

No. My inner wolf raged. *You're not giving up. Go and get that book and read as hard as you damn well can.*

I pulled myself to my feet, and crept into the hallway, listening hard to the clatter of dishes in the kitchen. Good, Rolf was working in there. I'd be able to sneak upstairs without him seeing me.

I crept across the hallway, and placed my foot on the first step. The wood let out a mighty creak. I froze, heart pounding, but the bangs and shuffles in the kitchen didn't cease. I crept up the rest of the stairs, crossed the landing and climbed up to the Rose Room. Even though she had strangers living in her house now, Bianca didn't lock her door. I pulled it open and ducked inside.

Bianca's scent hit me as soon as I crossed the threshold – a wall of spice so intoxicating it disoriented me. I stood like a fool, my nose in the air, drinking in the essence of her. This close to the full moon, I had to reel in my wolf before he escaped to bask in that glorious scent.

Once I had my wolf under control, I scanned the walls, admiring how she'd began to plaster the rose-covered wallpaper in tattoo posters and old vinyl record covers. I stared at the rumpled, unmade bed, remembering what we'd done there this morning, how Bianca's back had arched as I entered her from behind and—

Get a grip on yourself, Robbie. You don't want Rolf to catch you in here. Find the scrapbook, and get out.

I scanned all the surfaces for the leather-bound book. It wasn't buried under the piles of makeup on the dresser. I moved to her bedside cabinet. There, hidden under a stack of tattoo magazines and a copy of some book called *On The Road*, was Silvia Sinclair's scrapbook.

I grabbed it and bolted to the door. As I passed the bed, I noticed something sitting in the middle of the sheets. I peered closer.

A small bouquet of blood-red roses sat on the duvet, wrapped with black paper and ribbon. A short note stuck out the side. I squinted at it for a few minutes, trying to read the curly red lettering. FROM YOUR ADMIRER, the note said.

Blood boiled in my veins. *Rolf.* It could only be him. No one else had been in the house apart from us and the guests. The flowers had only one purpose – he *was* trying to take Bianca from me.

I grabbed the flowers and note, tossed them into the rubbish bin at the end of Bianca's dresser, hiding them beneath a bunch of used tissues. *Take that, Rolf,* I seethed. *Two can play at this game.*

I took the diary up to the attic. Somehow, knowing that Silvia had spent much of her time up there with Hattie made it the perfect spot to try to solve the mystery.

I flopped down on the bed and opened the book to the first page. My heart sank when I squinted at the handwriting again. Silvia wrote in a loopy, romantic cursive that made my eyes hurt just looking at it.

I shut my eyes. *Come on, Robbie. This is your job. You have to do this.*

Slowly, as though I was a scholar mulling over a particularly difficult Latin passage (I assume), I worked my way through the words. I had a children's dictionary app on my phone alongside the useless screen reader that gave me simple definitions for all the words I didn't understand, which were quite a few. As I figured out each sentence, I wrote it down on a pad next to me. My crooked, childish writing wouldn't win any calligraphy awards, but at least I could read it back to myself.

My stomach growled as I struggled through each page of the scrapbook, trying to decipher every single word to make sure I didn't miss a thing. Something meaty and delicious wafted up the secret staircase from the kitchen below, but I wasn't about to go downstairs and give Rolf the satisfaction of feeding me.

Some time later, I heard footsteps on the stairs. "Bye Robbo," Rolf called from the first floor landing. "I'm off to get naked for Bianca. I will return for dinner tonight. Good luck with that ring!"

Go to hell, you wanker, I thought, but didn't say.

A few moments later, Rolf's footsteps descended the main staircase. The front door slammed, and I was finally alone.

I slammed the book shut, and raced down from the attic. I returned to Bianca's room, grabbed the flowers from out of her rubbish bin, and flung them in the kitchen bin, where Rolf would be sure to see them.

Looking around, I noticed Rolf had left several pots in the sink. He must've made himself something for lunch. I flung open the fridge. A large pot of chilli sat on the shelf. It smelled delicious, packed with glorious spices. I pulled it out, ladled myself off a generous bowl, and placed it in the microwave. While I waited for it to heat up, I took the rest of the chilli and dumped it into the bin on top of the flowers.

"HONEYS, I'M HOME!" Bianca yelled from downstairs.

I flung the book and my pad onto my bed, hiding them under my pillow, and flew down the stairs. Rolf hadn't come home yet, and apart from the journalist, the other guests were all out. I wanted to talk to Bianca before Rolf had a chance to get to her first.

"How was your day?" I asked as I clattered down the stairs, my heart leaping at the sight of her.

"My hand has cramped up so bad, I can't feel my fingers anymore. I had wall-to-wall clients all day. First, that reporter Serenity came in to get a massive dragon on her shoulder. I just managed to get the outline done before Rolf came in for his touchup—" She stopped. "What's wrong?"

"Nothing's wrong."

"You have your serious face on." She stroked my cheek.

"I have to show you something." I grabbed her hand and dragged her into the kitchen, lifting the lid of the bin to show her the crumpled flowers.

"Roses," she said, bending down the touch the petals. "They're pretty."

"They're for you."

"Then why are they in the bin, covered with chilli?"

"I found them on your bed." Bianca glanced up at me. "I didn't put them there."

"Oh, Robbie—"

"Rolf is trying to win you," I said. "He knows that I've claimed you, but he thinks he's got the right to swoop in and take you—"

"Whoah, whoah, whoah!" Bianca grabbed my shoulders. "What's all this bollocks about claiming me? I thought we cleared this all up. You and I are together, but we're not *together*. This isn't the dark ages, Robbie. I'm not anyone's to claim."

"I ken." My cheeks flared with heat. "It's just ... what it's called in shifter society when you find your fated mate and give her the mark."

Bianca rubbed her neck where I'd bitten her. She sighed. "Let's get this clear right now. There's nothing going on between

Rolf and I. He's hot, okay? I'm not going to deny it. But I'm hardly going to go after him, especially not now that we've agreed to be exclusive and *especially* now that I know how much it affects you."

"Okay, but—"

"No buts. So, can we drop this? I'm going to start regretting my decision if you continue to give me this lip."

"What about the flowers?"

Bianca glanced down at the bin. "Flowers? I don't see any flowers. Only a giant pile of chilli. Although, why is all this chilli in the bin? It doesn't smell off. In fact, it smells kind of delicious."

"Oh, no reason." I slammed the lid down. "Go have a shower and I'll order some takeaways."

23

BIANCA

Rolf didn't come home for dinner. He texted me to say he was going to meet up with Caleb and Irvine for beers at *Tir Na Nog*. His next text read:

I'd invite you along, but the boys don't want Robbie there tonight. Caleb's still pissed at him.

Feeling infuriated on Robbie's behalf, I snapped my phone shut and tossed it aside. When Caleb left here, he'd seemed fine and he'd reiterated his trust in Robbie. If he'd said all that, but was still holding a grudge, then he was being a dick. I tucked into my pizza, and decided I wouldn't tell Robbie about the text. He'd cheered up so much since we made up. I watched Robbie and Hans swapping beers and chatting about something or other. Unfortunately, that left me to make conversation with the models, who picked at a limp salad and snarled at each other in German. Serenity just looked on with curiosity, and chewed on her third slice of pizza.

After dinner, I left the guests in the drawing room playing Settlers of Catan, grabbed Robbie's hand, and hurried him up to the Rose Room. I threw open the doors to the balcony, and led him out into the crisp night.

"I thought we could enjoy a little time alone out here," I said, as I poured us both a shot of absinthe. We clinked glasses, and leaned side-by-side over the edge, peering down into the darkened trees. The electric energy sizzled in the air around us, taking the edge off the cold breeze.

"I feel like the Queen, surveying her domain," I said.

"What an amazing view," Robbie said, staring out over the forest. "I never see the trees from up high. They're usually just a wooden blur flying by."

I pointed up at the moon, which was waxing its way to full. "How long until the full moon?"

"A few days." He sighed. "I hate the idea of leaving you alone for so long."

"I backpacked across Europe on my own when I was fifteen. I think I can survive a few days in my *mansion* by myself."

"You need to talk to Rolf about the protocol," Robbie said. "He might not know that he needs to go away into the forest when he changes. And he'll need to stay far away from here, because in my wolf form I don't know if I'll be able to resist the urge to tear his throat out."

"Can't you just ... not do that?"

"It's not that easy. Usually, I'm able to control my mind when I shift, but on the full moon, I'm a wild beast. I operate completely on instinct. For a wolf, instinct is tied up with scent. And right now, my instincts are screaming that Rolf is my rival, and anything with his scent on it is a direct challenge to me. For example, if I smelled you wearing clothes that had Rolf's scent on them, in my wolf form, I'd think you betrayed me, and I'd probably attack you. That's why it's so important we all – especially Rolf – go far away."

"Can't you talk to him? I'm not exactly qualified since I don't turn into a flesh-eating beast on the full moon."

"I'm not going to do it," Robbie growled, throwing his arm

around my waist and wrapping his body around mine, so my back pressed against his chest. "It's nothing to me if he ends up a mangled wreck."

"Don't say things like that. It's not very nice."

"Oh yeah?" He nuzzled his mouth into my neck, his teeth scraping across my skin. "What are you going to do about it?"

I opened my mouth to reply, but Robbie claimed my lips with his, and I forgot what we were talking about.

The electricity in the air coiled around us. Robbie pressed his body against mine, the warmth of him drawing out my desire. I reached behind me to cup his cheek and pull his mouth to mine, but he took my hand and placed it back on the railing, knitting his fingers in mine.

"Don't move," he whispered, his breath tickling my ear. "This is all about you tonight, my Queen."

An ache rose between my legs, settling just above my stomach. If that's the way he wanted it, I was all too happy to oblige.

I gripped the railing, while Robbie put his amazing hands to work. As he kissed me, his hands trailed all over my body, lifting my old Slayer t-shirt up and tugging my bra aside so he could knead and pinch my nipples. The sharp pain against the cold wind only inflamed me further.

Robbie nibbled on my ear, and his hardness pressed against my thigh. I rammed my ass up against him, grinding myself into him, letting him know just how badly I wanted it. He growled in my ear, a low rumble that coursed right through my body. I loved him like this, so wild, so untamed.

I gripped the balustrade as Robbie tore at the buttons on my jeans, slipping them down over my thighs from behind me. He dropped down beneath me, crawling between my legs and sliding up so his back was against the balustrade. With one hand reaching up to grasp my nipple, he plunged his tongue inside me.

"Oooh," I moaned, as his tongue slid along my entire length, stroking me just the way I liked it. He found that little bud and lapped at it like a kitten, sending me wild with desire. The energy thrummed through my veins, lighting my whole body on fire.

Instead of closing my eyes or looking down at what he was doing, I kept my gaze fixed on the tree line and the empty space right in front of me. The vertigo made it all even more exciting. A sharp breeze blew up from below, caressing my naked chest. If anyone turned down the driveway right now, they'd get quite a show.

Robbie thrust a finger inside of me, and I didn't even care anymore. Hell, let someone come up the driveway and see what good fucking sex is all about.

Not good ... Robbie's tongue flicked over me, and the ache inside me spread out through my limbs ... *dead pure brilliant sex. The best sex I've had in my whole damn life.*

He thrust a second finger inside of me, and his tongue swirled faster, and the ache inside me exploded through my body. Red welts danced in front of my eyes, and I had to steady myself against the railing as my legs gave way beneath me. The orgasm tore through me, and I tossed back my head and howled for the sheer joy of it. My voice rippled through the night.

Robbie' gripped my legs as he continued to lap at me, softening his strokes while I recovered, before battering me with his tongue once again. His finger inside me pressed right up against my wall. This time, it only took a minute or so before I came again, even more intensely than before. My vision swam, and for a moment, I lost complete sense of where I was. I lost all feeling in my legs, and it was only Robbie's grip that kept me from toppling over the balcony.

Before I'd even properly finished coming, Robbie stood up

and caught me in his arms. "Don't you squirm away now," he whispered against my ear.

"I wouldn't dare," I tried to simper back at him, but the words came out as a choked gasp. My whole body sizzled with energy, ready for more of what only he could give.

He moved around behind me again. I gripped the balustrade, arching my back and thrusting my ass up into the air. Robbie leaned into me, gripping my thighs with thick fingers. With a groan of pleasure, he plunged himself deep inside of me.

A groan escaped my lips as he slid deep. He felt so good. Robbie started to thrust into me, slow and steady at first, but as his own pleasure mounted, he pounded harder. With each stroke, I rose up to meet him, thrusting back with my hips to grind his length deeper.

That's it, Robbie, unleash that inner wolf. Be the beast I know you are.

Robbie's fingers dug into my thighs, sending a shiver of exquisite pain through me. His teeth grazed my neck, but if he bit me, I couldn't feel it for all the pleasure flooding my veins. As he came against me with a shudder, my neck arched, and my eyes flew open, swinging through the view of the deep blue sky and the darkened tops of the trees. My breath fled my body as my own orgasm claimed me, and the blue of the sky stained my eyeballs, a vision so perfect I never wanted to forget it.

So ... this is what it's like to fly.

24

ROBBIE

I left Bianca tucked up in bed, snoring heavily against the pillow with Macavity pressed up against her cheek. Being out on the balcony with her, with the scent of the forest thick in the air, and her thrusting her gorgeous ass against me, had made me desperate to go out to the forest again. I'd been cooped up in the house all day with Rolf's disgusting smell, and my body itched to run under the moonlight again.

I snuck down the stairs, careful to avoid the most creaky boards so as not to wake the other guests. A faint glow from the hallway told me the kitchen light was still on. Thinking Bianca must have left it on by mistake – she was terrible at forgetting about those things – I went in to turn it off, and was surprised to see Serenity sitting at the table under the window, her laptop open in front of her and a look of intense concentration on her face.

She jumped when she noticed me. "Robbie, you scared me! I couldn't sleep, so I thought I'd come down and get a midnight snack and do some work."

"Aye, hello Serenity. I didnae mean to startle you. I was just ... getting some water."

"Don't let me stop you," she said, turning back to her computer, her fingers a blur as they whizzed across the keyboard.

I wondered what she was writing with such ferocity in the middle of the night. I peeked at her computer screen as I filled my glass, but it was all a mess of gibberish to me. The moon shone through the open window, extending a shaft of pale light across the kitchen floor, like a beacon calling me into port. Clutching my glass of water, I moved back into the hall. As stealthily as I could, I set down the glass on the hall table and crept into the ballroom, shutting the door quietly behind me. With slow jerks, I eased the sash window up high enough so I could leap in and out. I took off my t-shirt and boxers and tossed them on a chaise lounge, then forced my shift.

As soon as my paws hit the rug, my wolfish senses took over. Rolf's scent swirled around me, forcing my throat closed so I could hardly breathe. I leapt out the window and cleared the sill, landing on the wooden porch with a dull thud. I bounded down the path, through the flowerbeds and leapt into the primroses that marked the boundary between the garden and forest.

Trees rose up around me, like giant pillars in a church's nave. Moonlight dappled the dirt below my paws, moving softly as a breeze caressed the trees to create striking ripples through the forest, so the world appeared to be submerged in a shimmering lake. It wasn't long before Rolf's scent was replaced by the myriad of sweet smells of the forest. Animal paths crisscrossed my tracks as the night creatures scurried about their business. I could read whole migrations through those whiffs of scent – a world that hummed with life completely unfazed by all the goings on in the village.

I ran deeper, not worrying where I was going, only enjoying the breeze ruffling my fur and the soft dirt beneath my pounding paws. Sweat streaked my fur, and my tongue hung from my mouth, relishing the chance to completely let go.

I scurried down a clearing, and came up across a scent that stopped me short. *Rolf.*

He'd been out here recently, within the last twelve hours. But why had he come all the way out here? I put my nose to the ground and sniffed, trotting along as I followed his path deeper into the woods, before turning back toward the village.

Where is Rolf? Why didn't he come back to The Prim tonight? Is he up to something? Is he doing something to betray our pack?

I needed answers, so I followed his trail back toward the village. I expected it to head toward the other side of The Prim, but instead it emerged right in the heart of the village itself. I exited the forest at the back of Marshell House, where Eric and Elinor lived. I darted past the old mausoleum at the back of their property, being careful to remain in the shadows in case some wayward pedestrian should see me. As I skulked in the shadows of the enormous house, I noticed their downstairs lights were on, and metal music wafted through an open window, punctuating the silent night with pounding double bass. Rolf's path continued down the street, and I followed it, leaping from garden hedge to picket fence until it stopped at the corner, right in front of *Resurrection Ink.*

Of course you smell him here, I told myself. *He was here this afternoon, getting his tattoos done.*

I sniffed again, trying to separate out the different trails. Rolf had two, one leading into the shop door, and the other leading down the street. Both of them could have been from this afternoon. On the concrete, it was too difficult to tell.

I couldn't follow him deeper into the village without a huge risk.

Disappointed, I turned to head back to the forest. As I did, I noticed Eric emerging from the fish-and-chip shop, a large parcel wrapped in newspaper clutched against his chest. A late-night snack for him and Elinor. His eyes met mine, and he waved. I lifted a paw to acknowledge him, then turned on my heel and headed back into the trees.

I still hadn't got any closer to solving the mystery of where Rolf had got to, but now that I had run out the nervous energy in my veins, all I wanted to do was curl up next to Bianca once again.

As I dashed up the garden path and leapt back into the window again, my mind whirred with possibilities. *Why is Rolf heading so deep into the forest? Did I miss somewhere where he veered off his trail to speak with some other wolf? Is he meeting another wolf outside the Lowe territory? Why hasn't he returned?*

He's up to something, but what?

25

BIANCA

The next day, my alarm rang as usual. I moaned, opening my eye just wide enough to discern a blaring line of sunlight streaming through the crack between the curtains. I jammed my eyes shut again and buried my face in the pillow. How could it be morning *already?*

Robbie reached across me and slammed his hand on my phone, hitting the sleep button and shutting the damn thing up for another fifteen minutes. I grinned, and rested my head back on his shoulder. Having a man in my bed was definitely good for some things.

Many things, actually. My legs ached from last night's balcony romp. The things Robbie had done with his tongue ... if he was trying to make a case for me agreeing to be his ... his *mate,* then he was off to a roaring start.

The phone buzzed again. Robbie lifted the screen. "Elinor," he mumbled.

"Ignore it," I mumbled, running my fingers down his chest, as the ache between my legs pulsed for attention. "I'll talk to her later."

ROBBIE and I stayed in bed for another hour, alternating between dozing and languid, lazy shagging. The phone rang again while I was riding him like a cowgirl, but we both ignored it. Eventually, I hauled my ass out of bed, found some clothes that were only slightly rumpled, and stumbled out the door.

I was grinning from ear to ear as I pedalled hard down the village high street, my legs aching from their workout last night. My fingers drummed a merry tune against the handlebars as I pumped harder as the road sloped around toward the shop.

Robbie. Last night ... I'd never had sex like that before. Sure, there had been tender sex, and orgasms that blew my head off, but this was something else. It felt like we'd ascended to another plane of existence.

Is this what he's talking about? This ... fated mates thing. When I thought about it, I'm sure I remembered Alex mentioning something about it. I tended to tune out when the other girls talked about their love stories. It was all too nauseatingly sappy for me, like the plot of some trashy romance book. But maybe I should've listened more carefully. I made a mental note to chat to Alex later.

As I rounded the corner next to *Resurrection Ink*, I was surprised to see Elinor standing on the footpath, her head bent low as she chatted to a policeman. She ran over to me as I pulled up.

"Where have you been?" she cried. "I've been calling you frantically since eight!"

"Sorry," I said, my heart hammering against my chest as her tone registered. Something was seriously wrong. "What happened? Are you okay?"

Elinor's face paled. She gestured toward the shop. My stomach twisted as I saw what had happened.

My beautiful shop window had been smashed in, scattering

tiny shards of glittering glass across the waiting area. I dropped my bike and stepped closer, my heavy Docs crunching on more broken glass strewn across the footpath, and peered inside.

The place had been utterly trashed. The framed tattoo art we'd hung on the walls lay across the floor – the frames smashed and paintings shredded. The padded benches and seats had been torn open, leather and stuffing hanging from them like ribbons. All our supplies lay scattered across the debris – hundreds of once sterile needles ripped from their packages and stuck into the chaise lounge like hedgehog quills, pots of ink thrown at the walls – splatters of colour dribbling down the Victorian wallpaper and staining the black tiles in a rainbow of destruction.

"It looks like some wild animal did it," the police officer said. "So far, we don't have witnesses to the break-in, but we haven't finished canvassing the village."

My stomach twisted. *A wild animal.* I knew exactly what kind of animal would have done this. A wolf. A werewolf.

But why? It couldn't be anyone in the Lowe pack. But if this was about pack politics, why attack me? I'm not exactly heavily involved in Caleb's plots. I'm really only in the pack because I helped Elinor rescue Eric, and I'd seen too many weird things to be written off. But why would anyone want to do this to *me*?

My knees wobbled. I tore my eyes away from it, before I started to cry. Elinor gripped my hand and pulled me away from the window. "I've called the insurance company. They say we're covered, but they won't pay out until the police finish their investigation. Can you call your tattooist friend in Crooks Crossing, see if we can work out of his shop for a while?"

Her words flowed through my ears, but I couldn't make any sense out of them. I kept staring at the ruined window of my precious shop.

"Bianca?"

"Call Caleb," I said, my hands shaking. "Someone is trying to send us a message."

26

ROBBIE

Rolf still hadn't come home. I checked his room as soon as I got up, but he hadn't slept there all night. Weird. I wanted to bring it up with Caleb, but after what Rolf had said, I didn't want to appear too suspicious until I had some solid proof that Rolf was up to no good.

Macavity curled around my feet, begging for his food. Normally, cats are pretty wary around shifters, but Macavity was cool. He didn't care who you were or what you smelled like, as long as you came with a bowl of tinned mincemeat on the end of your arm.

I was just setting up his bowl when Hans and his models trooped down the stairs, shouting each other in German as they dragged their heavy suitcases down the stairs. "What's going on?" I asked.

"We are leaving," Hans announced, throwing his skinny arms around me and squeezing me just a little closer than I was comfortable with. "We've greatly enjoyed our stay, but it is time for us to return to the motherland."

"You don't want some breakfast before you go?"

"Robbie, Robbie, Robbie." Hans clapped me on the back.

"You are a man of many talents, but cooking is not one of them. No, we will go to the delightful bakery of your Asian friend, and have pasties and cake." He patted the nearest model's ass. "We need to pack a little more onto this delightful specimen before we return to Germany."

The model pretended to pout, and I laughed. "Don't leave without stopping by *Resurrection Ink* to say goodbye to Bianca."

"Oh, I wouldn't dare. And also say *auf wiedersehen* to that delightful journalist too, when she rises from the dead."

"She isn't awake yet?" Serenity was usually the first one up in the morning, tapping away at her laptop, coffee in hand, as she watched the sunrise from the back porch.

"*Nein.* We heard her come in last night, very very late. But not a peep from her *Schlafzimmer* all morning."

I remembered that she'd been up working when I came down last night, and the kitchen light had still been on when I went back to bed. I didn't blame her for wanting a sleep in.

I waved goodbye to Hans, then went back in to start my work on the ring once more. I was just going through the last cabinet in the study, when Bianca called. "Someone's broken into the shop," she sobbed. "It's completely trashed."

I tossed down a pewter monkey statue and raced for the door, not even stopping to lock up. I barely registered driving into the village, but I probably broke several laws getting there.

As soon as I stepped out of the car, I could smell Rolf's scent. It wasn't as strong as it had been last night, but it lingered, seeped into the footpath, clinging to the ruined furniture. Rage burned inside me as Bianca sank into my arms and I got a good look at the mess that had once been her shop.

"I can't believe someone would do this," she sobbed into my shirt. "Why would a wolf want to target me? Why not Caleb or Luke?"

"There's only one wolf smell here," I said. "It's Rolf's."

Bianca glanced up at me, her blue eyes studying me carefully. "Of course you can smell him here. He came into the shop yesterday to get inked. So did a lot of people."

I pointed through the shattered window at what had once been the leather massage table, now a broken pile of twisted metal, the fabric torn to ribbons. "This was done with serious muscle, and with claws. A shifter is responsible to this. And I'd be able to smell any shifter who came here. I'm telling you, there's only been one."

"Can't some shifters disguise their scent?" Elinor said. "I remember Luke saying that the shifter who attacked Anna had been able to do it."

"It's pretty advanced magic. There cannae be that many shifters who would be able to pull it off."

"It's a pretty serious accusation," Elinor reminded me. "You want to be careful before you make an enemy of Rolf. You'll be putting Caleb in an awkward position. He's not going to be happy."

My stomach twisted. I knew it better than she did. But what choice did I have? If Bianca was in trouble, I had to act. "You don't think Rolf did it? Who else could have?"

Elinor held up her hands. "Calm down, man. I'm just trying to play devil's advocate. I was a lawyer, remember? That's what I do."

Bianca's face was set in a hard line. She didn't take her eyes off the carnage. Elinor grabbed the handlebars of Bianca's bike, and started trying to lift the wheels into the boot of my car. "Confounded contraption," she mumbled under her breath.

"Here." I took the bike off her and slotted it into the Lada's boot, then opened the door for Bianca. She slid in, her face fixed with rage.

"Take her home and calm her down," Elinor said, patting my shoulder. "Hans stopped by before, so I know the house is mostly empty. Get her some scotch, she's going to need it. I'll deal with everything else, including talking to Caleb."

"I will. Thanks Elinor."

I slid into the seat and slammed the door shut behind me, giving the destroyed shop one last furious glance. How could Rolf do this to Bianca? And why? Had he heard us on the balcony last night and realised he didn't have a chance? Was he one of those insane guys who couldn't handle losing so he lashed out at the woman who shunned him?

At least now you don't have to worry about him winning Bianca over.

Bianca didn't say a word as we drove back through the village and out along the country road toward The Prim. "I'll call Caleb as soon as we get back," I said, as I pulled in the driveway. "I know Elinor said she'd do it, but I think it would be better if I … wait here in the car. I don't want you to go inside until he leaves."

"Until who leaves?"

"Rolf. I don't know if he's home, yet. He can't stay with us anymore. I thought that would be obvious."

Bianca gave a hollow laugh. "Rolf didn't do this."

"He did. He's obsessed with you, Bianca. He put those flowers on your bed."

"He didn't. I texted him to ask about them last night. He swears he didn't."

"And you believe him?"

"He doesn't have any reason to lie. Besides, if he was obsessed with me, why would he destroy my shop? It doesn't make any sense."

"Then who else could it have been?"

"I don't know, Robbie!" Bianca yelled, throwing up her hands. "Some rogue wolf trying to stop Caleb, some other rival pack who hate you guys because of a stupid ancient grudge.

Hell, it could have been someone from within our own pack who secretly hates my guts, for all I damn-well know."

"Hey." I reached across to her. "We'll punish the person who did it, don't you worry. We'll just go in and grab your stuff and take you up to Ryan's—"

She turned away, pushing herself out of the car and slamming the door behind her. She stalked toward the house, her Docs kicking up a spray of pebbles from the drive.

I buried my face in my hands. Why, just when things were going so well, did this have to happen? Why couldn't Rolf just give it a rest?

27

BIANCA

My shop.

The raw pain of seeing everything I'd built over the last five years torn to shreds cut through my body like a blade. My skin itched, like it was covered in open sores.

I sat in the least lumpy chair in the drawing room, my feet on grandmother's prized Turkish tea table, and a glass of scotch gripped in my shaking hand. I'd already sent two drams down to fuel my twisting stomach, and the few drops left in my current glass were about to join them.

I hadn't seen Robbie since I got home. He'd stormed through the house, searching for Rolf. But the big werewolf was still gone. Briefly, I wondered if that was an admission of guilt, but I just couldn't believe Rolf had done this. He had a lot riding on the successful alliance with Caleb – it just didn't make sense that he'd risk it all on a senseless act of destruction. Anyway, Robbie had headed out again, probably to look for him, so I guessed we'd find out sooner or later.

If it wasn't Rolf, then who did it?

There was a knock at the door. I stared at the frowning

portrait of Grandmother June above the fireplace, and poured myself another scotch. Maybe if I ignored them, they'd go away.

Knock knock.

Just go away. Please go away.

Why had I even decided to make this place an art house, anyway? The last thing I needed right now was some smelly poet begging for a room.

Knock knock.

Fuck them, they can stay out in the cold. I just lost the first business I built up from scratch, the one thing I loved doing even more than shagging.

"Who didn't lock this door?" Caleb's voice echoed through the hall. "Bianca, it's me. Are you here?"

"Back here," I called out, swallowing the last of my drink. I had to focus hard to set down the bottle and my glass on the table without dropping them.

Caleb burst through the drawing room, with Eric right behind him. Caleb wrapped his arms around me. "Elinor told me everything. I'm so fucking *pissed* this happened to you. We'll get the bastard, I promise."

"Thanks, mate." I accepted the hug, grateful I had these guys in my life. At least when you were surrounded by werewolves with super strength, you feel at least a tiny bit invincible.

After a final squeeze, Caleb and Eric sank into the chairs opposite me.

"Elinor and I talked to the police," Eric said. "They're pretty stumped. They definitely seem to think it was a wild animal. Of course, they're connecting it to the creature who sometimes attacks people in the forest." He gave me a small smile. Every time there was an incident involving shifters in Crookshollow – which frequently involved members of our pack – the police would write it off as a rabid dog or some other kind of animal attack. It was better than them stumbling on to the existence of shifters, but still seemed ridiculous given the facts. In this case, the "Crookshollow monster" was a scapegoat. It meant that the police wouldn't do any more work into investigating who trashed *Resurrection Ink*.

"You can imagine the press are having a field day." Caleb rubbed his temple. "They're starting to put together all the different incidents. We're creating an urban legend. I saw a headline in the Crookshollow Chronicle about 'The Monster of Crookshollow Forest'."

"Even that woman from the London Underground was hanging out taking pictures," Ryan said. "I thought she'd have gone back to the city by now."

"Serenity? She wanted a tattoo first," I said. "I've just got a bit of colouring to finish on her sleeve piece. Although," I frowned, "I guess that's not going to happen now."

"Elinor's been on the phone with the insurance company all afternoon." Eric grabbed the scotch from the table and pouring a dram for Caleb and himself. "She'll have your money in no time, and you'll be back up and running before you know it."

"Is Robbie around?" Caleb asked, glancing toward the entrance hall. I thought he looked a little nervous, but then my vision blurred and it was gone. I rubbed my temples. The alcohol was already making my brain all fuzzy. *Good.* I wanted to erase this horrible day, and if alcohol could get me there, so be it.

"I haven't seen him since we got back. He thinks Rolf did it, so he's gone into the forest to try and find him. He was mumbling something about following Rolf's trail from last night. You should probably send someone after them. Robbie and Rolf have some kind of intense rivalry going on, and I'm not sure how long your alliance will hold up when Robbie's through with him."

Caleb and Eric exchanged a look.

"What?" I drowned my glass and slammed it down on the table. "I know Rolf didn't do it, okay? It would be stupid given your alliance."

Caleb knitted his fingers together.

"Fuck." I reached for the bottle. "Do *you* think Rolf did it?"

Caleb shook his head. "No. Rolf would be risking too much. Besides, he was with me and Irvine and the rest of the pack at *Tir Na Nog* last night. I can't say for a fact I watched him every second, but I doubt he would have had time to duck out, trash the store, and get back without anyone noticing."

I remembered Rolf's text to me last night. I hadn't realised the rest of the pack had been there, too. "How come you didn't invite Robbie and I along?"

"Because Robbie has made it clear he can't stand Rolf, and I didn't want it to be difficult for him."

So Rolf had been telling the truth. Caleb really was losing faith in Robbie. I met Caleb's eyes, pouring my rage into my words. "I want you to find the person who did this. I want them to pay."

"The police will—"

"The *police*," I growled, "will do sweet fuck-all, and you know it. As you pointed out, they're gonna pin it on the 'Crookshollow Monster' so they can go back to stuffing their faces with dough-nuts. I want the kind of justice the Lowe pack dishes out. I want you and Luke and Robbie to get this prick and tear his throat out."

"That's what I came here to talk to you about." Caleb picked up a backpack he'd dropped beside the floor. He pulled a piece of fabric from the bag, and handed it to me. "Do you recognise this?"

I took the fabric in my hands and turned it over. It was a black v-necked jumper, a £1 sticker from the charity shop still stuck to the washing instructions. "Yeah. It's Robbie's. Why?"

"We found it at the shop," Eric said.

I frowned at the jumper, my foggy mind struggling to understand. "He must've left it there the last time he came by—"

Eric leaned forward. "Bianca, I was out last night, around midnight, getting some takeaways from the shop across the road from *Resurrection.* You know how Elinor gets after drinking – she was begging for a greasy burger. I saw Robbie behind the rubbish bins, in his wolf form. He even waved at me."

"Robbie was there last night? He never said anything about going out." My head throbbed. The alcohol burned in my veins. All the strings of these clues dangled in front of me, but I couldn't seem to grab them and put them together. "He must've gone for a run in the forest after I was asleep. It is near the full moon—"

"Bianca." Caleb set his drink down. His face was grave. "Eric and I think ... we're worried that Robbie might've done this."

"What? Why would he have—"

"That's what we were hoping you might be able to tell us." Caleb said. "There are only two wolf scents by the shop – Rolf and Robbie. We know Rolf was there getting inked by you during the day, but we have no evidence he was there last night."

My heart pounded in my ears. *It can't be true. Robbie loves me. He wouldn't do this to me.*

And yet ...

Robbie has been so jealous of Rolf. He hated Rolf being at The Prim. He'd been unable to control his shift when he'd seen me kiss Willow, and his rage over Rolf was so much more intense. If he'd thought I'd been giving Rolf a chance, what would he do to ...

My heart broke. The pain gripped my chest like a vice, tearing at my skin, ripping through sinew and bone.

Robbie did this. He destroyed my shop. He did this to control me, just like my parents tried to destroy me so they could control me.

"Bianca?" Caleb leaned forward, placing his hand on mine. "Are you okay?"

I should've know this was too good to be true. I should've seen that it would end with Robbie betraying me and me being alone. No one does anything for love. It's all about control.

"I have to go," I whispered.

Caleb reached over to squeeze my arm, but I yanked it away. I tried to stand, but my vision swam, and I lost my balance, toppling back against my couch. Tears sprang in my eyes.

"Stay here with her," Caleb told Eric. "Call Elinor. I'll go find Robbie. We need to sort this out—"

Caleb's voice faded away, replaced by a loud ringing in my ears. The room spun, the drab wallpaper bleeding into a dark cloud that drew up around me like a fog. Strong hands gripped me under the arms as I fell into a void of black despair.

28

ROBBIE

Caleb found me stalking through a remote corner of Crookshollow forest, my nose to the ground, so intent on Rolf's scent that I didn't even notice him approach until he leapt out in front of me.

What are you doing out here? His gravelly voice fell into my head. *Bianca's upset. She could use you now.*

I am helping, I shot back, pawing the ground. *I'm looking for Rolf. That bastard destroyed her shop and now he's trying to run back to his pack. Look, his trail from last night leads all the way out here. He's had a decent head start, but if I keep going, I'll—*

Rolf isn't running away, Robbie. He's hiding from you, because I told him to.

What? Why would you—

Caleb's lips pulled back around his teeth. He stood with his paws wide apart, a stance of power. *Because I've noticed you becoming more and more obsessed with him and his presence, and I was worried about his safety. Now I know that my concern was completely justified. Look at you, you're ready to tear him to pieces. I can't have you destroying the alliance, not when we're so close.*

Dammit, I don't care about the alliance! I don't even want to have an alliance with the Wulfrics—

Careful, Robbie, Caleb growled. *I know you're angry, but don't say anything you can't take back.*

I snarled, but dropped onto my stomach, showing Caleb that I was acknowledging his superior status. *He hurt Bianca, and you just let him get away.*

Of course not. I will speak to him soon. If he did this, which I don't believe he did, I will find out, and I promise I will punish him for disrespecting our pack. But that is my role as alpha, not yours.

I need to do something.

Exactly. You need to return to The Prim with me. You need to be with Bianca. She needs you now. As her mate, you should sense that. There are some things she needs to discuss with you.

I slumped down in the dirt, the rage in my veins cooling as his words sank in. I hated the fact that Caleb was right, but he was. Bianca was my first priority. I never should have left her like that, all alone with the pain of losing her shop.

Caleb trotted over, nudging my cheek with his muzzle. *Get going.*

I ran with Caleb back to The Prim. He didn't say much else along the way, and I noticed he walked much closer to me than was normal, at many times brushing his shoulder against mine. Usually, an alpha would walk at the front, setting the pace, and it would be up to me to catch up with him. But it seemed as if Caleb didn't want to leave my side.

A nervous jitter crept through my veins. Was something up? Was Bianca in trouble? Was that why Caleb was marching me back here like a naughty child?

We emerged at the back of The Prim's garden, surrounded by the delicate primrose bushes that spread beneath the trees. I glanced up at the house, the white weatherboards luminous in the grey glow of the overcast sky. Lights were on in the downstairs rooms, as well as in Serenity's bedroom, but Bianca's turret was dark. Caleb escorted me right to the porch.

As soon as I entered the house, I forced my shift, my bones snapping and my fur retreating into my skin and I transformed back into my human form. Behind me, Caleb did the same thing, blocking the front door with his naked body.

I picked myself up off the floor, not even worrying about the fact I had no clothes on. I raced across the entrance hall and called out, "Bianca, I'm home. I'm so sorry I ran away."

"I'm in here, Robbie." Her voice slurred from the drawing room. I cursed myself for my selfishness. *You ran away and she's been drinking alone all afternoon. She needed you.*

I raced into the drawing room. Bianca was sprawled in a chair beside the fire, an empty scotch glass in her hand. Her head snapped up when I entered, and the flare in her eyes stopped me in my tracks. She didn't look upset. She looked pissed as hell.

"Bianca, I—"

Bianca threw a black object down on the table in front of her. "Recognise this?"

"Hey, that's my sweater. I thought I'd lost it in the laundry—"

"No, Robbie. You didn't. You left it in the shop last night while you were there trashing it."

It took a few moments for her words to sink in. "You can't possibly think that I—"

"We know it was you." Her eyes flashed. "You lose control when you feel threatened. You showed me that when you shifted at our wedding. And now you felt threatened by Rolf, so you planted those flowers so I would think he was obsessed with me and then trashed my shop so I'd think it was him."

"I didn't do either of those things!"

"Well, Rolf swears he didn't either. He had no idea about the flowers, and he was out all night with Caleb and the others, so how could he have trashed the shop? But you were there. Eric saw you. And you knew that Rolf was coming to get his tattoo done in the afternoon, so his scent would be all over everything."

Shit. I'd completely forgotten about seeing Eric. "Yeah, I was there. I needed to go for a run in the forest and clear my head. I caught a weird scent trail from Rolf, so I followed it to the shop. I just wanted to find the guy, learn what he was playing at. That's all, *honest*—"

"And it's just a big coincidence that you're seen at the store around the exact time it was trashed? You were in the house too when the flowers were put on my bed, if they even were."

"They were. I saw them!"

"You're the only one who saw them!" Bianca screamed, leaping to her feet, her hands balled into fists. "Because you were the one who put them there. *You.*"

"Bianca, you don't know what you're saying ..."

She slammed her hands against my chest and shoved me toward the door.

"Get out of this house," she growled at me. "I don't want to see you ever again."

29

BIANCA

I watched from the window of my bedroom as Robbie packed his boxes into the back of his car, his shoulders hunched. He glanced up at the house, and for a moment, his stricken face captured me. My arms ached to slide around him, to feel his warmth against my chest. I hugged myself, willing back the tears that threatened to spill down my cheeks.

I can't believe it's over.

I'd been so ready to let my guard down, so certain that if anyone would be able to convince me a happily-ever-after was possible, it would be Robbie. But it had all been a lie, of course. It was always a lie.

A hand landed on my shoulder. I jumped, whirling around in fright. It was just Elinor. She gave me a sad smile, and passed me a drink. "I'm so sorry. I really thought he was right for you."

I sniffed, wiping at my eyes with my sleeve. "Where did you come from?"

"Eric told me to come over. Apparently, Caleb confronted Robbie in the forest today, and told him to come back here. I guess he figured there was no worse punishment than seeing how much he hurt you." She cast a gaze over to the window, as

Robbie's car pulled out of the drive. "From the looks of it, he wasn't wrong."

I sipped the drink, the alcohol burning my stinging throat. Add a heavy dose of heartache on top of a day of depressed drinking, and you ended up with me – an empty shell of a person who felt as though her whole body had been attacked by a giant potato masher.

"You don't have to stay. I'm not exactly great company right now."

Elinor shook her head furiously. "That's not how this friendship thing works. You were there for me when I thought I'd lost Eric, remember?"

"You were so drunk that night," I said. "So drunk and angry. The bartender at *Tir Na Nog* asked you if you wanted ice in your G&T and you gave him a ten-minute lecture about why he should never date a ghost."

"Exactly. And you held my hair while I threw up in the pub toilets, and possibly in the taxi, too. So consider us even."

I stared out the window. Robbie's car disappeared down the road. My chest split down the middle as a deep wound opened up inside of me. Beside the gazebo was a pile of junk – all bits and bobs from the house Robbie had been using to make his "sculpture."

I turned away from the window, squeezing my eyes shut. I couldn't bear to think about it. Thinking made the wound sting hot, like I was pouring acid into my chest. There was only one thing that would make it better. Oblivion.

I raised my glass to my lips, and toasted Elinor. "Here's to true love," I spat. "Here's to family."

30

ROBBIE

I met up with the M1 outside of Crookshollow, and followed it for a little way before turning off into some backwater village. I drove and drove until the roads blurred into one endless stream of black measuring tape stretching out in front of me.

I lost Bianca.

Raw fury beat out the hopelessness of Bianca's final words to me. Of all the things that could have split us up, of all the crazy fucked-up pieces of our past that could have come back to haunt us, of all the stupid things that could have split us up, why did it have to be this?

I didn't do it. If you really knew me, you'd know I would never do it. If you're willing to believe Rolf over me, then you two deserve each other.

My hands tightened around the wheel. I wanted so badly to believe there was some way to fix it, but I couldn't see how. Even if I could come up with some convincing proof that it wasn't me – and I didn't see how – and I convinced Bianca and Caleb to take me back, I wasn't sure I could ever go back, not now, not when they'd thrown everything they claimed to love about me back into my face.

The road narrowed, and I rounded the corner, and came to a dead end. Roaring with frustration, I slammed on the brakes, halting the car in the middle of the road. *Fuck it, it's not like anyone was coming.*

I'm completely alone.

I slammed my head against the steering wheel, jumping as the horn honked. Howling with frustration, I drew my fist back and punched the dashboard, cracking the plastic shell and sending a sharp pain through my knuckles.

The pain drew me back, reminding me what I was – a wolf without a pack, a cast-off from what would soon be the most powerful shifter clan in the entire world. Word would get around that Caleb had kicked me out, and I'd never find another pack to take me in.

I'd left my father's pack in order to join up with Caleb. I'd trusted him and believed in his vision. I'd tried my best to help, to do my bit to make the pack a success. I'd done nothing but care about Bianca, try to protect her, try to be kind. But all of them had just assumed the worst. They believed Rolf over me. When they looked at me, all they saw was a criminal who would hurt those he loved just to prove a point. *If that's what they believe I am ... I was never part of their family in the first place. I was always alone.*

I'd thought I'd found a family, a real family that would support me through horrible times, the way the families in Mum's storybooks always did. I thought I'd finally started to understand what all those fairytales were talking about. But it had all been a lie.

Family, love, trust ... it was all a lie.

I'd burned all my bridges. I had nowhere left to go.

I DROVE UNTIL NIGHT FELL, then pulled the car over to the side of the road, parked up, and tipped the seat back. My back ached from being in the seat all day. My stomach growled. I hadn't eaten anything since ... I couldn't remember when. The idea of turning the car around and heading back to civilisation made my stomach turn.

The moon shone in the window, taunting me with its hypnotic pull. It would be full tomorrow night. I'd need to be far away by then. My inner wolf was already desperate to be free, chomping at the bit to return to Crookshollow and fight Rolf. But without the support of the pack, that would only end in death. I longed to be outside, running in the moonlight, sleeping in the soft leaves or in the hollow of a tree. But I couldn't leave the car. It would be just my luck that it would get stolen. And I could smell other wolves on the breeze. This was already some-one's territory. I'd be safer in human form, for now.

I closed my eyes, hoping that exhaustion would wash over me and grant me a few blissful hours of oblivion. But as soon as my eyelids closed, Bianca's face danced across my vision, her blazing eyes burning me as she banished me from the home we'd built together.

My fingers flew to the wedding band on my finger. The metal felt ice cold.

Bianca. How could you think I would do such a horrible thing? How could we be so close, and yet you didn't know me at all?

LIGHT BLARED in front of my eyes, pounding inside my skull. I opened my eyes, and immediately wished I hadn't. Blinding light blared through the windscreen. The sun had well and truly risen.

I tried to roll over. A cramp arced down my side. The gear shift dug into my thigh. My temples throbbed. I used to sleep in a hollowed-out car when I lived in the forest, but then, I'd mostly stayed in my wolf form. Clearly, Ladas weren't designed with the comfort of humans as a forethought.

I leaned over the backseat, searching through my backpack for a muesli bar. *I know I have a stash from when I went to the library ... maybe they're buried under my clothes ...* My hand brushed something hard and square.

Silvia's scrapbook.

In my haste to throw as much stuff as possible into the car, I must've picked it up by mistake. Guilt sliced through me. Bianca loved that scrapbook, and it rightfully belonged to her. I pulled the volume out and rested it on my lap while I tore the end off the wrapper of a muesli bar and shoved the whole thing in my mouth. I opened the book, sniffing the edge of the page. A pang shot through my chest as a whiff of Bianca's spicy perfume wafted past my face.

I slammed the book shut again, and tossed it on the passenger seat, the rage rising in my gut once more. But after a few moments, I dragged the book back onto my lap and flipped it open to a random entry. Right now, Silvia Sinclair was the closest person I had to a friend.

I didn't bother reading the entries – I knew most of them by heart. Instead, I stared at the illustrations and scraps of fabric and lace that had been lovingly glued into the pages.

I paused on one particular page – the entry where Silvia had first declared her love for Hattie, and alluded to their night together in illicit discovery. The image printed on the page was of a woman's silhouette, her hair rendered in an elaborate period style. Silvia had use a scrap of ivory lace and a blue ribbon to create a bridal dress. Another scrap of lace formed a veil. Silvia had coloured in the bride's hair with golden pastels. I knew from the portrait that Silvia's hair was brown, so I guessed she was trying to draw Hattie. I noticed Silvia had made other doodles on the page with ink and pastel. She'd even drawn in a choker around the bride's neck, and a ...

Hang on.

I squinted at the picture, wondering how no one else had ever noticed it before. On the hand of the bride in the image was a beautiful ring rendered in tiny, perfect detail – two coiled snakes and a red stone.

The Benedict Ring.

Silvia drew Hattie wearing the Benedict Ring.

Excited now, I turned the pages, forgetting the words entirely and just focusing on the many tiny doodles Silvia had made on the pages. There were so many details we hadn't even looked at, like little hands reaching out of cupboards to pluck cakes from the kitchen while the cook's back was turned (Hattie, I presumed), or a funny doodle of a boy carrying a huge stack of groceries and bags down the street, while a girl walked next to him and laughed. I wondered if the boy was meant to be Ben, the gardener's son.

I noticed a couple of the other female silhouettes had been turned into Hattie, with their hair coloured golden and their lips drawn on in blood-red.

I couldn't believe it. Everyone who'd looked at the book, even me, had been so focused on the words that we completely over-looked the hundreds of images that brought to life Silvia and Hattie's relationship. There were love hearts and lips and kisses, cakes and card games and teacups, hands reaching for each other and gift boxes tied up with string.

I came to the page where Silvia wrote about Hattie's death.

My book fell open on my lap. My fingers dug into the seat as I focused on the image.

The printed figure on the page was a woman holding a bouquet of flowers, the obvious idea being that the scrapbooker would place a posy of dried flowers over the space. Here, Silvia had placed a single white dried flower, now grey and brittle with age. The girl's eyes had been crossed over with black ink, and Silvia had drawn a long cloak around her body, or perhaps it was a shroud. A thick black line around the picture formed the distinctive shape of a coffin, and a dove flew overhead.

Bloody hell, she's drawn Hattie in death. How did I never noticed it before?

I squinted at all the details, taking in the love and devotion that Silvia had rendered her lover. My heart pounded as I noticed that Silvia had added jewellery to the image. At the nape of the woman's neck, hanging from a string, the edge of a tiny ring with a red stone peeked out from the edge of the cloak.

The ring ... it was around Hattie's neck when she died. Somehow, Silvia had it buried with her.

Find Hattie's grave, and you find the Benedict Ring.

I reached across the seat to grab my phone. Wait until I told Bianca. She won't believe it—

As soon as my hand grazed the edge of my phone case, I remembered. I couldn't call Bianca. She hated me. I couldn't call Caleb, either, and by now word would have spread to everyone in the pack. Not one of them would take a call from me.

You don't owe them anything, I reminded myself. *You could just toss the book out the window, and drive on. After all, you're the one who's been wrongly accused, and if you're caught near Lowe territory in your wolf form ...*

Sighing, I set the seat upright, tossed the book onto the seat beside me, and jammed the key in the ignition.

Looks like I'm going back to Crookshollow.

31

BIANCA

The night passed, and so did much of the morning. Sunlight blared through my window, its warmth like a punch in the face. I lay in bed, squinting into the glare but unable to draw the energy needed to get up and shut the curtains. Instead, I counted the roses on the wallpaper and wished they would come to life and envelop me in their thorny embrace. Any pain would be better than this.

I'd been so sure that I could trust Robbie. I let down the defences I'd built for so many years to hold back the influence of my parents. But it had all been a lie.

Elinor appeared in the doorway, a *Bewitching Bites* takeout box tucked under her arm. "Rise and shine, sleepyhead. I've brought you sustenance."

My head pounded. I sat up and rubbed my temples. Elinor perched on the edge of the bed, opening the box to reveal two still-warm Cornish pasties. "Fresh from the oven," she said. "Belinda made them special."

"She's a doll." I reached for the pastie, wincing as a sharp pain attacked my temple. Instead, I changed course and grabbed my water bottle from beside the bed. Elinor had placed a bottle of painkillers next to my bed. I popped two in my mouth with a huge gulp of water.

"I've called all the clients booked in for the next week and explained what happened. Most are willing to wait to hear from us to reschedule."

"Mmmm." A stab of guilt hit me behind the eye, or perhaps it was just the hangover. I knew I should be helping Elinor. After all, it was *my* shop and my heartache. But ever since I found out what Robbie had done, I just couldn't bring myself to care about the shop, or The Prim, or anything else.

Elinor continued. "I've also called Dave over in *Inked Insanity* in Crooks Crossing. He's willing to lend us some space so we can keep working while the shop's repaired. I told him I'd head in tomorrow to knock out a few clients, but that you'd still be out for a couple of days."

"It's fine," I said. "I should start working again."

"It's not fine, Bianca. You've had your heart broken. It fucking sucks, and you need to take some time to process it. Hell, we all do. This is a huge shock. Robbie was such a good dude. It just doesn't make sense that he would betray all of us like this."

No, it doesn't. But he did.

With a heave of effort, I shoved the blankets aside and kicked my legs out. "No, I don't want to lie here anymore. It's not a big deal, really. He's just a guy. "

Elinor nodded toward the rubbish bin in the corner of the room, overflowing with balled-up tissues. "That's an awful lot of tears for someone who didn't mean anything to you."

"I think I need coffee. Coffee will make it all better." I rolled onto the ground, fumbling around in the piles of clothes for my jeans.

Strong hands lifted me under the shoulders and dumped me back on the bed. "You need to stay *here*, and wallow," Elinor scolded. She shoved the bakery box toward me. "Eat your pastie and I'll get you your coffee. I'll bring you your sketchbook and some pens as well, so you can draw some flash if you get the urge. I've got the laptop here if you want to answer some emails or watch a trashy movie. But you are *not* leaving this house, and that's an order."

"Thanks, Elinor. You're amazing."

"I know." She bounced toward the door, leaving me alone with my misery.

I pulled over the laptop, biting into my pastry as I checked through my email. The attack on my shop must've hit the local ink grapevine, because hundreds of messages of support flooded my inbox from old clients, fellow tattoo artists and other friends. Someone had even started up a "Resurrect *Resurrection Ink*" crowdfunding page, and people were donating money to help fund the repairs. Tears welled in the corners of my eyes.

So much support, so many kind offers of help, and yet ... I wanted none of it. The only person I wanted was *Robbie*.

I wiped the tears threatening to spill down my cheeks, and slammed the laptop shut. It was too much to think about right now. I flopped back down on the bed, fresh tears springing from my eyes.

Robbie, wherever you are ... I hate you for doing this to me. I hate you for how weak you've made me, and I will never, ever forgive you.

32

ROBBIE

"Fuck, fuck, fuck!" I slammed my first against the steering wheel, cursing at the top of my lungs as I crawled along behind a massive lorry.

There would have to be a huge accident on the M1, so of *course* all traffic was in gridlock while they funnelled us into one lane so they could clean up. At this rate, I wouldn't get to Crookshollow before nightfall. Which, given the way my inner wolf was scratching to be free, would be *bad*.

My hand on the wheel turned into a paw. I gritted my teeth and forced the wolf back inside me, turning the paw back into fingers again. I couldn't get the fur to retract, but as long as I made it to Crookshollow before I turned, I'd be okay driving with furry hands.

Come on, Robbie, just a little bit longer.

MY WHOLE BODY shuddered as I crossed the scent trail that marked the boundary of the Lowe territory. I whipped the car around the corner as quickly as I could, heading for the flat that

Anna and Luke shared near the edge of town. My cheeks itched from the fur poking through my skin, but I didn't have time to worry about it now.

Just a little longer.

Their house loomed up ahead. I whipped the Lada into their driveway, ploughing it straight into the back of Anna's family wagon. Metal crunched. My head whipped back against the seat. As the Lada rolled back from the impact, I could see their back bumper had been completely caved in.

Shite. Anna is going to kill me.

"Robbie, what are you doing here?" Anna cried, running out of the house as I shoved the door open and toppled on to the grass. Little baby Colin gurgled as he bounced on her hip. "You're not supposed to be back in Lowe territory. If Caleb catches you here—omigod, what did you do to my *car*?"

"Help me," I cried, dropping to my knees as the shift started. The scrapbook toppled from my arms, landing on the grass and opening to a random page. I tried to flip the pages, but my paw wouldn't grab the edge of the paper. The page tore with a loud rip. "You have to show this to Caleb. Show him the page about Hattie's death. Sylvia buried the ring with Hattie! It's right here in the picture. You have to show this to him, Anna. I promise I'll leave just as soon as you—"

Anna screamed as my face contorted. "Robbie, you're shifting. Get the hell out of here before you hurt my son!"

I opened my mouth to tell her that even in my wolf form, I'd never hurt Colin, who was part of our pack. But all that came out was a tormented howl. I was a wolf once again. Pain arced through my whole body as my bones snapped and my organs rearranged themselves. The world around me exploded with new smells—trails of animals, Anna's dinner from the night before, Colin's dirty nappy ...

Anna screamed. I bolted away, heading for the woods. *You've done as much as you can do now. Get away, before Caleb catches you.* I turned back to look over my shoulder. Anna was bent over my clothes. The scrapbook was shoved under her arm and she was fishing around in my pockets for something. *She's probably looking for the keys so she can move the car. At least that might bide me a little time before Caleb realises I'm back—*

But Anna held up my mobile phone, the screen flashing that I'd received a message. Anna's eyes darted across the screen, and her whole face collapsed, first with confusion, then with some kind of grim realisation.

I growled, baring my teeth at her. If she came too close to me, Caleb would smell me on her and his instincts may make him do something dangerous. I didn't want to put her or baby Colin in danger.

"Robbie," Anna yelled, hiking Colin up against her hip and holding my phone in her hand. "Stop running and listen to me. I think Bianca's in trouble. We've got to get to Primrose House right now."

33

BIANCA

My eyes fluttered open. The room was dark, a pale sliver of moonlight cast across the bed. Rubbing my aching temples, I rolled out of bed and pulled back one of the curtains, admiring the bright orb that blared through the window.

The full moon.

My eyes darted to the trees at the edge of the forest that bent toward the house. Somewhere out there, Caleb and Luke and Rolf and Robbie were hiding, hunting, their rational minds warped by their animal instincts. Caleb and Luke and Rolf would be stalking through the Crookshollow Forest, on the prowl for a tasty snack, whereas Robbie would be somewhere far away by now, somewhere I could never hope to find him again, even if I wanted to.

Which I didn't. Not at all.

Robbie. I hoped he was okay. I wondered where he had gone. Did he go back to his father? Surely he wouldn't, not after every-thing that's happened—

No, I shook my head, trying to shake away the thoughts. *You don't get to worry about Robbie any longer. Whatever he does from now on is his business.*

I grabbed my phone and checked the time. 8:12 p.m. My stomach growled. I stared at the bakery box Elinor had left beside the bed. The end of the pastie had crusted over, and the lemon tart had melted into an unappealing yellow puddle.

That won't do. My stomach rumbled. I needed food before I could begin another night of drinking away my pain. I grabbed a hoodie from off the floor, and threw it on over my pyjamas. The *tick tock tick tock* on the grandfather clock punctuated the still silence of the hallway. I had no idea if Serenity was out, and I didn't particularly care. I shoved my hands into my pockets, and made my way down the darkened staircase.

I didn't turn on a light until I got to the drawing room, where I clicked on one of the garish carved lampshades and slumped into the chair by the fire. My bottle of scotch still sat on the table from where I'd been drinking with Caleb and Eric. Three dirty glasses sat next to it. I grabbed one of them and filled it, sipping the burning liquid while I dialled *Pete's Pizza.*

"Hey, Pete."

"Hey, Bianca. Sorry to hear about the shop. I hope they get the wankers who did it."

"Me, too." I winced as my chest tightened. "Can I get a delivery up to The Prim?"

"Sure thing. Do you and Robbie want your usual?"

Another sharp pain jabbed into my chest. I sucked in a breath, willing myself not to break down. I kept my voice even. "No, it's just me tonight, so you can hold the Meatsplosion with the extra BBQ sauce. Just hit me with a double Hawaiian, and an extra order of those lemon pepper wedges."

"You want sour cream with the wedges?"

"Sure. You only live once, right?" A tear spilled down my

cheek. Pete continued with my order regardless, as if ordering pizza for one was the most natural thing in the world, and not a sign that I'd lost the only person I'd ever really cared about. I garbled my way through my credit card number, and hung up with a promise from Pete that he'd arrive within a half hour.

I leaned back in the chair, raising the glass to my lips. As I tipped the liquid down my throat, a shadow in the corner moved. I darted around, and noticed a silhouette in the doorway, the outline of a person's head drawn by the bright moon.

My blood turned cold. *Someone's in my house.*

It's okay. It's probably just Serenity coming home, or some other artist wanting to crash at Prim. The website does say, "Open all hours."

"Hey," I called into the darkness. "Don't just lurk in the shadows. Let me get a good look at you."

"As you wish," a familiar voice simpered back. The figure took a step forward, her face falling under the warm glow of my lamp. I relaxed when I recognised Serenity. "Hello, Bianca."

"Oh, hey." I gestured to the sofa opposite me. "I thought you had gone out. How did you get in here?"

"Oh, the door was open. I thought that was your policy here at The Prim – anyone is welcome." She took another step towards me, an odd, lopsided grin spread across her face. She had her hands clasped behind her back, like some cheeky kid about to present his mother with a live lizard he'd found in the garden.

"Well, since you're back, come on down and have a drink with me." I held up the bottle. "Are you still in town for anything in particular? I know we discussed some more ink but with my shop destroyed, I won't be able to take any bookings until I've got the okay to go back to work. Which given some personal setbacks, might be some time yet."

"Oh, I'm afraid you won't be going back." Serenity grinned wider, stepping right in front of me, so she loomed over me the way my mother did when I'd done something naughty. She whipped her hands from behind her.

The lamplight caught the glint of a long, sharp kitchen knife.

A nervous itch blocked my throat, and I choked out a weird, strangled laugh. "What's that for?"

"It's for you, Bianca."

"I'm sorry?" I tried to inch around her, but she shuffled closer, her gaze never leaving mine. "You're trying to give me a knife? That's nice, I guess, but I'm not exactly a master chef—"

"You still don't recognise me, do you?" Anger flashed in her eyes. "I can't say I'm surprised. For all your big talk about being *different*, you never cared about anyone but yourself."

I stared at her face, willing the features to knit together in a memory, to connect the dots to the familiar feeling I'd had from her since the moment she arrived. And suddenly ... it clicked. I remembered where I knew her from.

"Sally Smith," I moaned, my lip trembling. Sally Smith, the mousy girl in my high school class with no friends, a girl I'd taken pity on at a party once and snogged in a cupboard. A girl who I'd "dated" for about a week before Mother caught us together and chased her away and I'd been sent off to get reprogrammed by the nuns and then got distracted by a hot football player at another school and never talked to her again.

But if this really is Sally Smith, what is she doing here, in my house, with a knife? Why did she have a new name and pretend to be a reporter?

"You *do* remember." Sally's lip curled back. "I am touched. Of course, I've had a bit of a makeover since high school. New name, a bit of work done, a new outlook on life. A great job, where I have freaks like you yapping at my heels for just a bit of attention. Now, I get to be the person who decides what's cool. I can't tell you how much fun it's been to watch you the last couple of weeks, knowing you didn't have a clue who I was."

"But why? I don't understand why you pretended—"

"I didn't pretend anything. My name is Serenity now. I had it legally changed. If you'd confronted me about my identity, I wouldn't have denied it. I was just waiting to see how long it took you to recognise me."

"Well, colour me impressed," I choked out.

"This isn't really a joking matter. Now, hand over your phone."

"Sally, I—"

"I don't want to hear what you have to say, Bianca. You never once listened to me, you never took the time to care about me. I worshipped you in high school. I thought you were fucking perfection in Docs. But you were just as bad as those snotty bitches you hated *so* much. You let me get close to you ... I confided my deepest secrets, my darkest fears. I opened up in a way I never had before. You gave me the courage I needed to consider coming out of the closet. But then, you crushed me. I wasn't alternative enough for you, so you let your mother terrify me and then discarded me without a single thought. Do you think I'd just forget that?"

"No, I didn't know—"

"Of course you didn't know. You didn't even think to ask how I felt. It was always about *you, you, you*. Now you'll see how it feels to be betrayed. How it cuts you, right here." She mimed jabbing the tip of the blade right into my chest. I shrunk away. "Phone, if you please. Next time I won't ask so nicely."

Numb with shock, I handed over my phone. I expected her to smash it, but instead, Sally held it up to her face, expertly texting with one hand while keeping the knife – and her eyes – trained on me.

"What are you doing?"

She flipped the phone around, showing me the text she'd just sent Robbie. A text telling him to come over, that I needed him.

My heart sank to my knees. *Please, don't bring him into this.* "Why do you want Robbie?"

"You mean you haven't put it all together yet?" Sally laughed. "It doesn't surprise me. You always thought you were so clever. But you're really nothing special. Not like me. People don't notice me, because I blend into the background. You haven't noticed me following you for the last week, and your boyfriend didn't notice me standing right in the hallway while he changed into a werewolf the other night. But it doesn't matter, because I got the whole thing on video."

Shit.

"I'm going to be the first person to break the story that were-wolves are real. I'll be giving a harrowing eyewitness account of how I went to visit my old girlfriend, Bianca Sinclair. And how I was just in time to witness her being torn to pieces by her ex-boyfriend, who had transformed into a vicious werewolf and who was also probably responsible for several recent animal attacks around the Crookshollow Forest area."

"Sally, you can't—"

She grinned, shuffling closer, that knife raised to her shoulder, ready to strike. "I'm about to become the most infamous journalist in England, probably the world. And you're going to help me do it. After everything you did to me, it seems only fair that you could give me this."

"If you want me dead, you're going to have to stab me. Robbie would never lay a hand on me. You'll never get him to kill me."

"I don't have to." She whipped out her own phone, and swiped the screen a couple of times. Robbie's voice echoed through the room, high-pitched and tinny through the tiny speakers. "... on the full moon, I'm a wild beast. I operate completely on instinct. For a wolf, instinct is tied up with scent. And right now, my instincts are screaming that Rolf is my rival, and anything with his scent on it is a direct challenge to me. For example, if I smelled you wearing clothes that had Rolf's scent on them, in my wolf form, I'd think you betrayed me, and I'd probably attack you ..."

"You've been spying on us." I remembered Robbie's paranoia about Rolf, that he was sending me flowers and watching me. I'd thought he was just trying to get me to throw Rolf out, but it was Sally all along. And the person who wrecked my shop ... that must've been her, too. "You destroyed *Resurrection Ink.*"

Sally clapped, her grin exploding across her face as she broke into terrifying giggles. "Well done! Ten points! Yes, I've been following you ever since you sent the press release about The Prim to my boss. I was just going to write a gloriously unflattering piece about this place and destroy you that way, before your business could even get off the ground. But then your boyfriend transformed into a werewolf in the middle of the party, and I got an even better idea. Why not destroy you *and* break the story of my life at the same time?"

"But you said in your piece that it was just special effects." *Keep her talking. You can find a way out of this.* I inched my way along the sofa, my eyes fixed on the gleaming blade. If I could shuffle her around, maybe I could run for the door before she had a chance to catch me. The heavy table lamp sat on the table between us. If I could grab it, maybe I could knock her out ...

As slowly as I could, I shifted my weight to my back foot, ready to spring into action.

"Of course. I wasn't about to give your place that kind of free publicity. I'm not here to *help* you by bringing a horde of werewolf hunters down upon your doorstep. No, I need to break this in a way that will give you just as much pain as you gave me. And you've given me the perfect excuse—"

I lunged for the door. My shin slammed against the coffee table, sending it flying. A cascade of magazines and empty absinthe glasses cascaded to the floor. I grabbed the lamp and hurled it at Sally. It hit her in the chest, sending her flying back.

My fingers grasped the door doorframe. I swung myself into the hall, scrambling for the front door. *Run run run—*

Something hit me in the side, knocking the wind out of me. My right leg collapsed, and I fell heavily, banging my knee on the hardwood floor. My hip ached, like someone had punched me. I rolled over and turned around, and saw a wide grin spread over Sally's face as she yanked the knife from my hip.

She stabbed me.

A pool of blood spread across my leggings, staining the fabric a deep pink. As soon as the blood registered, the pain came – a great sweeping tide that flowed through my body, driving out all breath and thought. It was as though the knife had twisted right inside of me, and wriggled its way through my veins.

"No!" I grabbed at my hip, trying to stop the bleeding. Blood soaked through my fingers. Panic rose inside me. *I'm bleeding. I'm going to die.*

Sally's face faded, wobbling into the wallpaper behind her head. Dull roses and grinning portraits spun around me. The panic rose up, overwhelming the last vestiges of rational thought. I tried to crawl away, but I had no idea what direction I was moving in.

Another punch hit my shoulder. Dully, I realised she'd stabbed me again. She slashed at my head, and I pulled back just s the knife darted in front of my eye. Something stung my temple, and my vision blurred with red.

I toppled backward, my head bouncing on the carpet. The last thing I heard was a thud of the door hitting the wall, or maybe it was my body as it slammed into the ground. Then the whole world wobbled again, and went black.

34

ROBBIE

I bounded across The Prim's front garden, my paws slamming into the damp earth. Panic seized my chest, making my breathing shallow.

My inner wolf's rage propelled me forward. Rolf's smell rolled around me, a putrid stench emanating off the house and gardens. *Rolf, if you've hurt Bianca, I'm going to tear your heart out.*

Another smell mingled in with it. The scent of blood. I poured on speed.

Behind me, Caleb's paws pounded against the drive, his hot breath panting in my ear. As soon as Anna had told me what was in that text message, I was ready to bound over to The Prim. But Anna had told me to wait. She called Caleb back from the forest. He was ready to kill me, but then I explained through the call what had happened, and he sprang into action. Even if I was no longer part of the pack, Bianca still was.

A car screeched to a halt on the drive, narrowly missing us. I dived out of the way, in time to see Ryan and Marcus leap from the back. Anna sat behind the wheel, waving at us to move.

The front door was open a crack. I fell against it, my heavy paws crunching against the wood. The door crashed open, slamming against the wall, and I scrambled into the hall.

What I saw turned my wolf blood to ice.

Bianca lay on the floor in a pool of blood. Her eyes stared at the ceiling, wide and glazed. One whole side of her face as drenched in blood, and more blood pooled from deep wounds on her shoulder and hip. The journalist from the *London Underground* blog stood over her, a knife raised high above her head, and an expression of wild glee in her eyes.

Everywhere, all over the walls, scrawled across the balustrade, seeped into the carpet, was Rolf's putrid smell, curling toward me in thick tendrils, driving my rage to the breaking point. Bianca's body had been covered with a shirt that looked suspiciously like it belonged to Rolf.

My teeth grated. My stomach rumbled. The blood blurred in my vision, until all I could see was red, red, red. The red of the vengeance I wanted for this betrayal.

Get control, Robbie. Rolf's not here. He and Bianca aren't together. It's her. It's Serenity. You have to get her away from Bianca.

But my wolf wouldn't listen. My thoughts fell into a dim, disjointed cloud, torn away by the force of my fury. I tried to pull my body back, away from Bianca, but instead, I crept forward, my head low, my teeth bared.

Your mate is seeped in your rival's scent. She has betrayed you. They both must be punished.

Serenity looked up when I rushed in, her eyes meeting mine with measured calm. "I'm so glad you could make it, Robbie. Please, take it from here. I know you must be hungry for justice. You can smell your rival all over this room. I've seem them together, Rolf and Bianca, fucking like animals."

The blood pulsed in my veins, the fury fighting to take control. I glanced down at Bianca's face, trying to see the woman I loved. But all that I could see was *red red red*.

She betrayed me. I growled out my anger, digging my claws into the hardwood floor. *She must die.*

Something slammed into my side, knocking me over. I tried to scramble to my feet, but a paw pinned my shoulder. *Caleb.* I snapped my teeth in his face, missing him by an inch.

Let me go! I screamed inside my head as I struggled against him. I pulled one leg free and swiped him across the face. Caleb howled as I drew blood, his claws flying at me but missing me by inches. Another animal slammed into me, sending us hurtling across the floor. Ryan pinned my arm again, sinking his claws into my flesh.

I wrenched my body around, trying to shake him off. But he held firm, his claws driving deeper into my skin. I howled again, flinging my body back to slam him against the wall. Marcus leapt onto my back, snarling into my ear.

Don't do this, Robbie. We're your friends. We're trying to help you.

You're all on his side. You let this happen. You all betrayed me. I sank my teeth into Marcus' shoulder. He screeched, scrabbling to free himself from my grasp. I lifted him from the floor and shook him roughly, tossing his body aside. I dragged my body, laden now with both Caleb and Ryan, closer to Bianca.

"Oh man, this is brilliant," Serenity breathed, her phone following my every move.

My foot landed in something wet. I lifted it to my face. Blood. Bianca's blood. *I'll spill it all for your betrayal.*

Robbie, you have to fight it, Caleb's voice landed in my head. *You are more than your instincts. You're everything to Bianca. You have to fight this, for her.*

I have to kill her! With a heave, I dragged my body closer. I no longer felt the teeth and claws in my body. My veins ran hot with the fury that would see my task done. I pulled myself forward another inch, so I was right beside Bianca's head. Her neck lolled to the side, her eyes glassy, her pale skin streaked with blood.

Serenity stepped back, gesturing to Bianca's prone body with one hand, while the other held her phone right in my face. "She's a horrible, filthy slut, Robbie. She must be punished."

Robbie, fight it. Remember who you are. Remember everything you've fought for.

I reached down, sniffing the rug, my stomach twisting as Rolf smell invaded my nostrils. I licked the blood, tasting its acerbic flavour on my tongue. My stomach rumbled. My teeth itched for the sweet, fresh meat.

Robbie, come back. You have to fight it.

Bianca's glassy eyes stared up at me. Blood speckled her cheekbones, and stained her favourite Ramones shirt. I bent down, my jaws wide, ready to tear her flesh from her bones.

I gasped as memories flooded me, forcing themselves through the red rage in my mind. Bianca tossing her head back as she laughed at something I'd said, Bianca and I sharing pizza and beer by the fireplace, Bianca and I at the altar, our hands entwined, Bianca riding my cock inside the tiny attic bedroom.

Her blood stung my tongue. Anger welled up inside me, but I couldn't remember why. I stared hard at her face, trying to see the slut who fucked my greatest rival.

Instead, all I saw was the woman I loved.

Bianca's eyes stared unblinking, her chest no longer rising with breath. The pool of blood around her body stretched right to the edges of the enormous hall rug. And *that woman* had done this to her.

I turned my head, my eyes meeting Serenity's. *You've taken her from me. She was my mate. I waited so long for her, and now she's gone, and you did this.*

Serenity kept the phone trained on my face. "Good boy," she cooed. "Now, tear her throat out."

I threw back my head and let out a roar.

Serenity screamed. I lunged at her, my jaw wrapping around her outstretched arm. She screamed as my teeth punctured her skin, and her body went limp in my arms. She sobbed as she brought up her other hand, still clutching the knife, ready to plunge it into my fur. I batted it away with my paw, and tightened my grip on her arm.

I'll break you in pieces. I'll tear your heart out while it still beats—

"Please, please, let me go," Serenity begged. Blood dribbled down her arm, splattering over Bianca's prone body.

Ryan leg go of my shoulder and dropped to the ground. He transformed into his human form, and lunged at me, grabbing my fur, shaking me so my teeth wiggled deeper. Serenity broke down into broken shrieks.

"Robbie, no," Ryan cried. "If you kill her, you'll never be able to see Bianca again."

Bianca's dead, I screamed inside my head, my teeth tightening around her arm. I tasted her blood on my tongue, hot and sticky.

She's not, Caleb cried back, his voice falling into my head. *Bianca's breathing, but she's in trouble. We have to get them both to a hospital.*

She stabbed Bianca, I screamed, that anger shuddering through my body.

I know, and I know you want to kill her. I know how that rage burns in your veins. Remember how I felt when you and Angus took Rosa? I know what you're feeling right now, Robbie. But if you kill her, we won't get away with it. Humans will always believe werewolves are brutal. We'll never get a chance to live a life of freedom.

I'll never be free, I growled.

You're free now. But if you kill her, I can't protect you.

I'm not free. Not really. I thought I'd found a family here, but I'm useless. I'm a waste of space, just the way I was when I was a

Maclean. If I'd even been able to do something simple like read, I'd have found the Benedict Ring by now. But I'm not smart like everyone else. I'm an idiot. That's why you don't want me, why you didn't believe me, why you kicked me out and replaced me with Rolf.

Robbie, you should've said something if you felt like this, Caleb growled back. *I would've told you you're being a complete idiot. Of course we want you here. I wouldn't have asked you to join us if I didn't. You're not an idiot, and even if you were, so what? Brains aren't everything. You're kind, and you're incredibly loyal. You are exactly the guy I want by my side in battle, because I know you've always got my back.*

I don't believe you. I shook Serenity's arm, and her femur crunched as it snapped. Serenity howled with pain, her body sliding to the floor and I held her arm tight.

Look, I'd love for us to discuss this in depth and find a way to show you that I really mean it, but I can't do it while you've got your teeth around a girl's arm and Bianca desperately needs an ambulance. So can you just drop her and come with me?

Caleb dangled his paw in front of my face, claws retracted – a sign of submission. I stared down at Serenity, wishing like hell I could eat her face. But Bianca ... Caleb was right. We had to get her to a hospital. If there was any chance that she could live ...

It took everything I had to unclamp my jaws. Serenity dropped to the floor, sobbing as she clutched her bleeding arm that now hung limp and bent at an odd angle.

She scrambled to her feet, blood seeping between her fingers. "You're going to rot in fucking hell for this," she snarled at me. "You disgusting animal. You were supposed to attack *her*."

"That's not how it works," Ryan said. The girl spun around, startled to see a naked guy blocking the front door.

"You're not supposed to be able to change during the full moon," she scolded him.

Ryan took a step towards her, his naked bulk towering over

her. He leaned in close, his face inches from hers. "Maybe … you don't know everything about shifters you thought you did."

I growled in assent. Serenity gulped.

Ryan held up a purse, and dangled a small wallet from his hand. "Well, it's nice to make your acquaintance. Serenity Jones, journalist for the *London Underground,* I see." He flipped to another pocket in the wallet. "Oh look, you have your full license, I see. And my, that's a very nice apartment you have – in Chelsea, very posh suburb."

Serenity grabbed for the wallet with her good hand, but Ryan held it out of reach.

"I know you're rethinking that article you were going to write. I'd hate for Robbie and I to have to pay you a visit at that *very nice apartment.* Now." Ryan stared at her phone on the floor. He picked it up. "I'll just keep this, and you can be on your way. Go on, the door's right here."

You're letting her get away! I screamed.

Caleb placed a paw on my shoulder. *If Bianca presses charges, the police will get involved. And I don't want them to have anything on you, brother. Look at her. She's had enough justice for one day.*

Serenity let out a moan. "I need to go to the hospital."

"Well, you can get there on your own. You're an independent woman. Go on." Ryan gestured to the open door. "Out you go."

Ryan thrust the purse into Serenity's good hand. She stared at him, her eyes wide, her whole body trembling.

"Get out," Ryan growled. "If we ever see you near Bianca again, we won't be so kindly."

"But—"

I growled low, baring my teeth. Serenity practically leapt out the door, tripping over the steps in her haste to get away.

I fell at Bianca's side, placing my paw on her shoulder. Caleb was right, I could just see the faint rise and fall of her chest. She was still breathing. Ryan raised Serenity's phone to his ear, and spoke to an ambulance dispatcher.

"You two need to hide," he said after he'd hung up. "They can't see any sign of wolves or foxes being here. Marcus, I've got a stash of clothes hidden in the garden behind the cherub fountain. Grab them for us. Quick now."

I lay my head down on Bianca's shoulder. *Please don't die on me. You are my whole life. I never knew what living really was until I met you. Please, Bianca. You have to stay with me.*

Bianca didn't more, didn't respond.

Behind me, I heard Marcus and Ryan scrambling into some clothes. An ambulance siren howled as it rounded the corner. "Robbie, Caleb, get out of here!"

No! I lay down in the blood beside her, my paw across her chest. *I can't leave her. She needs me.*

Yes, she does. Caleb's teeth sank into the skin on the back of my neck. He dragged me back. I scrabbled at the floor, but there was nothing to grab hold of. *She needs you to stay out of jail, and out of government testing. Come on, Robbie, there's nothing we can do.*

Caleb dragged me into the sitting room and pushed the door shut with his paw, just as the ambulance officers burst through the door. The last thing I saw before the door slammed shut was Bianca's cold, dead face as she was lifted onto a stretcher to be carried away.

35

BIANCA

Beep beep. Beep beep.

Fucking alarm clock. What bastard put that on?

I rolled over, my eyes determined to remain closed, and reached out a hand to shut the thing off.

Instead of my wooden bedside table stacked high with books and magazines and makeup, my fingers grazed a cold, metal surface. I couldn't find my phone anywhere.

Something tugged on the back of my hand, yanking me back into the bed.

Beep beep. Beep beep.

I fumbled for the thing on my hand, and felt a long, thin tube attached to my hand with a piece of tape. My skin stung from where the tube pierced it.

Beep beep. Beep beep.

If that's not my phone, what is it?

My eyes flew open, and I raised my hand to my face, trying to register the unfamiliar scene around me. Why did I have a tube in my hand? Why was I in this grey room, surrounded by beeping machinery? Why did my thigh throb with pain and my head feel as though it was full of cotton wool?

"You're awake."

I snapped my head toward the voice. Big mistake. Pain seared through my skull. The air hissed from my lungs, and I gasped for breath.

"Dinnae move so much." Robbie leaned over me, his warm hands settling me back into the bed. "You'll damage yourself more."

"Ow," I moaned, as my tender head hit the pillow. I caught a better glimpse at the beeping machine attached to my hand, and realised at last that I was in a hospital. I tried to cast my mind back to remember what had happened to land me in this lumpy bed, but everything was a fuzzy blank.

Everything except him. *Robbie.* Sitting as close to me as possible without actually climbing into the bed beside me, his kind eyes sparkled with relief, the corners of his mouth turned up into one of his gorgeous grins. The smell of him invaded my nostrils – rich and sweet against the sterility of the room.

I thought I lost you. I couldn't remember why, only that at the sight of him, a wave of joy surged through my veins. He took my non-tube hand in his, his touch sending that familiar shiver through my body.

"Stay still and never do that to me again, and you'll be just fine." His beautiful voice rolled over me, like a soothing drink after a bad day. If only I didn't feel like I'd just been hit with ten hangovers at once.

"What happened to me?"

Robbie turned his eyes away. "You nearly died, Bianca. That's what happened. Serenity Jones stabbed you. You lost a ton of blood. You've been unconscious for three days. It's been ... hard."

A sharp pain grazed my temples, and I cried out. Robbie winced, as though he was the one in pain. "Should I call a doctor?"

"No, I just ... everything hurts." Flashes of memory tugged at me. "Sally ... the reporter ..."

"You mean Serenity?"

"No ... her real name is Sally ... I knew her in high school ... that's why she looked so familiar ... she was my first girlfriend and she wanted revenge because I treated her like shite ..." My fingers brushed Robbie's. "Oh, god. I treated you like shite, too. Robbie, I'm so sorry."

"Hey, don't you go apologising to me. I'm not the one in hospital." Robbie lowered his gaze. "I tried to save you, but Rolf's smell ... it nearly did me in. I nearly tore your throat out myself. Bianca, I'm the one who should be sorry."

I shook my head. "You came to rescue me. That gets you an automatic pass on any transgression from now on. But how did you know?"

"Serenity ... er, Sally sent me a text message from your phone. She mustnae have known we were ..." He gulped. "You know, because it was too casual. I came back because I figured out where the Benedict Ring was, and then my full moon shift hit, but Anna read the text out to me and I just had this ... feeling, I guess ... that you were in trouble. I thought Rolf had attacked you. So I came, and she'd stabbed you and covered you in Rolf's clothes to get me to attack you."

"What?"

"She wanted me to kill you. She must've been listening to every conversation we had, because she knew all about the instinct I'd have when I shifted during the full moon. She wanted to film me mauling you to death and ... I guess use it to expose shifters to the world. I managed to get her off you, but you were already so ..." He gulped, looking away again. "I'm just so glad you're okay."

After a few moment he turned back, and I gazed into his beautiful, kind eyes. A lump rose in my throat. This man had saved my life. He mastered his own inner wolf, in order to protect me. "I'm trying to remember ... what did we fight about again?"

"It doesn't matter now." Robbie rubbed my hand.

"It does matter, Robbie. It matters because it was probably my fault and I need to apologise."

"No, Bianca. It was me. It was all my fault. I let Rolf get to me, and because of that, you'd naturally assume that I might've done the things—"

"Hey," I croaked, rubbing my finger across his knuckles. "I'm the one in hospital. If I want it to be my fault, it's my fault."

"Fine. It's your fault." He lifted my hand to his lips and kissed it, his lips like fire against my skin.

"So ... I've been here for three days?"

Robbie nodded. "Aye. Elinor hasn't left your side since they brought you here. I've been hiding in the bushes outside the window to be close to you until the full moon waned." He withdrew one of his hands to pull his phone from his pocket. "I'll text her, let her know you're awake. She'll want to see you."

I placed a hand over the screen. "In a minute, okay? I just want to ..."

Another memory tugged at my mind, of me screaming at Robbie that I never wanted to see him again. I squeezed my eyes shut, not wanting to believe that I'd thought Robbie, beautiful Robbie, could have trashed my shop. I've been so selfish, so consumed with The Prim and my own stupid problems, I couldn't see the wonderful man who was right in front of me.

I took a deep breath. I knew what I had to do. Once the thought came to me, I knew I'd never be able to rest easy until I got it out. I wondered briefly if I should be frightened, after all – it's what I'd been resisting for so long, what I'd been railing against my entire life. But one look into Robbie's eyes and I knew I'd never have to feel scared, ever again.

He leaned closer. "Are you okay? You look all weird. I'll get the doctor—"

"Robbie Maclean, will you marry me?"

Robbie blinked. "Don't take the piss," he said, sitting up with a stiff back.

I squeezed his hand as hard as I could. "I'm not even remotely taking the piss. There's nothing like being stabbed multiple times by an old high school hook-up to put your life into perspective. I was scared before, Robbie. I was so terrified that I'd open up to you, and then you'd turn around and throw it all back into my face, the way my parents did. But I was a fool, because you're amazing, and I was so, so selfish. I wanted all the best bits of you, without giving anything in return."

"Bianca ..."

I held up a hand. "Let me finish. I always thought marriage would be a chain around my ankles, forcing me to conform, to do things I thought were disgusting, like marry my cousin and live in a stuffy, loveless house. But now I realise it's the opposite. Because being with you – *completely* with you – gives me the confidence to be completely myself. Our marriage is not my parents' marriage, or your parents' marriage. It's exciting, and challenging, and filled with love and joy and all that good stuff. Just because we missed out on that growing up, doesn't mean we can't create that together."

Tears welled in Robbie's eyes. "Oh, Bianca."

My own fat, wet tears rolled down my cheeks. "I want to be the wife from your storybooks, because you're already the husband I was too afraid to dream of. I love you, Robbie, with everything I am and everything I want to be. So come on, will you marry me again, for real this time?"

"Aye, I will."

Robbie's whole face broke into a grin, the smile reaching right to the tips of his ears. *The grin that launched a thousand ships.* My heart surged as I received his answer. He threw his arms around me, and I sank into his warmth, ignoring the pain arcing through my body. I rested my head on his shoulder – and for the first time in my whole life, I knew exactly what it meant to be loved, and to love in return.

36

BIANCA

ONE MONTH LATER

"Ready to do this again?" Alex asked, standing back to admire the twisted black metal tiara she'd set into my hair.

I stared back at my reflection. The scar above my eye from where Sally cut me had been expertly hidden by Alex's deft hand. The rest of my makeup was similar to the last wedding – the smoky eyes, the lips a slice of jet blue. The only thing different this time was that my skin glowed with the promise of love.

"It gets easier the second time." I grinned back. "Especially when this time you know you've got the perfect partner."

"You had the perfect partner last time," Elinor reminded me. "You just didn't realise it."

"Well, even people as awesome as me are allowed to make mistakes." I stood up and smoothed down the front of my dress. "Bouquet, please."

Grinning, Alex handed me the short viking sword Willow had ordered in special from a blacksmith in Prague. "Here you are, my warrior woman. Willow promised she'd get some swords in the wedding this time."

"That girl is going to make someone an incredible wife one day." I checked out my reflection in the mirror, giving the sword an experimental swing. Robbie and I were going to present each other with our rings on the blade, the way they did in traditional Viking ceremonies. Later, we would use the sword to cut the epic cake Belinda had made us.

Yet another awesome thing about having two weddings. Two cakes!

Willow poked her head around the edge of the door. "Bianca, we're ready for you."

I expected butterflies to explode in my stomach. After all, this was it. I was getting married. The only thing that wasn't real was the paperwork. We'd already got that bit sorted. But this time, the rest of it was for real. I was chaining myself to another human being for the rest of my life.

I couldn't bloody *wait*.

I flung open the Rose Room door and practically ran down the staircase. "Bianca, wait for us!" Alex cried, as the girls crowded down after me.

I picked up the hem of my dress and tried to slow my pace. To distract myself, I glanced around the walls Robbie and I had painted together. This time, every wall of the house hung with new art. Each piece depicted the artist's interpretation of "family." Above the staircase hung my second-favourite piece – a wedding present from Alex and Ryan, who worked together on a scene of two foxes and four cubs playing together in the forest.

Other artists had contributed sculptures to line the sides of the driveway and front gardens. Robbie's piece – my favourite of the whole collection – stood proud right in the centre of the lawn. It was an amazing sculpture – a mother wolf and her cub made from scraps of furniture and crockery and some pieces of an old camera. The two wolves stood proud, ready to fight off any intruder who might come to harm our pack, our family.

I couldn't believe that piece had come from my Robbie's brain. He had real talent. We'd already had three offers to buy the piece, but no way in hell was I going to part with it. I told Robbie he could make a living as a sculptor, but he'd decided to get himself a building apprenticeship. "I want to help other families to build homes for themselves," he said, as he struggled his way through filling out the paperwork. "I never had a home until I came to live at The Prim. I'd like to be able to help others to create their own space."

I patted my smooth stomach as I took my place at the top of the stairs. Just this week, Robbie and I had decided to stop using birth control. Perhaps it wouldn't be long now until we had a cub of our own. At first, the idea had been terrifying to me, but now I couldn't wait to be a mother, and define my relationship to my son or daughter on my own terms.

But that was in the future. Now, all I had to do was walk down the aisle.

"Bianca," Willow whispered in my ear. "This is your cue."

Here we go.

The music swelled. I descended the stairs as slowly as I could manage, and glided into the ballroom. My eyes cast around the room, meeting the gaze of a hundred joyous faces, each one bringing a pang of recognition and love. How lucky was I to have this amazing family. There was Caleb, looking dapper in black tails, Rosa smiling from under his arm. There was Cole and Belinda, each with black raven feathers woven through their hair. My parents stood stiffly beside the bar, frowning at all the faux skeletons and fairy lights hanging from the priceless chandeliers.

Even Rolf stood alone in the corner, his handsome face daring a shy smile. He'd apologised to both Robbie and I for the way he acted, and even confessed he was a bit jealous of Robbie. Apparently, Rolf had been treated pretty badly by his parents, too, and as an only child, he always envied the way both Angus and Caleb stood up for Robbie. I think Robbie's head swelled to twice its normal size that day.

At the end of the ballroom, Robbie stood proud, looking as handsome as I'd ever seen him in his Maclean family kilt, with a new sporran to replace the one Hans had stolen at the last wedding. Behind him stood his mother, her face beaming with the same gorgeous smile I so loved in her son, my husband.

I don't know how she was able to be here, but Irvine had left for Aberdeen three days ago and returned with her. Robbie was Irvine's biggest fan after that.

I reached out to Robbie, and he took my hands in his. His eyes locked with mine, so full of love it made my chest tighten. Robbie's whole face broke out into a wide grin, the most beautiful sight I'd ever seen in my life.

Robbie tore his gaze from mine, and nodded to Clara. She began the ceremony, much the same way as she had before. Only this time, the words soared through the ballroom, lifting everyone up with the force of our vision.

We'd written the ceremony ourselves, taking out all the stuff about honouring and obeying, and replacing it with words that had meaning to *us* – about the kind of marriage we wanted. About how we'd fight by each other's side and give the other person the space they needed to conquer their own challenges.

How we would love, and be loved, and how it was this that set us free.

"We will now exchange rings," Clara said.

I held the sword out to her, and she slotted our rings on the tip of the blade and offered them to us. As I slipped Robbie's ring on his finger, the words flowed from my mouth, so simple, so perfect.

"With this ring, I bind my life to yours. Wear it, and know that I love you."

Robbie's eyes never left mine as he slid my own ring back on my finger. "With this ring, I bind my life to yours. Wear it, and know that I love you."

"Always," I whispered back.

Clara addressed the room. "Bianca and Robbie, you have reaffirmed your vows today. In front of your family and friends, you've declared your enduring love, and from your bond, created a new and thriving family. While it's a little odd for me to be doing a vow renewal a mere three months after the wedding—"

At that, the guests all tittered.

Clara continued. "I believe strongly that when a couple goes through a bad experience together, and that experience helps them to grow stronger, then this should be celebrated. Marriage is a choice – it's not a choice you make once, but one you make every single day. How wonderful it is to be chosen by someone you truly love, and to be able to love them in return. Bianca and Robbie, you've chosen each other today. Go now, with the love and support of your friends and family. You may seal your union with a kiss."

Robbie's grin lit up the whole room. He cupped my neck, bending toward me. His lips met mine, and the whole world exploded with pleasure.

I used to think marriage was for people who were weak, who were too afraid to make their own way in the world. But as Robbie's tongue brushed mine, I realised I'd never felt stronger in my whole life.

With this man at my side, there's nothing I cannot conquer.

THE END

Want another story from the world of Crookshollow? Willow Summers has a new haircut, a new name, and is starting her life over as Crookshollow's premier wedding planner. But what happens when Scottish hottie Irvine gets under her skin? Wedding bells are ringing in Crookshollow – see who gets their happily ever after in the final Wolves of Crookshollow book, *Wedding the Wolf* – READ NOW

Find out what Robbie and Bianca get up to next in a FREE BONUS EPILOGUE. Sign up to Steffanie Holmes' VIP Readers Club to read it, as well as free books, exclusive giveaways, and other fun stuff.

I should be running a mile from Irvine. Instead, I keep falling into his arms. He makes me uncomfortable. He sets my body on fire. He makes me want to spill my deepest, darkest secrets.

Irvine terrifies me. But whenever we touch, sparks fly. There's an ache inside me that only he can satisfy.

I know I can't have a happily ever after. But that doesn't mean we can't have some fun together. The old me would never have tried a casual fling, but the new Willow can totally handle it. Right?

Right?

Wedding bells are ringing for some of your favourite characters in Crookshollow, but Irvine Baird has his sights on the one lass he can never have. Find out who gets their happily ever after in the thrilling finale of *USA Today* bestselling author Steffanie Holmes' popular Wolves of Crookshollow series - *Wedding the Wolf.*

If you like hot Scottish werewolves (in kilts), smokin' chemistry, and a broken heroine discovering her own power, then this book will have you howling for more.

READ NOW: Wedding the Wolf

WEDDING THE WOLF

AN EXCERPT

"I just wannae help you—"

"Don't." I stepped back again, the panic rising up in my stomach as I leaned weight on my right limb.

The Scot held up his hands. "Okay, okay, I'm not gonnae touch you, I promise. I dinnae want to scare you. I just want to find out why you didnae run away. And also, because that kiss between you and Bianca is gonnae haunt my dreams."

A flush burned my cheeks. I lowered my head, tearing my gaze away from him. My whole face stung from embarrassment. He'd seen Bianca kiss me. *He must think ... oh, crap ...*

"I didn't—"

"Aye. I've been thinking about coming over to talk to you," he continued. "But now I ken you're nae interested in men. You saved me embarrassing myself, so I thank you for that. Although, I am insanely jealous of Bianca right now."

The Scot's words burned into my mind. He wanted to talk to me, *to kiss me ...* That didn't compute. *He must be joking. Probably Bianca or Elinor put him up to it. No way would a guy like this notice me in a party filled with exotic and sexually adventurous artists. It's just not possible.*

It didn't matter. Even if he *had* been interested, which he wasn't, I'd never have been able to talk back, let alone manage anything else. I couldn't maintain eye contact with someone that gorgeous—

What am I even thinking? He's a werewolf. As in, big scary teeth, sharp claws, lack of basic human morality. Inhuman urges to maim and kill. I came to Crookshollow specifically to get away from everything werewolf, and yet I seemed to have walked right into the thick of it.

As hot as he was, if this Scot or any of his friends knew who I really was, they wouldn't hesitate to tear my throat out.

The Scot waved his hand in front of me. "Hello in there? Are you all right? Do you need me to get you a pint—"

"I know you're one of them," I blurted out.

That caused a reaction. The Scot's grey eyes flashed with something like curiosity. He recovered quickly, and that grin was back. "One of what?"

As soon as the words were out of my mouth, I wished I could take them back. *I'm a fool. Why did I say that? He may be hot, but if I make him angry, I know what those claws and teeth can do—*

"A werewolf." I whispered the word, desperate for him to deny it, to find some reason that I was wrong about him. *Please let me be wrong about him.*

The Scot's gaze faltered. "Now, there's a curious thing. How did you ken that?"

He took a step toward me, his hands raised. I whimpered, shuffling back. I knew I should be terrified, but those eyes kept me transfixed.

READ NOW: Wedding the Wolf

ABOUT THE AUTHOR

Steffanie Holmes is the author of steamy historical and paranormal romance. Her books feature clever, witty heroines, wild shifters, cunning witches and alpha males who *always* get what they want.

Before becoming a writer, Steffanie worked as an archaeologist and museum curator. She loves to explore historical settings and ancient conceptions of love and possession. From Dark Age Europe to crumbling gothic estates, Steffanie is fascinated with how love can blossom between the most unlikely characters. She also writes dark fantasy / science fiction under S. C. Green.

Steffanie lives in New Zealand with her husband and a horde of cantankerous cats.

Steffanie Holmes Mailing List

Want to be informed when the next Steffanie Holmes paranormal romance story goes live? Sign up for the VIP Readers Club and get a free bonus epilogue to enjoy!

Come hang with Steffanie
www.steffanieholmes.com
hello@steffanieholmes.com

OTHER BOOKS BY STEFFANIE HOLMES

This list is in recommended reading order, although each couple's story can be enjoyed as a standalone.

Nevermore Bookshop Mysteries

A Dead and Stormy Night

Of Mice and Murder

Pride and Premeditation

Memoirs of a Garroter (available May 2019)

Briarwood Witches series

The Castle of Earth and Embers

The Castle of Fire and Fable

The Castle of Water and Woe

The Castle of Wind and Whispers

The Castle of Spirit and Sorrow

Crookshollow Gothic Romance series

Art of Cunning (Alex & Ryan) - READ NOW FOR FREE

Art of the Hunt (Alex & Ryan)

Art of Temptation (Alex & Ryan)

The Man in Black (Elinor & Eric)

Watcher (Belinda & Cole)

Reaper (Belinda & Cole)

Wolves of Crookshollow series

Digging the Wolf (Anna & Luke)

Writing the Wolf (Rosa & Caleb)

Inking the Wolf (Bianca & Robbie)

Wedding the Wolf (Willow & Irvine)

Fallen Sorcery Fae (shared world)

Hollow

Witches of the Woods

Witch Hunter

Coven

The Curse (coming in 2018)

Find out what Robbie and Bianca get up to next in a FREE BONUS EPILOGUE. Sign up to Steffanie Holmes' VIP Readers Club to read it, as well as free books, exclusive giveaways, and other fun stuff.

www.ingramcontent.com/pod-product-compliance
Lightning Source LLC
Chambersburg PA
CBHW031214120726
47905CB00002B/332